AVENUR

Heir of Wuli

Kei Khani

J. K. Hannans

To my family, for always believing, and to my friend and coach, Khadijah, for almost 3 years' worth of motivation.

CONTENTS

prologue

From the Desk of Julie Winor

In pure silence, academy officers awaited the arrival of the directors. Other than the tap of our feet, nothing could be heard. Everyone's posture was stiff, and their mouths silent. Their eyes were concrete, and their expressions were strong. Anticipating a command, none would dare move before it was issued. They had all been so well trained, obedience was now ingrained in every corner of their existence. By now, it was instinctual, only second to breathing.

The arena that held them was large enough to fit more than fifty thousand people. Though the room was dark, and everyone's combat suit nearly blended with the darkness, the officer's glowing badges made it easy to distinguish the seating. There was a tricolor arrangement that created an image of our flag.

The view was familiar and comforting. The badges themselves were nothing extravagant. Just two to four bars around the left arm of the suit. The top bar was gold, and the other three depended upon the unit the officer belonged to. They could be blue, white, or violet. For directors, all four were gold.

The other directors stood stony-faced in front of their seats. The empty podium beckoned me to take it. With my shoulders high and my eyes forward, I reminded myself to keep my words clear and my thoughts focused.

"Thank you, please be seated."

Everyone moved at once, and I waited for the rustling to settle before continuing.

"Hello everyone, my name is Julie Winor and I am your Director of Academy. Seated behind me is Nuet Numan, your Director of Intelligence, Freda Riv, your Director of Medicine, and Anais Ruid, your Director of Combat..."

Numan waved, slightly uncomfortable and slightly uninterested. He was a quiet man with a laser-focused mind. Riv created comfort in every person she met, so she gave a smile that was welcoming and warm.

But then there was Ruid.

As if he were in the middle of counting the seconds until dismissal, he only nodded. He wouldn't wave nor smile. He'd only nod, because he was a reserved man whose mind was usually elsewhere. Though their introductions were brief, the revelations were abundant.

"As I look out over this grand arena, I'm constantly taken aback by the constant triumphs of this academy...something that's only made possible by its worthy inhabitants. But, sadly, this assembly will not be filled with the praise of achievement. Recently, an academy mission was impeded, and it would be an unforgivable disservice if we were to simply forget those that dedicated all that they were to our team…"

That team had not simply been impeded. They'd been murdered. They were attacked while collecting resources on an unexplored planet, and were blown to bits just as they made it back to their aircraft.

"All unit-specific responses to this event will be explained by the unit directors. But, I implore every soul of the academy to observe this team's sacrifice with every move you make. They are truly deserving of it, and may they be forever honored."

After a few more announcements, I dismissed the room and joined the other directors. Soon, we were in the main hall, navigating through a sea of officers. The hall was large, and it wrapped around the entirety of the floor we were on. The main hall on each floor of the circular building all wrapped around in the same fashion. But, given the size of the academy, the curvature of the path was hardly noticeable.

Every officer walked with the robotic focus they had been taught to maintain. Their heads were forward, and their chests were out. Though it could not be seen, their minds were clear. This behavior is what protected them, and even a moment's lapse could end in catastrophe. Unfortunately, our fallen officers had served as a reminder of that.

We walked until we came to the door of the directorial meeting room. Respectfully, one of the Tier 1 officers in the hall opened the door and held it for us. He appeared to be quite young, though the scar through his brow indicated he probably had already seen more than he should have. But other than that, there wasn't much to him. Even after such a short time on Avenur, his identity already belonged to the Academy. It was a harsh, but necessary, reality.

After allowing the unit directors to pass through first, I thanked him and entered the room. The far wall held a large window that looked out into the arena. Now that the directorial address was over, it was dark and empty. Its main source of lighting were the emergency lights scattered throughout it, but they didn't provide much.

In the center of the room was a silver round table. There

were 16 seats with a small screen in front of each. Given that there were only three unit directors and myself, the table was never full. The center of it was cut out, and the open area was used to project holograms during our meeting. The intricate displays were created by a circular projector built directly over the table, with a receiver built into the floor below it.

The unit directors chose three seats on the opposite side of the table, and once they were seated, I cleared my throat.

"Well, let's begin. As you-"

The projector whirred to life but, soon after, the resulting hologram flickered and disappeared. Given how well maintained the academy was, it was the first time I'd seen such a thing.

For the briefest of moments, we stared at the spot where the hologram should have appeared, but then Ruid spoke up.

"We've been having quite a few...malfunctions with the YARA system lately."

Riv nodded.

"A few days ago, a surgical table shut off a moment too soon, and a revival bed wouldn't release an officer."

I turned my attention to Numan. Nodding, he spoke before I had to.

"We've ran 3 system scans in the last few weeks, but I will order another. Please accept my a-apologies on behalf of the Intel unit."

He quickly tapped around on the screen in front of him and, finally, a model of our T46 aircraft was pulled from the floor of the projector. The silver contours of it were smooth and its utility placements precise. As it slowly rotated, Ruid began to brief us on its progress.

"As you all know, the T46 reached its developmental completion long ago. We've already completed 5, and another two are in production. The only setback we have is the one we've had since the beginning of this process: Fuel."

Quizzically, I stared at the model.

"Director Numan, what is the state of progress on your division's fuel search? Has the intelligence unit found adequate reserves or are earlier promises now being ruled unrealistic?"

"Given the intelligence we've c-collected so far, no. Our

earlier promises of delivery are still realistic, however-"

Following another tap on his screen, the T46 projection was replaced with that of a planet. Much larger than the projection of the aircraft, it easily obscured the faces on the other side of the table.

"…they do come with drawbacks."

When Numan paused, I gestured for him to continue.

"Well, this planet is…"

"What? The same planet we've just lost a team on? Is that what you are afraid to say, director?"

He remained quiet, so I continued.

"Well let me remind you of the fact that you are a leader of Avenur, and there is no higher honor. If this is where we must return to fulfill our objectives, we will."

No one jumped in to say anything, so I continued once again.

"We may have lost a team, but that was a result of us rushing into an environment that we made assumptions about. We have now learned from our mistakes, and any officers that may be sent- that will be sent- will be given the necessary tools to ensure their success."

Numan looked down before bringing his obscured eyes back to meet mine.

"Director, I respectfully disagree. With g-greater intel or not, I do not believe our officers are prepared to face what lies on that planet. It is with great pain that I say that, but-"

His resistance was unsettling. One by one, I looked each of the directors in the face. I willed someone to object to what had been said, but no one did. They all remained quiet. Their unsureness was disgusting and though I tried to hide it, I failed.

"Well I'm sure they're capable of handling it, and I'm shocked at your lack of conviction when mentioning the capabilities of this academy..."

I paused, attempting to give the director a moment to defend his position.

When he didn't, I continued.

"Director, the fuel will be sought, obtained, and safely returned by our officers. Any local predators will be dealt with in an appropriate manner, and if you are unsure of what constitutes 'appropriate,' I will have no problem assisting you."

The meeting room was silent. When it looked as if no one else had anything to say, I moved on.

"Seeing as there are no objections, we can move forward and address our next topic. The area around-"

"Director, I fully object to your call for such an endeavor. Our academy was put here to be the guardian angels of younger societies. We shouldn't dine where we are not welcomed, and we certainly don't "deal" with locals. We don't kill and we don't take what's not ours. The actual truth, is that we went too far by even considering the development of a military vehicle. That alone should have never occurred, and your actions are eerily reminiscent of another director I once had the displeasure of knowing."

Riv's words caught me off guard. For a second, I was at a loss for my own. When her eyes wouldn't back down, I rose from my seat and walked over to the window that bordered the right side of the room.

The arena was empty but, in my mind, there was a sea of officers sitting. Waiting. Waiting for any words that I would utter or any commands that I would give. It took me two decades to get to the point that I'd made it to, and every moment of my position was cherished. I'd made hard decisions before, but I always stood by them because I trusted myself. I'd taught the officers to do the same. It was a reality that reared its head through every action and mannerism of the academy, and it was something to be proud of.

I turned back to the unit directors.

"Director Riv, I've already decided. This will be necessary for the growth and protection of our academy. It's unfortunate if you're unable to realize that but, despite any misunderstanding my unit directors may have, this mission will happen."

Riv and I stared at each other. I waited for her, Numan, or Ruid to challenge what I'd decided. But instead of repeating her objection, she acquiesced.

"Fine, director. But please remember, you're only the leader of this academy. You're an overseer, a manager. You are not a god. You are only a person, and people make mistakes. I just hope yours won't be tragically regrettable."

There was a glass of Okla on the table and I picked it up when I realized how parched I'd become.

"I don't regret my decisions, director. But if you've got a better idea on how to protect the academy, I'd be more than happy to hear it."

I took a sip of my Okla while the other directors collected their thoughts. When no one spoke, I placed the glass back on the table.

"Hmm?"

The room remained quiet. But then I realized I didn't feel as well as I had just a moment before. My stomach tightened and the nerves in my hand began to react to something. I heaved a little and, when I looked down, my hand was shaking uncontrollably.

Everyone rose, but only Ruid spoke.

"Director?"

I leaned away from the table and held my hands up to my face just as everyone began to rush over. Both of them continued to tremble, and my stomach continued to tighten. The room spun, and sounds blurred together. I almost lost my footing, but I was somehow able to catch myself. However, I was only able to catch myself once. Looking into the blurry faces of the directors as they rushed over, I once again lost my standing ability. As I collapsed, I lost my vision, and felt the hands of the directors catching me just before I crashed into the cold tile of the meeting room floor.

***

I found myself lying in a private room in the medical unit. The room was mostly dark, and the only bit of light was what came from the monitors that hung over my head. My mind was foggy. My head was heavy, and the world felt 'airy.' If I turned too fast, the room became deformed. Mushed together in a haze, it became unrecognizable.

I turned to the ceiling and closed my eyes. There was a low beep coming from one of the monitors, but the sound of it grew. Louder and louder, it grew until I was forced to reopen my eyes. When I did, I realized they'd been shut a lot longer than I thought. A medical officer had entered the room, and he quietly tapped around on the machinery next to the bed.

My mouth was dry and numb. As I stared at the medical officer, he calmly attached a needle to the machinery sticking out of the wall, emptied it, and then attached another one. Noticing I was awake, he leaned closer to my face, and studied my eyes.

"Hello, Director. I am Olsa, and I will ensure you have no worries. Soon, you will improve. You will be better."

His accent was striking. As he continued to work, I realized he was the Tier 1 officer that had held the door open. He concentrated as he attached, emptied, and removed a few more needles. Once he finished, he reached for a cup that sat on the table just below the machinery. Bringing it to my lips, he gently tipped my head, and I sipped.

He backed away with a smile and a nod.

"Good."

As I became oddly interested in the ceiling tiles, the door slid open. Ruid entered and walked over with a look that was a mix of worry and confusion. He slowed as he neared the bed, and then gently squeezed my arm.

"How are you feeling?"

I attempted to form words, but my mouth was too numb. Surprisingly, sounds came out anyway, but they vaguely resembled speech.

"…tire…d…what is wrong?"

Ruid answered with an expression that offered no answers. Turning to the medical officer, I willed him to speak instead.

"Well Director, a virus has found you. Its strength is unclear, but your body fights well."

"You've been unconscious for a few days. We were all afraid."

Ruid looked as though he himself had been the one who had gotten hurt. As his stare began to linger a few seconds too long, he looked away. The silence became tense, so the medical officer rushed to fill it with more information.

"Soon, you may leave. Treatment will continue, but you may leave. Soon."

I nodded as best I could. For a while, I just stared at the

ceiling tiles. At some point, Ruid left me, but that point in time was a blur in my mind. In fact, nearly every moment was a blur. People came and went and, all the while, I just lay still. It was as if the world was zooming past and, every now and then, I'd black out completely. Maybe it was regular sleep, but it could have been something else. Nothing felt normal anymore.

After enduring days that passed by in minutes, I was finally freed from the medical unit. No answers had been found and no theories proposed. Time moved a lot slower than before, but something about it still felt off. Almost fake. But I didn't care. My mouth was no longer numb, and I felt better.

I found myself in my office. Randomly, my eyes landed across the small hologram projector on my desk. It had been a while since I'd turned it on. After a light tap, it brought up the projection of a photograph. It was a relic of an infant society, but what it held was invaluable. It was a photo of a smiling child. Laid across a grassy field, his face beamed in a way that held nothing back. Sighing, I sank into my chair for a moment.

A panel of buttons was built across one side of my desk.

Without taking my eyes from the projection, I pressed one of the buttons, and waited to hear the usual beep.

"Combat Unit, this is your Director of Academy."

There was a pause before another beep was followed by a response.

"Hello Director, are you well? May we assist you?"

I paused, reconsidered, and then settled.

"Yes…I am in need of an officer. Preferably one of your finest."

"Yes ma'am, we'll send someone."

I stared at the photo, attempting to picture all that had happened before and after it. Hopefully, most of those moments had been fulfilling. If they were not, I'd be to blame. But the guilt I felt, my best kept secret, was already enough. I could handle no more.

My door slid open and, to my surprise, Talo stood in the entranceway. She was quick, cautious, and strong, and every choice she made was well calculated. But having her complete my task was possibly the best and worst thing that could happen.

After all, she was yet another well-guarded secret.

"Talo…"

Only stepping far enough inside for the door to close, she nodded respectfully.

"Yes, Director?"

I froze, unsure if I should go through with my request. It would be unprecedented, possibly foolish. But I'd already decided on what mattered more to me, and a glance at the projection solidified it. Talo had noticed it too, but she pretended she hadn't.

Looking back up at her, I spoke clearly for the first time in days.

"…I'm in need of a favor."

one

"Who are you?"

Silence.

"Allen? Will you answer my question, or will we spend this meeting just staring at each other? Who do you want to be?"

Angela's hair shook as she grew a little annoyed. Seconds passed before she realized I still wasn't ready to answer. Sighing loudly, she leaned back in her chair and relaxed, still staring at me. Lines of crow's feet cut away from her eyes, creating something that was a mix of exhaustion and patience. Angela was always patient. Even while stuck in a tiny office with a desk that wrapped around her, consuming her.

Initially, I hated visiting her office, but it was forced. Once a month for eight months. Either I would comply, or I would be forced into a room that was much smaller. One that showed no signs of empathy and that was inescapable without the permission of another person. So initially, I hated visiting Angela's office. But after ten months, I'd found comfort in it. So much comfort, I'd probably keep returning until she forced me not to.

It was odd. The comfort in the room was created by all the things that couldn't be seen, because the things that could be seen were bland. There were folders, binders, pens, and paper. Most of which carried no signs of life or personality. But Angela liked her job. So much so, she agreed to skip lunch to continue helping me.

"Okay, well, how about I tell you about the last month of my life instead? It's a bit repetitive, as always, but I'll share it if you want to hear about it."

Reassured with a headshake, she started her story.

"Last time we met I told you Paul had been in the hospital again. Well he's back out, and this time he got to go back to work within the week. His doctor still doesn't have all the answers we want, but he's trying. Apparently, the rate of his heartbeat…"

Angela's voice faded away, allowing her words to be replaced by the images they created. Her husband was a serial hospital patient, but no one knew exactly why. Each visit, the problem centered on a different part of his body, before seemingly disappearing and reappearing somewhere else. It was almost as if his body hated him.

Anytime she talked about him, her eyes would dart to the photo on the corner of her desk. It was hidden amongst all the blander things that surrounded it. Her glances were quick, but I noticed them every time. So much so, I tried to get a peak as I left my last official visit with her.

"I'm confident we're reaching a point where he'll start to feel better, permanently, because each of his hospital visits are getting shorter and shorter…"

It wasn't a photo of her husband. It was a photo of her son.

He was tall with dark skin and perfect teeth. In the photo, he had one arm around her and one grasping a football. A university cap donned his head, even though he hadn't started attending yet. Due to a drunk driver, he never would.

Every time Angela's eyes glanced at the photo, longingly, they would then dart up to meet my own. I looked a lot like her son. Similar in most features and age. But that's where the similarities ended. In every other way, we were nearly opposites. I didn't carry a name local fans cared to remember, and there were no parents who would attend any of my games, because both were stuck in whatever place Angela's son had been sent to.

"What do you think of that Allen? I think dinner would be nice, and I'm sure Paul would like to meet you."

Lie. Not only would such a meeting likely pose a threat to her job, but it was unlikely her husband wanted to share a table with me anyway. On the day of meeting number nine, I'd noticed him coming out of Angela's office just before it was my time to go in. Even from down the hall, he'd glared at me. Maybe he blamed me for invoking intense memories of their son once every month.

Maybe he blamed his health and took it out on me. Maybe it was a combination of both.

Angela had stopped talking, but it took me a few seconds to notice she wanted an actual answer. She would probably just skip over it if I sat silent for long enough, but then I realized I could give her one.

"I don't know, I'll think about it."

It wasn't what she wanted to hear, but it got the job done. Without pushing it, she just nodded and continued.

"Okay, time to talk about you. I know you left your parents-"

"Foster."

"Foster parents. So, tell me, where have you been staying? Have you found work or school or…?"

"I live with a friend."

"Well have you found work or decided on school?"

"I have a job."

"Doing?"

Silence. My silence used to be followed by warnings,

almost threats. But I'd already finished my required term with Angela, so there were no longer threats to give. I was free to answer and not answer, show up and not show up.

She was obviously done with trying to pull things out of me for the day. Now she just looked tired. As she waited for me to answer, her eyes glanced at the papers on her desk. She would never rush me out, but I knew she had work to do, so I stood up to leave. Halfway to the door, she stopped me. With her hand outstretched over her desk, she offered a stack of paper and tiny booklets that had originally been hidden from sight.

"Here. Take these with you and look over them."

Every paper or book cover was somehow related to college. Some were university-specific, but some were not. One was labeled, "Making the Transition," and its cover featured photos of people who were supposed to appear as if they had troubled backgrounds.

Angela didn't give me the chance to protest. As soon as I was done skimming, she started talking.

"Take them and read them. Next time, this is what we will

talk about. No exceptions."

I nodded and headed for the door.

"Allen? You're young but you need to understand that you have to figure out at least part of who you want to be. You've got a whole canvas to draw on, so make it count...and know that petty theft takes a lot more than it gives."

I shook my head.

"I never did that again. Promise."

She stared for a moment, trying to decide if she believed me, before nodding and smiling to lighten the farewell.

"Good. Now get to reading."

The sun was doing its last bidding as I walked outside of the building. Even in the evening, it was brutal. It lashed me across the face, neck, and chest. But I'd grown used to it. So much so, I didn't bother to remove my coat and sweatshirt. Mostly because they were all I had, and I had nowhere to put them. But also because I knew there was no escaping the heat anyway, ever. Even in the night, the heat found a way to grab you. A month of sleeping on the street had taught me that.

It was a quick walk to Marion Street, but mostly because I'd learned to take it physically, but not mentally. Initially, there were a few awkward stares, given my dirty and unruly appearance. But you can't see the stares if you don't look, and you can't feel them if you don't think about them.

Often, I avoided thinking about them by daydreaming about possibilities. In my own thoughts, I could give to, and take from, the world as I pleased. There were no consequences in doing so. At the whim of my thoughts, I could be someone worth something. Every city was my playground, and no gate, real or imagined, could keep me outside of them.

Within my thoughts, I could have parents and a home. I'd lived with my father until the age of seven, but there were no memories of my mother. I usually just assumed she would be someone who was caring. Caring was always the way my dad had described her when I was younger, so that's what stood out. She would do 'this' because she cared, or she would say 'that' because she cared. There were other things, but that's what stood out the most.

She was mysterious. My parents met in a diner and, according to my father, something about her was otherworldly. He also said she was a secretive person, yet he still trusted her. He wasn't sure why, but something about her made him. He sometimes said that if he looked hard enough, he could see the outlines of the secrets behind her eyes. For the shortest of moments, her doors would open, and light would begin to pour out. But then they would close again.

I'd loved listening to my father's stories when I was younger. If he were still around, I'd still be listening, even to the retellings. Those stories were nearly all I had of my mother, Julie. The only other thing to cement her memory was a single photograph. In it, she had just given birth and was looking both excited and exhausted. I was held in her arms and, contrary to her tranquility, my mouth was gaped open in a wail.

I carried the photo everywhere I went. Even if I had no memory of Julie, the photo felt familiar. It was almost as if I could remember the exact moment. Vaguely, I could even hear her voice calling out to me.

Hello, Allen. Allen? Who are you, little Al?

Any time nights fell too silent, those words would come whispering. Surely, I couldn't really remember that far back. It was likely I'd just filled in the blanks over the years, but it didn't matter. Those were the only words, real or fake, I'd ever heard her speak.

Lost in thought, I made it back to the part of downtown where all the homeless congregated. Most sat around and talked, sharing stories of things that had happened to them. A few kept to themselves, only sitting with the group so they didn't have to feel so alone on any other street. Most of their names were a mystery to me, but some I'd actually grown fond of.

One in particular was Mr. Ganders. His thin grey hair and sagging skin was an unapologetic sign of age, and he always wore a black windbreaker, khakis, white tennis shoes, and a baseball cap. A green tote bag never left his side, and its contents were always different from what they had been the last time I saw him. It was usually whatever he had managed to collect as he wandered around during the day.

"Good evenin', Al."

"Hey. So, what's the city looking like today?"

I took a seat next to him. He held a small pack of crackers, and his frail hand shook as he ate them. I once offered to help him do things, due to his age, but I quickly learned to never do that. He hated it. So instead of acting like a nurse, I waited patiently for him to finish eating.

"Well Al, there's not much happening right now. The birds sung their morning tune and Mr. Richey Rich is still talking about putting a hotel on the parking lot next to that arena, but that's about it."

He constantly kept up with everything happening around the city. Usually, he would report it all to me whenever we saw each other. There was never much to tell, but he always kept an eye out anyway. He was a veteran and he once told me he was continuing his service by being the city's 24-hour watchdog. But truthfully, his homelessness, health, and pride didn't provide many other options.

"So how did ya meeting with the counselor lady go?"

"Angela isn't my counselor. I don't usually say much anyway."

"Hm. I don't know, Al. I think she's a counselor. You're calmer when ya come back like…ya know, I don't know what she tells ya, but I think it may be good. Hopefully it's something that'll take ya far from here, 'cause you're a lot younger than me…"

I rolled my eyes, but he ignored it and continued.

"Ya can't live out here forever. See, me, I lived already so if I'm stuck here, so be it. But you're different. Ya have to find yourself."

I nodded without turning to him. Even after he stopped talking, his gaze burned into the side of my face. What he wanted was obvious, so I gave in and acknowledged him the way I should I have. With another nod, I looked him in the eye.

"I understand."

"Good."

I looked away, but I felt him pat me. When I turned, his hand was outstretched, holding a pill bottle.

"Here?"

"What's that?"

"Medicine for ya."

I shook my head.

"Not much of a pill person."

"I know, but they're from a doctor. Here, take them. They'll help ya get some sleep."

I shook my head again.

"That's okay. But thanks."

"Fine, suit yourself."

The rest of the day's hours blended together. The further away I got from Angela's meeting, the less time mattered. That's how it always was. A familiar rumble in my stomach became the background noise for every moment, and the pain of hunger was something that grew exponentially. But soon, it reached a plateau. From that point forward, every second felt just as numb and distant as the one before it.

The night was quiet. The sky was clear, but light pollution kept all its wonders hidden. Few people walked about, and there was a light breeze that made the night just that much more bearable. But I couldn't sleep. I rarely could. The concrete of the sidewalk didn't provide much comfort, and neither did my thoughts.

Mr. Ganders and a few other people were lined up next to me, sleeping. With his tote bag secure under his head, he looked content. Four years of his life spent on the street, and he'd nearly accepted it. It was sad. I'd been in the same position for a fraction of the time, and part of me was already coming undone. He was right. I needed to find myself.

With sleep evading me, a walk through the night beckoned me away from my bed of stone. There weren't a lot of cars on the road, and everything along the street was quiet. The wind blew gently, disturbing the tops of the palms trees and, lost in thought, I walked two blocks before even deciding on a destination. The riverwalk. It actually sat over the water, and the calm of the river was enough to quiet a talkative mind.

I turned on East Twiggs, which would take me directly to where I wanted to be. Just after the last block before the water, I crossed the street and walked through Curtis Hixon Park. A museum sat opposite the path I was walking, silently watching. The top part of it was a silver box that sat out farther than its first floor, which was completely wrapped in glass. There were lights built into the silver part, and tonight it was lit a glowing purple. Its innards were a mystery to me, but its appearance always caught my attention. I stared as I passed it, promising myself a visit when it was no longer likely I'd be more of a spectacle than the art.

Bordering the other side of the park was the river and, on the other side of that, a university. It was quiet, but a few people were already hanging out along the riverwalk. Most were laughing and enjoying the night. Some had children with them, so I kept my distance. Experience had proven they'd grow uncomfortable if I were to walk by.

Once, a small child whispered to his mother, asking why I smelled so badly. His tone was one of concern, but his mother's was the exact opposite. She told him, judgingly, it was because that's how I wanted to be. It was a response that cut deeper than I'd have liked, so I vowed to avoid families along the walk altogether.

Claiming a spot of my own, I grasped the rail of the riverwalk and attempted to calm the voices in my head.

Ya can't live out here forever. Ya have to find yourself.

You're young… figure out at least part of who you want to be…make it count…

I was alone. At least in every way that counted. Standing tall, I closed my eyes and took a deep breath. The intention was to free all the thoughts rambling in my head and, as expected, the world grew quiet as I exhaled. But it was too quiet.

When I opened my eyes, the people that had been along the walk were a lot farther away. The sound of their good time was no longer heard. Gaining composure, I took another deep breath. I needed sleep, even if I had to find a way to force it.

Giving the rail a final squeeze, I turned to leave, but stopped. Standing behind me was a woman in a complete head-to-toe bodysuit. The skin of the suit had a reptilian pattern and a subtle reflection effect. The entire thing was black, save for the soft glow that was emitted from four bands that wrapped around her left arm. The top band was gold and the bottom three were purple. There was a place on the mask that seemed to be made of plastic, but it was also blacked out. Whatever eyes lie behind it were completely hidden.

She rolled a closed fist and threw something. It was small, and almost felt like a bullet. With the world feeling a bit wobblier than before, I braced against the railing and mentally begged myself to wake up from whatever nightmare I was having.

Stuck to my chest was a red orb. Much like a marble, it was mostly clear with a colored filling. However, unlike a marble, the filling emitted light and swirled around. Soon after I looked at it, the glowing stopped, and my ability to stand or move began to abandon me. I attempted to run, but the battle was lost before I'd even thought to fight it.

I fell to the ground. The world grew dimmer, and the seconds that passed lasted longer and longer. A pair of feet walked over to me. Part of my face stared back at me from the dark of the suit, and I became aware that it was probably the last time I'd see myself.

As everything was consumed in darkness, I slowly rolled

over and stared into the face of the mask. It was uncaring and merciless. My breath had quickened. Another deep breath was my last-ditch effort to live, but it was ineffective. With my mind finally clear, the last thing I heard was the rush of my final exhale.

two

Everything was dark and cold. A headache thumped its way into my conscious, but I ignored it. I'd been attacked, probably mugged. But there wasn't much to take, so that had likely been a waste of time. It was weird, but part of me felt a little disappointed, almost angry. I couldn't even get mugged properly.

I lie in a bed. It was a feeling I hadn't felt in a long time, but I recognized it. It was warm, almost comfortable. My thoughts were foggy, but the realization cleared it fast. Pushing the cover back in a panic, I bolted upward. As suspected, I didn't find the concrete of the sidewalk I usually slept on. Instead, I lie in a windowless room. The only lighting present was what was emitted from the base of the walls. Never had I seen a room lit in such a way.

I wasn't alone. Other than the bed, the only thing in the room was a chair to my left. Sitting in it was an older guy. Almost bursting from his clothes, he looked like a muscle milkshake. His face called for a shave, his bald head begged for a slap, and the size of his arms and chest assured me he could remove my larynx with little effort. I'd never met him before, fortunately, but he looked at me with a disdain I'd never felt. For a moment, I only stared at him.

His posture commanded respect, and he wore a suit that was exactly like the mugger's. The only difference was that he wore four gold bands around his left arm, and he wasn't wearing any sort of mask. His Caesar-cut hair had started to gray, but his expression wasn't one that was worn by a kind old man. He was the opposite of Mr. Ganders. His eyes were void of any kindness, and I could tell he probably wasn't good at telling jokes.

Without breaking eye contact, he raised his left wrist to his mouth.

"Medical Unit, this is your Director of Combat. The captive has awakened and is ready for cleansing."

With that, he stood up and headed for the door. There was a small light above it that switched from yellow to green as he approached, and the entire panel just slid away. The hall on the other side was brightly lit. Lots of people rushed by, and most were dressed in a similar fashion to what he was wearing.

Just as the panel slid shut, the bed began to move backwards through a space in the wall. The space was only as large as the headboard, so I ducked to avoid getting decapitated as I passed through.

The room on the other side was lit from the ceiling and resembled more of a hospital. It was at least four times the size of the one I'd woken up in, and there were two levels to the open space. The way the two levels were set up reminded me of the way prisons are always set up on TV. The only difference was that there were beds that slid into the room instead of prison bars.

The center of the room had a white circular desk with the words **Medical Division 3** written across it. There were people sitting behind the desk and they were all busy with something. Their movements were calculated, and if one moved, the others knew without looking. Repeatedly, they crisscrossed the large desk area without crashing a single time.

Around the room were a few people who were in the same situation I was in. Dazed and confused. Each one was being addressed by someone who would periodically scratch things on a tablet as they spoke. There was one that stood out in particular, because she was like nothing I'd ever seen. She was covered in thick brown fur, and sat with her legs crossed. As the tablet holder spoke, she rolled her eyes and ignored everything that was being said. When her eyes landed on me, she stared as if I were the odd looking one.

As I looked on, a guy my age walked up to me. He held a tablet of his own, and wore a uniform like the others I'd seen. The only difference was that his stripes were white, not violet.

His skin was tan, and his hair was short. So much so, he

was nearly bald. There was a scar that ran from his temple to just below his ear, and it was surprising whatever had caused it hadn't killed him.

"Allen Winor. How are you feeling?"

"...huh?"

He shrugged.

"Good. Now, stand up."

When I didn't move, he pressed something on his tablet, grabbed my arm, and yanked me out of the bed himself.

"Follow me."

He walked toward a door that looked like the larger version of the one Muscle Milk had disappeared through. The only difference was that this door was made of glass, and it had two halves that slid apart as we approached. On the other side of the door was a room that was the same size as the one we'd walked out of. There were stalls lining the room, and each had multiple showerheads that ran down its walls. They were all empty, yet we walked halfway across the room before stopping in front of one.

"Step into the stall and remove everything you're wearing.

Then, place your belongings on the outside, turn on the shower, and it will do the rest of the work."

He was obviously used to giving instructions. So much so, he expected me to move immediately. But I couldn't. The clothes I wore weren't even mine. It was amusing, but the tension of the moment kept the laugh from escaping my lips. When it became apparent I wasn't budging, he sighed. After walking back to the entrance, he pressed the only button on the wall next to the door.

"Combat, I'm going to need reinforcements."

He started to turn around, but then pressed the button again.

"But DON'T send Saav."

He turned back to me, placed his clipboard between both of his hands, and waited. Within seconds, the door slid open and two uniformed guys walked in.

One pointed at the shower.

"Get in."

When I didn't move, the other guard reached across, wrapped his fingers around my throat, and drove me into the stall.

Hard. For a moment, I struggled to breath. Grasping at his arms, I managed to force him off. His partner responded with a punch, but I dodged it by mere centimeters.

As both started swinging, the door slid apart again and more ran in. I attempted to fight back, but my efforts were futile. There were too many to fight and, within seconds, I was on my back receiving an award-worthy pounding to the face. Each punch was executed just as good as the one before it. Seconds felt like hours. But then a voice screeched across an intercom system, interrupting what was likely a near-death experience.

"STOP IT! BRING HIM TO ME NOW!"

Instantly the fight stopped. Mid-punch, everyone just froze. A few of them even looked as though they were suddenly afraid of me. I was yanked to my feet and pushed in the direction of the door. Scarface put his hand up before we passed through it. After studying the results of my beating, he smiled.

"Good."

Silently, the uniformed troop escorted me back across the hospital room. On the other side was another door, and this one led into a hall. It was brightly lit, and everyone we passed seemed to be busy and on their way to something that couldn't wait. No one looked happy.

We passed a lot of doors, and when we finally stopped at one, I took a deep breath. It was glass just like all the others, but it was blurred to the point of being opaque. In large print, it read **DIRECTOR OF ACADEMY**.

One of the guards reached to knock, but it slid open and a voice called out.

"Come in, Allen."

Tentatively, I stepped into the room. It was a large, yet cozy, office. One wall held a massive screen that showed camera feeds from multiple places in the building. From the looks of the feeds, there were hundreds of people rushing around the place. All carried overly-serious expressions, and all wore the same dark uniform.

While I peered at the camera feeds, the person that called me in cleared her throat. Her short hair hugged her scalp, and her skin was smooth, almost perfect. Her eyes gleamed with life, and everything about her glowed with authority. As I approached her desk, she stood up and I got a clear view of what she was wearing. The first thing I noticed was the four bands of gold wrapped around her left arm. They glowed and almost looked as though they were attached to her skin.

Thick folds ran down the front of her white dress, and they smoothed just at the top of a large sash. Matching the jewelry on her arm and in her ears, the sash was gold. Overall, she was striking, but her clothes weren't what held my attention.

When she stood up and looked me in the face, I almost stopped breathing. She was someone who was nearly a stranger, yet I knew all too well. It was as if the photograph in my pocket had somehow managed to manifest into something that could actually be touched.

When she spoke, her voice shook a little, and each word was delivered on a plate of anxiety.

"Hello…Allen…"

I couldn't stop staring. Someone who was supposed to have been a pile of dust stood in front of me, breathing. I always thought that if I ever met her, it would be joyful. But that was from the point of view of someone who thought he never would. Now that I was looking at her firsthand, I didn't know what to do.

There was a second of silence that lasted longer than anything I'd ever experienced. The world ceased to exist, and the only thing I could hear was the marching band of my heart. She handed me a tissue to clean up the bloody proof of the beating, and gulped. As I cleaned up, she pointed to the seat across from her in a palm-up fashion.

"Please, sit."

I slowly lowered myself into the seat, which brought a smile to her face. She responded by taking her own and pulling up to her desk. For a second, there wasn't a word to be spoken. There was only a silence that was laced in questions we were both aware of. My face begged for her to say something and, after enduring seconds of us staring at each other, she finally did.

"Allen..."

Her eyes dropped as she said my name. For a moment, she just stared at her desk, before abruptly looking back up.

"I went over an entire blueprint of how I would have this conversation, and all of the things I would say…But now I don't know where to start…"

My mind rattled with questions, yet none of them made their way out of my mouth. So badly, I wanted to speak, but couldn't. I could only stare Julie in the face as if all the answers would suddenly appear in the depths of her eyes. When words finally did come, my voice was low.

"…What is all of this?"

"You're at Avenur…"

Silence.

"…you're 3 million light years away from anything you've ever seen."

She paused. When it didn't click in my mind, she continued.

"…Our officers are taught to counter any forces that may cripple the growth of infant societies, and they are skilled in every documented form of combat, medicine, and intelligence that we have encountered and…"

After another uncomfortable silence, she shook her head as if to clear it.

"Well…relative to most things in existence, we're a very big academy with a very little footprint."

Opposite the camera feeds was a large window that covered the entire wall. On the other side was a decagonal-shaped arena with a stage in the center. At full capacity, it looked as though it could hold thousands of people. Sighing, she stood up and walked over to it and, at first, she just stared out into the empty arena. But then she turned to me.

"I grew up here. It wasn't always the easiest place to be, but I got used to it…Once, while I was on a long-term mission, I fell in love with someone and it led to an illegal marriage…and a tiny child…"

She stopped and just looked at me as if she expected me to interrupt, but I didn't. I didn't know what to say and everything she was telling me was overshadowed by the fact that she was even alive. When she saw I wasn't ready to speak, her eyes dropped again.

"…There are so many things I have to tell you, but I'm struggling to tie it all together…"

As my shock lessened, my words came out low.

"I don't believe you."

"…what?"

"I don't believe you."

I shook my head.

"I was hit too hard, and now my mind has created all of…this."

"Allen, no. I am telling you the truth."

"So why am I here now? You've died already, why are YOU here?"

She shook her head.

"I never died. That was only a ploy to get me back to the academy. I didn't want to leave with you and your father going on to belie-"

She paused, as if afraid.

"…to believe I'd suddenly just run off somewhere."

"But that's what happened…when dad died, did you know

about that?"

She shook her head. For a moment, there was a silence that was thick with dread. When she finally defended herself, her voice rocked.

"Unfortunately, getting what we want isn't easy here. There are guidelines for our behavior, and there are consequences and I…it just wasn't that easy."

She let out a sigh.

"Recently, I began to feel ill. I locked myself in my office, and I just sat and thought about everything that had happened over the last two decades. You weren't apart of any of the memories, so naturally my thoughts all seemed to start and end with you…"

She paused for me to speak, but I didn't. Her expression grew more hurt and, when she spoke again, her voice was even lower.

"Allen, I'd like for you to join the academy. I'd like for you to stay here. With me."

She nearly fell apart as she waited for a response. I wasn't sure what joining, 'the academy' would entail, but I wasn't entirely concerned with it either.

"…It's been twenty years and within the last five minutes I've realized I know you even less than I thought."

She looked as though the statement had cut straight into her soul.

"It was a hard decision to make, and answers will come in time, but right now…I would like for you to stay here. With me."

Her watered eyes pleaded but, oddly, I felt nothing. Confusion maybe, but not much else. To me, she was only a carcass of a person, and the academy was only a figment of my imagination.

Her breath came out in quick, successive puffs. She fought within herself to keep from crying, and it was clear that if she fought any longer she'd lose. Attempting to compose herself, she offered her hand.

"Please, Allen…"

Slowly, I stood up and made my way across the office. Part of me wondered if touching her would make her disappear again.

As I reached for her, she nervously reached back and, upon contact, she didn't disappear. Dream or not, she felt real yet, still, I felt nothing.

As soon as her arms were wrapped around as far as she could force them, the battle that she held inside came rushing out in a nearly silent stream. Every tear created a path that fell from her cheeks and seeped into the threading of my shirt.

Slowly, I backed away and looked at my mother. She had a few tears on her face, and she reached up to softly touch my cheek. I only stared at her, still feeling just as empty as before and, when she noticed, she quickly withdrew her hand.

She clasped her palms together and looked around the room for something to save her from her moment of embarrassment. When she didn't find anything, she looked up and hugged me again. But even after the second hug, I was unable to give her even the smallest smile and, after a moment, her own faded as well.

Through a look of suppressed hurt, she took a deep breath. Exhaling, she stepped back.

"...Okay. I'll give you time."

three

Avenur was a place that never stopped breathing. Over the course of a few hours, I witnessed people rushing around endlessly. It was as if no problem was ever truly solved and no task was ever complete. There was always work to do. Every second felt like the one where something major was about to happen, and each second it was moved to the next second.

In the halls, people marched and raced about as silver platters flew above them. I never saw what was in the platters, and Julie never said what they were for. Unattached to anything, they freely headed for wherever they had been sent. They moved silently, almost invisibly, appearing and disappearing through slots in the tops of the walls. Like the people they passed over, their movements were coordinated, and they seemed well aware of each other's path.

The officers below them were rarely seen speaking. In fact, many were just as robotic as the platters. But hearing them speak didn't do much for me either, as most used languages I'd never heard. Some of them were soft and musical, while others were loud and jarring. But, either way, all conversation stopped anytime Julie passed by. With silence and a nod, they would acknowledge her, before picking up their conversation once they were no longer facing her. Some received a nod in return, some didn't. If she was in the middle of saying something, she wouldn't bother, but no one seemed to mind.

They all wore the weird reptilian suit. They also had the large bands around their left arm like Julie, but theirs weren't all emitting the same color. Julie's were all gold, whereas the officers wore only one gold band. The others were either blue, purple, or white. None of them were wearing a mask, and the ages ranged from early twenties to maybe late forties.

As we walked, Julie's topic of discussion bounced around between unrelated subjects. At one point, she spoke of a military vehicle, and at another she was naming places I'd never been to or heard of. It all sounded complicated, but I did my best to follow along.

Julie didn't seem to notice my struggle though. She just continued to pour out information, minute after minute, subject after subject. Surely, my lack of understanding should have been obvious, but it seemed she hadn't noticed.

We ended up in an empty banquet hall. The room was circular and expansive with a high roof. White banners fell from the ceiling, donning a light gray academy emblem. The emblem was a simple, unfilled circle, with three bars in the center. The same emblem was plastered in random places throughout the building and, when in color, both the circle and bars were gold.

A light draft of air left a feeling of openness. The room sat at the very top of the academy, and we'd entered using stairs that wrapped around its edges. With room to spare, it housed a seemingly endless army of round tables. Enclosed in glass, it also allowed a generous view of the world outside.

Avenur was nearly perfect. The building sat above a blanket of treetops, but there were no signs of birds or anything else outside. Just a sea of leaves that rose and fell across large hills. It extended away, rising and falling, until it was no longer in view. At that point, it was met with the arms of a clear sky. On one side, a moon much bigger than normal faintly hung in the air.

The liveliness of the academy was contagious. Even as we sat in a quiet, empty room, there was still an air of anxiety. A feeling that almost whispered in your ear, ordering you to move. As I scoffed down whatever foreign soup was in the bowl I'd been given, part of me wanted to move around and live like the officers we passed. But then the indifference would return once again.

Across the table, Julie watched me. She looked concerned with how fast I was eating, but she was also unaware of when my last full meal had been. Undoubtedly, it had been too long. It was to the point where I might open my eyes any second and realize she and the academy was just an elaborate hallucination.

"I'm happy you've taken to the Rumin. If you like, I can have more brought out for you."

"Yeah well I can barely taste it."

The comment made her eyebrows raise, but then her face softened. The moment was uncomfortable, so I turned my attention back to the Rumin.

"I'm sorry, Allen."

"Call me, Al. And don't be sorry. It's not your fault…I guess."

Again, she watched me eat for a second before continuing.

"At the academy, we're not supposed to have children. The species we bring here are seen as being a part of one universal family, and our population is maintained with the addition of newcomers."

Not caring to say anything, I nodded without looking at her.

"Anytime we visit a new world, we're supposed to visit with the objective of protecting its people from extinction. When you were born, I was on a mission. I was given orders to watch and study, not mingle."

Her voice lowered.

"But I failed."

I paused.

"Oh."

"But I don't regret you, I just… I've always wanted to bring you here, I just couldn't. I wasn't supposed to."

"I understand…I guess."

The bottom of my bowl was starting to show, but I plowed through it anyhow. Just as I was about to lap up the last of the soup, our eyes met. She'd been staring at me with an expression that was a mix of many things. There was both sadness and pity, but also intrigue. Once again growing uncomfortable, I opted to finally give her a response.

"I've definitely broken a few rules myself, so I know what a hard decision feels like…but I can't say I've ever done anything this big."

"Have you never had the chance to see beyond the stars? A

lot of time has passed since I was last with you but, surely, humanity has reached that point by now."

"No. But I've never done a lot of things though so who knows."

She glanced away. In silence, I finished my soup, marking the end of the meal with my spoon's final clink against the bowl. Julie stood to leave, and officers I hadn't seen came over, nearly running, ready to clean up after me. My bowl was placed on a flying silver platter, which flew away before they were done wiping the table. When one of them caught me looking, he nodded in the way so many had done to Julie.

"From the looks of what happened in the shower room, I believe you'll fit comfortably in the combat unit."

"Yeah, okay."

As we descended the stairs leading away from the banquet hall, I looked down into the room directly below it. Thick glass curved parallel to the stairs, so the room was in view the entire time. It was the same size as the banquet hall, but nearly twice the height. It mostly looked like a warehouse, and within it were seven large aircrafts.

They were the length and height of navy ships, but more triangular. All of them were black, and every curve looked carefully crafted. A control area was near the top and front, but it was dwarfed by everything else. Each of the ships rested upon three legs. One was discharged from beneath the control area, and the others from each of the last two sides of the 'triangle.'

Other than rows of vents stretching across the bottom of their underbellies, everything was sleek and smooth. Each had an entrance lowered to the ground, and it provided further support for the aircraft to stand upon. Save for two of the ships, they were all open with people running in and out of them. The two lonelier ones looked as if they weren't completely built yet, and there were parts still laying near each of them.

Julie had been silent, but she jumped at the opportunity to say something.

"Those are our T46 aircrafts."

"What are they for?"

"Protection. Though they're currently inoperable. The

academy is in the middle of a fuel search and it isn't exactly going as planned."

It didn't look as if she was the biggest fan of the search, and a roll of her eyes solidified it. But then she shook her head as if she were clearing it.

"No matter. I'm sure the search will soon end in success. Academy officers aren't ones to fail."

The stairs ended near the entrance of the aircraft warehouse. The doors were open, so all the noises bled into the hall. Though it couldn't be seen, something was being hammered in the distance, and something else was creating sparks not too far off. Voices called out to each other, and feet jogged across the floor. Somehow, the room managed to appear both chaotic and harmonious.

"Hopefully, I'll soon be able to show you the inside of one. All things considered, it may be our biggest accomplishment yet."

More hallways, an elevator ride, and another flight of stairs eventually brought us to large double doors labeled **Combat Division 1**. Just as we approached, the doors slid away. A look inside revealed a sight like what I'd seen in the medical area, but smaller. There was the familiar circular desk in the center of the room, complete with officers that were all busy. Unlike the ones in the medical area, these officers didn't crisscross each other. They just sat with their eyes glued to their screens and their hands tied to their controls. But that wasn't what stood out the most.

Amongst the team was a single officer whose appearance was peculiar, to say the least. It looked as if we were about the same height, but that was probably the biggest similarity between us. Shockingly, her skin was a pale purple color, and oddly smooth. She had a nose that rose ever so slightly from the rest of her face, and her eyes were large and shiny, as if she were eternally excited. Her body was more lean than lanky, and she sat with perfect posture. She was also hairless, and, despite her striking appearance, she looked friendly.

The officers stood when Julie came into view, and she acknowledged them with a nod.

"Thank you, please, take your seats."

As they sat, I couldn't help but stare at the purple one. For a moment, she stared back as if I were the one who was out of place. But then she looked back at whatever she was working on, and it was as if I were no longer in the room.

There was a large window that sat opposite the entrance. On the other side of it was a completely blank room. Nothing but white walls that were oddly sectioned off into squares. In front of the window was a beefy figure, staring out into the nothingness. I wasn't sure what he saw or what he was looking for, but he turned around when he heard Julie ask the officers to take their seats. Once he'd turned to face us, I easily recognized him. Muscle Milk.

Julie began the introductions.

"This is our Director of Combat, Director Ruid. Ruid, this is Allen."

"This captive was just brought in, no? Why isn't he in Division Three?"

"He is not a captive, and he'll be staying. I wanted to show him around a bit."

He took a second to size me, and his glare told me Julie must have been joking about me staying. No part of him wanted to take me seriously. To be fair, I probably wouldn't have either. But his eyes carried such contempt, I was sure he thought I wasn't even worthy of his air.

"You plan to work in Combat?"

"Looks like it."

"Well, let's see what you can do then!"

As soon as he'd made his challenge, one of the officers behind the desk pressed a control in front of her. A part of the far wall slid away, and Muscle Milk gestured toward it. Where the wall had been, there was now an aisle with reptilian suits hanging on either side. Without being told, another officer stood up, signaled for me to follow her, and briskly headed into the room.

She walked until she came to a suit she assumed would fit me. But without stopping to check, she took it down and handed it over.

"Suit up."

It took a second to figure the suit out, but I hurriedly started changing from the black jailhouse attire I'd been dressed in. Almost tripping over it more than once, I wondered how anyone could comfortably wear the suit for an entire day. It was a single step above being too tight.

When I reemerged, the same officer walked over and placed me in front of a blank part of the wall. Using a small device that resembled a tiny smartphone, she pressed a button and it flashed in my face. I wasn't sure if I was supposed to smile or not, so I chose to keep it bland and uncharacteristic. She then handed me a mask. Without waiting for me to put it on, she pointed toward an elevator next to where we stood.

"Go down and we'll tell you when to begin."

I started toward the elevator, but Julie interrupted.

"You can't just send him into his first session alone."

Muscle Milk waved his hand dismissively.

"He'll be fi-"

"I'll go with him."

The voice had come from the control center. When I looked to see who it belonged to, I froze. It was the purple lady. I couldn't stop staring, even after we awkwardly locked eyes. She'd stood up, and her gaze jumped between both Julie and me, before settling on Julie.

"I've only recently arrived myself, so I'll understand his position a little better."

Her eyes begged like that of a child. Julie turned to me, but I didn't know what to say so we only stared at each other for a moment. Finally, she waved her hand.

"Please. Thank you."

The purple lady took this as her cue to move, and nodded in my direction.

"Let's go."

Still shocked, I didn't move. When she saw I was still standing in the same place, she remained patient.

"Let's go."

I followed her into the elevator and stared the entire way down. Now that she was closer, everything was clearer. She had a few strange markings on the sides of her face, indented but not painful looking. They were only slightly darker than the rest of her, so you'd have to be close to make them out. Their meaning was unclear, but they were mostly lines and circles that led to her eyes.

At first, she didn't notice I was staring and, when she did, she just stared back for a moment.

"I'm Alora."

I nodded, still staring. When the doors opened, she had her hand out, waiting for me to shake it. I hadn't noticed before due to how much I'd been staring, but I mumbled an apology. The hand felt smooth, but strong.

There was a short, dark hall leading away from the elevator. On the other end was another set of sliding doors that opened as we approached. On the other side of that, the blank room. It was about the size of both areas of the medical division combined. There was nothing discernable about it, and spending more than an hour inside of it would likely drive someone insane.

As we stepped out, loud spraying sounds came from the ceiling. Alora eyed me curiously.

"Are you not afraid?"

"I don't know. Should I be?"

She didn't get a chance to respond because the walls of the

room suddenly dissipated as if they'd never actually been there. Within moments, everything was replaced with thick fog and tall trees. I looked up to see how far up the trees went, but I couldn't tell. In all honesty, the forest seemed to reach for the clouds. When I gave up and brought my attention back to the ground, I realized I also couldn't see that far in front of me either. Everything was just foggy and gray.

There came a loud roar that could only come from the throat of something that was deadly. It shook the trees and filled the air, and part of me hoped I'd imagined it.

As I stood in fear, Muscle Milk's voice came from an intercom system that couldn't be seen.

"Begin."

four

Another roar came from the forest. This time, it echoed in my chest. Much closer than the first, it was paralyzing. For a moment, my limbs were frozen and my eyes didn't blink. When I tried to move my fingers, they nearly creaked.

Alora was fine. With her hands on her hips, she was upbeat, almost excited to fight for her life. Even when she finally noticed I was wide-eyed, she looked unbothered.

"Kylo."

I scrunched my eyebrows, which earned me a look of

disbelief.

"As in Kylohin?"

Still nothing.

The sounds of small animals and birds could be heard in the trees. Shadows dashed to and fro, and the noise built until it was as if the whole forest was moving. Louder and louder, the scurrying and squawks became more frantic. As my heart rate increased, the invisible intercom clicked to life again.

"Welcome to your first session. Your objective is to stay alive for at least ten minutes. Here is my first and only pro-tip: Put on your mask."

Suddenly remembering I'd even been holding one, I shoved it on. Shockingly, it suctioned itself to my skin as if it were alive. My heart raced. For a moment, it felt as if the mask itself had begun to nibble my neck. But once the suctioning stopped, an overlay appeared. Some of the information came and went, while some remained in view near the edge of my peripheral. Invasively, it told me more about myself than I'd ever been aware of. In one corner was my heart rate and, below it, my blood pressure.

In the center of the overlay was a faint glow. With each second that passed, it grew larger. When it was nearly the size of half the overlay, it grew brighter and pulsed. My heart rate quickened. It became clear that whatever the glow represented was getting closer. The closer it got, the brighter it glowed and the faster it pulsed. Just as it had brightened to the point of being nearly white, it disappeared.

For a moment, the forest was quiet. There were no roars, and scurrying amongst the bushes had ceased. Even the distant shadows had stopped moving. We were alone. But then, a low, heavy growl came from one direction, followed by the snap of a branch. Trees gave way. One by one, they fell, creating a path that led to the clearing we stood in. Between them all, a large shadow came closer. The air grew warmer, and my palms sweated.

The head of the beast was elongated and topped with curved horns. Its jaw was large and filled with a bed of teeth. Covered in skin that was scaly and lizard-like, its limbs were close to that of a person. With claws almost as sharp as its teeth, it nearly cut the thin trees in half with each grasp. As it neared the clearing, it got lower. Behind it, a thick tail waved slowly, as if introducing itself separate of everything else. Though its back was hunched, it stood about twenty feet in the air. The arresting smell of its breath was warm as it seized us.

It leaned until it was about two yards from our faces. Up close, its jaw was large enough to squeeze both me and Alora in at the same time. My heart rate fell to nothing but, again, Alora went unbothered.

"Definitely a Kylo."

Her eyes traced over the Kylo as if she were studying it. It even looked as if the beast were studying her too. But then, its head withdrew before shooting toward us. Again, it roared.

I could only stare.

Its eyes were malevolent, numbing. Shaken, I mentally begged my legs to move. But when they didn't, I reached for Alora. She looked at me strangely, before starting to back away, pulling at my arm.

At first, my feet were made of stone. But then they regained their abilities and I dashed for the trees. Hurling the rest of its body into the clearing, the Kylo roared again. As soon as our feet entered the forest, he lunged after us. He was quick, but the forest stood in his way.

The ground was disgustingly moist, and every step felt like the one that would leave me in the dirt. But over roots, on dirt, and through heavy fog, the suit gripped the ground. Within the mask, my hearing was improved, and the world appeared clearer than normal. Constantly shifting focus as I moved, my overlay highlighted things to avoid.

At one point, the treads of the suit failed to be good enough and I slipped. But Alora was right behind me and, without slowing down, she pulled me back into motion. Just as I was yanked forward, the Kylo's mouth snapped at where my body would've been. Another second and I would've been devoured.

The trees and fog began to thin. There was a stretch up ahead that looked to be nothing but a barren field. With no trees to cover it, it was soul-crushing. I'd have to move faster. The run became painful, but I gritted my teeth and pushed harder. A voice in my head beckoned me to give up, but I couldn't. I pushed harder.

As we approached the clearing, I prepared to give the stretch everything I had, but nothing about it was as expected. Instead of a clear patch of dirt or grass, it was a cliff. There were also no signs of being able to get across it. Fog poured off the side, and deep moans echoed from the darkness. We almost came to a stop, but Alora abruptly changed course.

Farther away, a tangle of roots extended from one side of the cliff to the other. Making it to the roots, I hesitated. They looked weak. It looked as if a single touch would bring them crashing into the abyss. But still, the trees behind us were falling fast, and few stood between us and the Kylo.

Alora grew impatient. With a light shove, she forced me toward the roots.

"No time to think. Just go."

Tentatively, I lurched for them. They shook, threatening a fall. But after a moment, the motion stopped, and I started crawling across. I bit my lip, likely splitting it. With eyes clenched, I avoided looking to whatever lie twenty-thousand leagues below.

As soon as I crawled enough to give Alora room to join, she threw herself onto the roots. They shook as she landed and, for a moment, it felt as if they'd pop. But, fortunately, they didn't.

The Kylo tore its way through the trees and lunged into the clearing. When it realized we were nearly the entire way across, it beat the ground with a thump that rumbled and echoed throughout the forest. Giving a vicious roar, it stood up to its full height, raised one of its claws, and swung, splitting the root.

Left in a freefall, I wrapped my arms around and prepared for impact. We fell toward the opposite side of the cliff, where we crashed into the wall. Again, the beast roared and beat the ground. Pacing in anger, he repeatedly cried out after us.

Below me, Alora yelled out.

"GO!"

I began climbing. Alora wasted no time following me up, and we quickly made it to the top. When I pulled myself back onto level ground, I turned around and helped her over. Panting from our efforts, we looked to the other side. Seemingly taunted, the creature gave a throaty growl and walked back a couple feet. For a moment, it looked as he would retreat. But then he turned around again. After crouching, he took a short gallop and threw himself across the clearing.

Without waiting for the landing, we dashed for the trees. There was the sound of commotion as the Kylo made a sloppy landing, followed by the thump of its gallop. As we ran, the fog thickened, flowing against us. Just after we made it into the forest, Alora stopped and yanked me in a different direction. Behind us, the noise of destruction echoed.

To my dismay, we approached a hillside. Agitated, I started up the mound, but Alora grabbed my arm and pulled me back. Instead, she pointed at a small opening near the base of the hill. It was nearly closed off by the land sliding in front of it, and it was partially blocked by a boulder.

Hurriedly, she rushed over and pushed the boulder another foot. She then beckoned me to her, and forcefully squeezed me through the small space. Sliding in sideways, I made it into the cave and fell to the ground, panting in the dirt. Shortly after, Alora fell to the ground next to me. In unison, we both snatched off our masks. Taking a second to catch our breath, we sat up against the walls of the cave, facing each other.

Fighting to breath, I looked to Alora.

"I don't like this."

She only gave a grin. For a moment, everything was quiet, but the peace was short-lived. Outside, there came the thump of feet. The ground shook and the vibrations grew stronger as the beast came nearer. When it stopped just outside the cave, I looked to Alora. For a second, there was another silence. But then there came a violent thrashing from the beast as it attempted to move the bolder. When light finally poured in, I looked into the face of the monster and, somehow, it appeared more violent than before.

There was a patch of light at the other end of the cave. It shined through like a path to salvation, so we crawled for it. As we did, the Kylo beat at the side of the hill. The ground shook more and more until the cave began to collapse in on itself. All around, dirt fell faster with every blink of the eye, threatening to trap us.

I was the first out of the hole, which only led back outside. But even in the foggy, open air of the forest, I was trapped. Not too far off, the beast beat the ground, looking for us. When it realized we were no longer inside, it stopped. We had no chance, and the distance was crossed within a few blinks of the eye.

At one point, Alora and I became separated and I wildly scanned for her. But the fog was too thick, making everything a cloud of near nothingness. The Kylo had managed to remove many of the trees in the area so, within moments, I stood amongst tattered branches and broken stumps. I'd be dead within seconds, but I couldn't run. I was alone and there was nowhere for me to hide.

It slowed its movements. It knew I had lost. Circling me, it swung, knocking me to the ground. As I rushed back to my feet, its eyes were taunting. Seemingly bathing in satisfaction, it raised its claw again. With no way out, I closed my eyes. My breath came out sharp, and my fists clenched for a fight I couldn't fight. But just as the claw fell, I was abruptly tackled to the ground. The wind of the swing swooped within inches of my face, but the beast had missed.

Alora lay next to me, panting. There was no time to ask

where she'd been, and she immediately pulled me up. Nearly

dragging me, she dashed through the forest. Dodging swings, we

ran with no sense of direction. We ended up in yet another

clearing, but it turned out to be the same cliff we'd just been across

a few minutes ago.

With no way to get across a second time, we held our

breath as the beast approached. Within moments, it attacked. We

dodged its first attempt. Fortunately, the force of its swing drove it

toward the edge of the cliff. It fought to stay over, but it failed.

Desperately, it grasped at the dirt.

Nearly over the edge, it took one last swing, almost taking

me along for the ride. As I was nearly over the cliff, Alora grasped

for my arm, but her help was a second too late. We both slid over

the edge, and the only thing keeping us from falling was her

latching onto a broken root. Slowly, the root weakened, and I

closed my eyes as I waited for the fall.

The sound of a snap cut through the air, but was only

followed by a second's worth of free fall. Beyond that, there was

nothing. No moisture of the dense fog, and no wind rushing past us. In that moment, there was nothing at all.

I opened my eyes, but didn't find the forest or the bottom of the cliff. There were only the blank walls of the training room. The quiet, empty, and safe training room.

Somewhere above me, the intercom system came to life again.

"Mission complete."

Sprawled across the floor, I just lay there. Blood drummed in my ears and an eerie ringing grew louder the longer I waited. When a scuffle of feet approached, I somehow knew who it'd be.

"Are you okay?"

I wasn't. A headache had begun to brew and, even though the training had ended, my heart was nearly jumping from my chest. I was sweating, and the feeling of danger wouldn't go away. I was afraid. Julie kneeled next to me, attempting to stare into my soul. Her face was one of comfort and security, yet I felt neither.

The ringing in my ear continued as she watched me, waiting for an answer. My mouth moved to respond but, at first, no words came out. I wasn't sure of what I wanted to say. My thoughts were unclear, but when words finally escaped my mouth, I believed them.

"…I need to leave."

I shook my head as I stood. Julie remained silent, confused. Alora started to say something, but when her mouth opened, she changed her mind. Without a second look, I turned my back on Julie and headed for the doors. Her eyes tore into my back, but her voice didn't call out until I was halfway there.

"Al, where will you go?"

I stopped. I didn't have an answer. There was nowhere I could take myself. It was impossible, because I'd gotten trapped within a dream that had begun to feel all too real. When I turned, Julie and Alora were both staring with equally confused faces.

"…I don't know. But I want to go home. I want to wake up."

Julie stepped forward, speaking softly.

"Why? You were never in any danger."

I started to shake my head.

"Sweetie, you're not in dan-"

"You're dead!"

Julie fell silent. For a second, neither of us spoke. Hurt was strewn across her face, and Alora just looked uncomfortable. When I finally spoke again, my voice was lower.

"Dead people don't just come back. People don't fly between planets and rooms don't just drop you into a land of monsters…and you're dead. So at some point, I have to wake up."

Julie's mouth opened and closed, but no sounds escaped. She trembled a little, but it didn't seem to reach farther than her hands. Whether she was angry or sad was unclear, but it looked as if she were seconds away from coming undone. Her eyes had begun to water but, as if she remembered we weren't alone, the tears receded.

Behind me, the doors slid open and an officer stepped out. Her expression was concrete and her movements brisk. She had short, curly hair and looked to be around sixteen. When she entered, she walked directly to Julie, but Julie was too busy analyzing me to notice her approaching. When she saw the look on Julie's face, she slowed her walk.

"...Director?"

Her tone was a mix of fear and surprise. She almost looked as if she wished she hadn't walked in. Julie only continued to stare at me for a second longer before finally turning to the officer. When she spoke, she sounded defeated.

"Yes, Talo?"

"There was a malfunctioning on one of the T46 warships and you are needed. Director Ruid has also left."

Julie only looked at her without saying anything, then glanced at me before looking back.

"I can't right now, but I'm sure Director Ruid can handle it."

Talo's eyebrows raised. She stared Julie in the face for a second, waiting for her to say something different. But when Julie didn't, she looked at me and gave a look I couldn't quite place. It lie somewhere between curiosity and disgust. It was blatant, but Julie didn't seem to notice.

Turning to leave, Talo shot me another look and headed for the elevator. Just before the door closed behind her, she gave me yet another glance over her shoulder. Again, Julie didn't notice.

By the time Julie and I locked eyes again, my anger had faded.

"I'm sorry."

"Don't be. It's okay to feel anger, confusion, fear...I owe you that freedom."

I nodded and she beckoned me over.

"I have something to show you."

It no longer looked as if she were on the edge of tears, but her tone was sad. Before, she had been upbeat, maybe even playful at times. But now she gave off an air of seriousness and authority. Without her having to say it, I knew I had no choice but to do and go wherever she was about to ask me to. She hadn't even waited on a response. She just turned to Alora.

"I would prefer manual control of this session."

I'd forgotten she was even there. With a nod, she jogged to the doors of the elevator. Just as they shut behind her, Julie looked at me and paused before finally relaxing her face.

"You have eyes like my father."

The comment was unsettling. In the moment, it was almost too innocent of a thing to say. My father once told me Julie's family was dead, and I believed him. But I no longer knew what to believe. For all I knew, maybe he was alive somewhere too.

Again, top to bottom, the walls of the training room disappeared. When the change was complete, Julie sighed.

"Lovely."

five

We stood in a dimly lit hospital hall. There were no people nearby, but voices could be heard in some of the rooms. At the end of the hall, nurses walked back and forth, oblivious to me and Julie. Like most hospitals, everything felt cold, distant, and impersonal. But the feeling was heightened. Unlike my training session, it did feel as though we weren't really there. There was an invisible divide between me and everything I saw, and it left me feeling as though I were a ghost roaming around the building.

Julie had already started moving. She was a few steps

ahead when I realized I was being left behind, and she never bothered to make sure I was following. She knew exactly where she wanted to go. Her eyes never darted into any of the rooms, and she didn't seem the least bit curious about what each may hold. Near the middle of the hall, light poured from one of the rooms.

Julie led me to the door before abruptly stopping. Gesturing inside, she allowed me to pass into the room first. It was lit by a single lamp, and there was a beep coming from a machine next to the bed. The uneasiness created by the machinery ran contrast to the comfort that was created by a single baby balloon on a table next to the hospital bed.

Completely alone, a single lady lay quietly. As I neared her bedside, I stopped. It was Julie. Dressed in a hospital gown, she looked tired. Connected to a machine next to the bed, a single needle pierced into her arm. Her breath was slow and steady, and her eyes were closed. But it didn't look as if she were asleep. Above all, she just looked tired.

When I turned to the Julie that stood beside me, she

remained silent, staring down at herself. But then, her eyes darted to the door. Standing in the middle of the door frame, wearing scrubs and a lab coat, was muscle milk. But oddly, he was smaller. He was still fit and strong looking, but he wasn't the tower of muscle he had been when I met him. He even had hair. His face was plain, but something about it also looked lost. Within his hands was a child wrapped in a blanket.

For a moment, he just stood there staring at bed-Julie. But then he took a deep breath and walked over. His steps were light, and he adjusted his grip on the baby so he could tap Julie on the shoulder. When her eyes opened, and she saw the child, she sat up. Nodding enthusiastically, she reached for the infant.

"Thank you."

As she kissed the forehead of the child, young Ruid sighed.

"It's time to go."

"I know."

"As in right now."

Finally, Julie looked up from the baby.

"I know. But I need more time."

"We don't have time. His father is down the hall and will be back soon."

"I don't care."

Annoyed, Ruid sighed and reached out a hand, demanding Julie's arm. When she raised it, he lightly tugged out the needle, and placed it on the bed beside her. As he worked, Julie kept her face nestled into that of the infant. Still asleep in its cocoon of blanket, the baby lay silent and unmoving. Every so often, Julie would place a peck upon his head, but she also remained quiet.

Reaching into his coat, Ruid pulled out a different needle. It was filled with a blue liquid that nearly sparkled in the light of the lamp. Taking the place of the first needle, the new one was lightly stuck into Julie's arm. Still calm, Julie remained still while the needle was emptied into her bloodstream. Once complete, it was pulled out and the first was placed back in its original position.

"Okay, hand him over so I can take him back."

Julie's fingers tightened around the child, which drew another sigh from Ruid.

"We can't keep him. He belongs here, with them."

There was a moment of silence, but then Julie nodded. As she handed the infant over, she looked as if she were liable to snatch him back at any second. But she didn't. Alone in the bed yet again, she just looked defeated. Next to me, the other Julie finally spoke with a tone that was far off.

"It was the hardest thing I've ever had to do."

Then she turned to me.

"This is the nightmare I'm forced to relive nearly every hour of every day...I can never give you back the hours between then and now, I understand that."

She glanced at the child. When she turned back, her voice was lower.

"But I'll give you a thousand more if only you let me."

I didn't know what to say, so I stayed quiet. Ruid had left the room and, seconds after, another person walked in. My father. Having not seen him since I was seven, it was weird being in the same room as him. Even with my mother standing right next to me, part of me almost cried at the sight of the only parent I'd had growing up. He looked strong. He was young, and his movements were brisk. Given how easily he got around, it was obvious this was well before his diagnosis.

He walked over and stood in the same place Ruid had just been standing. Rubbing the top of Julie's hand, he forced a smile.

"Are you feeling any better?"

"Not really…"

"Ah Julie, you can fight this."

Crouching down, he kissed her hand.

"I'm sure. You've always been the strongest person I know, and now we have a child. There are so many things we'll have to teach him together and, despite what any lab coat says, I know you're not going anywhere. Your strength won't allow it."

He kissed her hand again, and then wrapped his around it. When he squeezed, Julie squeezed back. In the hall, Ruid had come back, but he stopped just before the door. At the sight of my father being in the room, he just paused for a moment, before continuing down the hall. Bed-Julie noticed him the way I had, and she squeezed my father's hand once more before letting go.

"Do me a favor and go have a look at him. I miss him already, so I need you to tell me what he looks like."

My dad chuckled.

"Yeah, I miss him too. I'll be right back."

With a smile on his face, he left the room. For a moment, Julie remained upright, staring at the wall. She looked as though she wanted to cry. But then she took a deep breath and lay back flat. Seconds passed with the only sound in the room being that of the medical machinery. But then, her muscles tightened.

Though she tried to remain calm, bouts of pain tore across her face. Her fingers grasped at the bedsheets, and she wiggled around under her covers. Next to her, the machine measuring her vitals began to beep. Her heart rate was speeding up, and it was obvious that things were no longer normal.

Within seconds, nurses were coming through the door.

"Mrs. Winor? Mrs. Winor?"

Still writhing in pain, Julie failed to respond. Next to me, present-Julie quietly headed for the door. I followed behind, but the entire time I watched bed-Julie. Even once we were outside the room, I still caught glimpses of her face between the bodies of the nurses.

My father darted from somewhere down the hall. With nothing but pure fear on his face, he paused at the door. A nurse noticed him and gestured for him to stay calm. It looked as though she were going to ask him to remain outside, but she didn't. Once he was inside the room, she just rushed over and shut the door. With the room now closed off, all of the noise on the other side fell silent.

Present-Julie reached over and rubbed the back of my head.

"I'm sorry for scaring you. Maybe it was too early for a training session, but know that the thought of us leaving each other is my nightmare."

She started down the hall. Following after her, I made sure to keep my tone light when I spoke.

"But why couldn't you just stay? Why couldn't you ever come back?"

"Because whether I liked it or not, I had a job to do."

She stopped.

"It may not be the answer I want to give, but it's the truth. This was not my home. It was my job. In the academy, we show up to societies on the brink of extinction and do damage control. Then we leave. Sometimes we do things we shouldn't, but our entire existence has always centered on protecting others."

The hall of the hospital faded away, but we didn't end up back in the training room. Instead, we now stood in a small room much dimmer than the hospital. But even in the terrible lighting, it looked as if it had been torn apart. The wooden floors were covered in dirt and dust, and there was a single couch that likely provided less comfort than standing. It was old, worn, and broken. The only other thing in the room was a wooden table placed in the center, and it looked as if it was covered in dried up juice and mold. The light hanging above it wasn't bright enough to give a clear view, but maybe it was for the better.

Julie stood behind me and when I turned, she'd moved next to a window. Without looking, she waved me over to her. The blinds were dusty, and I reluctantly adjusted them to get a better view outside. As I breathed in the smell of death, I made sure to not put my face too close.

The world on the other side of the glass was grim and abandoned. We were a few floors from the ground, and the street below was lined with five-story buildings that all appeared to be empty and left behind. Something about them struck me as weird and unsettling. It was as if they looked familiar, yet they weren't. They were imaginative in design, but also practical. The road looked as if it could have been made of cement, but the amount of dirt everywhere made it unclear. The only thing differentiating where it was and wasn't was the slight indentation created from the curb.

For a moment, there were no sounds being made, but then a small child came rushing down the empty street. He was wrapped in a dark, hooded robe, and he traveled alone. When his hood fell, his wavy shoulder-length hair was tangled and slightly matted. Undoubtedly, a closer look would've confirmed he hadn't bathed in no less than a week. Still alone, he disappeared between a couple of buildings across the street. I turned to Julie inquisitively, but she only peered back for a second.

There came the sound of an explosion. It was deep and monstrous, and was accompanied by a loud twang similar to the sound of banging two large pots together. Dirt and dust rushed out of the alleyway the small boy had just ran into, and part of the buildings on either side of it looked as if they had fallen in. Where I had previously heard nothing but silence, I now heard voices screaming and calling out in a language I didn't understand.

As I stared, Julie spoke.

"This was a war that went on for so long, it became unclear who was fighting who. Their population dwindled over the years, and it began to look as if the fighting wouldn't stop until there was no one left to wield a weapon..."

I listened to Julie, but I couldn't look at her. I was only able to focus on the destruction outside. The view was no longer clear because of the dirt in the air, but I continuously tried anyway.

"Families were broken apart or destroyed all together, and there was no place they could escape. The child you saw a moment ago watched the bodies of his own disappear under rubble, and he's been wandering alone for days."

"Well, is he okay?"

Julie's eyes dropped to the ground, and she turned away from the window. Behind us, a door on the opposite side of the room burst open and a group of people rushed in. There were three men and one woman. They all wore tattered clothing, and the third guy to enter the room carried the small boy I'd just watched rush down the street. My breath caught in my throat when I realized one of his small feet was missing.

He was placed in the center of the table, and the four adults gathered around him, speaking frantically. Some of his hair was stuck to his face, and the man closest to his head brushed it back and mumbled something to him. The boy didn't respond, and only stared up with eyes that were nearly devoid of life. I felt a pang in my chest, but it was also at this moment I noticed the piercing color of their eyes. They were all hazel, but strikingly so. It was as if they were almost glowing, but not quite.

Another person rushed in, and everyone adjusted to give her room at the table. Unlike everyone else, she calmly, but quickly, looked over the child. When she saw one of his feet were missing, she made a pained expression and looked into his face. She gently lifted one of his eyelids, as if she were checking if he were truly alive, and nodded to herself. She had to be a doctor, given how everyone else just stood around quietly. When they were addressed by her, they listened attentively before rushing out of the room.

Once everyone was given instructions, the only one left with the child was the doctor. She grabbed a few bottles from beneath the table and began pouring them all into one. She then shook the single bottle to mix it, and leaned down into the boy's face. She stared into his eyes and whispered something I couldn't understand. I wasn't sure why, but my ears ached, and it felt similar to the feeling of pressure building just before they pop. Everything quieted, and when the pressure was finally released, all of the sounds returned. At this moment, I clearly heard the doctor's words.

"This is going to burn, sweetie."

The child didn't respond and just continued to stare at

nothing in particular. When no response was uttered, the doctor leaned away, whispered, "Okay," and began to pour the liquid onto the boy's wound. A small bout of smoke rose. I'd have thought the boy would cry out, but he didn't. He lay silently and expressionless until a single tear rolled out of his eye and down the side of his face. When he and the doctor faded away, the image of his small body and empty eyes remained clear.

I looked away and peered at Julie, but she didn't say anything. She only jerked her head back in the other direction, motioning for me to continue watching. When I turned back, everything was silent and calm again. The doctor was leaning against the table, facing the lady that had come into the room with the three men. The lady sat on the couch with the child on her lap, and his legs stretched across and into the lap of the man sitting next to her. His wound was bandaged, and I felt relief at the sight of his healing.

There was a moment of everyone staring down at the small child before the doctor finally spoke.

"We can stay no longer."

No one reacted to her words. They all just stared at the boy, until the lady holding him finally broke the silence.

"I know."

"So we should leave. No matter who warns us to turn around or attempts to shoot us down, we should leave."

The lady looked up, a slight fear torn across her face. She eyed the doctor and then turned to the man sitting next to her. They stared at each other, before coming to an agreement without actually saying anything. The man then turned to the doctor.

"The regime doesn't have many working ships left, but I'm sure I could get a few pilots together to take what they can. I have some friends on the inside."

The doctor nodded, and the room fell silent again. When someone finally spoke, it was the lady holding the sleeping child.

"…I don't think he has anyone."

"So we'll take him with us."

The man's voice was sincere, and his suggestion was silently agreed upon. Beside me, Julie finally spoke again.

"This is the most important moment in our history. The

child's name is Nazaahr, and he'll live to be our first and greatest

director of academy. He motivated the minds of this society to

escape, and therefore he is the reason for our creation."

She motioned me over to the small boy. Turning back to

the group, I nervously took a few steps. I expected the people in

the room to notice me, but they didn't. It was as if I wasn't even

there. Even once I was standing between the doctor and the

others, no one glanced in my direction.

Though I was afraid of what I'd see up close, I stared down

at the small child, who breathed softly. Surprisingly, he looked

peaceful. He was dirty and wounded, and it was obvious he'd had a

long day, but he didn't look troubled. He looked peaceful.

His head moved slightly, and his eyes slowly opened. They

looked into the faces of everyone surrounding him, and he

remained expressionless as he took in the room. I wondered if he'd

speak, but he didn't. He just looked around and in a moment of

unforeseen intensity, his piercing eyes landed on me.

He looked me directly in the face and, for a moment, I held

my breath. I waited for him to say or do something, but he didn't.

He just stared at me and communicated a message I couldn't decipher. After a moment of us staring at each other, he and everything else faded to nothing. Once again, I found myself back within the walls of the training room.

The eyes of the boy were still burned into my head, but Julie's voice interrupted my thoughts.

"Those moments say more about us than we could ever say about ourselves. If you want to know who we are, that is it."

Her expression was concrete and unmoving. It brought about an uncomfortable tension, and I nervously nodded my head to force it away. When she finally turned, she looked up at nothing in particular.

"Officer Yiani?"

"Yes, ma'am?"

"I have duties that I must tend to, so I would like for you to finish showing Officer Winor around. Following that, I ask that you bring him back here for another session... I take it you're best for the job."

"Yes, ma'am."

She then turned to me.

"I will finish as quickly as possible, and then we will continue our reunion."

I nodded. She started to walk off, but suddenly she stopped. Briskly walking back over, she paused as she neared me. She looked nervous. But pushing through it, she leaned over and wrapped her arms around me. The embrace wasn't unwelcomed but, still, I felt nothing. I couldn't even bring myself to hug her back, but she didn't seem to care. Backing away with a smile, she finally turned and walked away.

As she entered the doors leading to the elevator, Alora walked out. Oblivious to the moment before, she smiled.

"Let's get started."

six

Alora knew everything about everything. She was purple, bald, and knowledgeable. As she gave her tour of the academy, her explanations were all but brief. Most things I didn't even understand, but it didn't matter anyway. She explained everything from academy technology and history, to the origins of the very people, and things, we passed. It all just came out in a constant stream with few breaths in between. One of the common things mentioned was Julie's name. She was involved in every little story she told.

"Director Winor is the single reason most of the academy is still here. I'm the most recent officer to be inducted so, honestly…"

She lowered her voice.

"She's even saved me."

But she didn't expand. Which was odd given the fact she gave the details of everything else. But when it came to this, she stopped and gave nothing more than the declaration itself. After a short pause, she changed the conversation completely and went back to pouring out words after word, details after detail.

"You know, Avenur is barren and would've been uninhabitable if it weren't for terraforming. But there are all sorts of things that need to be considered. Like exactly what are you replacing and what will grow in its place. The beginning is important and some of the smallest organisms can make the biggest differences…"

My mind wandered. Her words just blended to the point where it became easier for me to just stare into her face and ignore everything she was saying. Her odd appearance easily overshadowed her words, but it wasn't something that made me afraid. It was something that interested me.

Her limbs were strong, but her mannerisms were gentle. The markings of her face and the smoothness of her skin were unusual and, so far, we hadn't passed anyone else like her. She was intriguing. More than once, I even came close to asking about the markings. But that might've been rude.

We ended up walking down a dark, somewhat narrow, hallway. We'd gotten there after walking through one of the medical divisions, but Alora hadn't explained the area. That, or I missed it as I spent my time staring rather than listening. The lights were placed in intervals across the ceiling, but they hardly did their job. The secondary lighting at the base of the walls wasn't much help either considering it was red.

The entire area was nearly silent, other than Alora's voice. There were small sounds being made, but they were mostly faint. Rumbles, gurgles, and murmurs that could've easily been blamed on imagination. At one point, there even came the sound of a scream. But again, it passed low and far away, straddling the line between a dream and reality.

We passed a lot of rooms with large windows, but most had blinds or curtains shielding them. All the ones that went uncovered were empty. Room after room, I nosily looked around for anything that could've been making the noises. At first, there was nothing but dark spaces. But then, we approached a window that actually had light shining out of it. Its single spot of brightness stood out in the darkness, and my curiosity was piqued.

It was no bigger than a room at the clinic. There was a table with various items placed across it, and a large bed that folded in the middle. The bed had a muscular guy laid across it and he was being addressed by a medical officer. There was another medical officer standing right next to the window, but his back was to me. Even as I stood in the open, no one on the other side noticed. They were all too preoccupied.

The guy on the bed nodded to something the medical officer was saying. The second officer then walked over, and both began helping the guy undo his combat suit. When the suit had been undone and rolled down to his waist, one of the officers strapped his wrists to the bed, while the other prepared a needle at the table. The entire time, the guy remained still. Without a single objection, he allowed them to prepare for whatever they were about to do to him. At one point, he made eye contact with me. But it only lasted briefly before it was cut short by one of the other officers saying something to him.

When he nodded in response, the officer grasped one of his arms and pressed the needle into it. The needle was completely emptied into his arm, but he didn't even flinch. After it was removed, he sat still for a moment, but then he began to look a little uncomfortable. The medical officer must have sensed it, because her eyes became concerned. Though the sound in the room was contained, her lips were readable.

"Are you okay?"

The officer nodded, but he was obviously lying. His hands and feet twitched, and he started to breathe harder. Within seconds, red blotches formed across his arms and chest. Blotches of all sizes, flat or slightly raised, reaching across his torso and up to his face. At first, there were only a few. But then they appeared so fast, he was nearly covered within seconds.

As the blotches covered more of his body, he twitched harder. The discomfort was undeniable, and the medical officer quickly reached for another needle and stuck it in his arm. But the second needle didn't make a difference, and the blotches only grew larger and darker.

He began to yell out. Veins bulged from his neck, and his mouth gaped open and closed, spraying small bouts of spit each time. To my ears, his voice was silent. But to my mind, the sound was excruciating. He'd started to sweat. His pain managed to grab me through the glass, but no matter how hard I willed myself, I couldn't look away. With his screams echoing through my thoughts, I was trapped.

The medical officers in the room panicked. When one turned around and noticed me watching, he rushed over and shut the curtain. Abruptly, everything fell silent again. For a second, I stared at the wall of curtain and wondered what I'd just watched. Next to me, Alora appeared.

"May he be forever honored."

She walked off without checking to see if I were actually following again. As I rushed to catch up, I called after her.

"Wait! What did they just do to him?"

"It's not about what they did to him, it's about what he did for the academy. He gave his life testing a serum for Director Winor."

I stopped.

"What's wrong with her?"

She'd kept going a few paces, but froze at the sound of my comment. Turning around, she looked at me quizzically.

"The director isn't doing well at the moment. She's sick. Very much so."

She tried to walk off again, but I ran over and stepped in her path.

"I think she mentioned it, but I don't know the details. Tell me."

"Because you and most other people aren't supposed to know."

She tried to walk away again but, again, I stopped her.

"Well I want to know. So tell me."

She stared, seemingly searching for something. I wasn't sure of what she was looking for, but I didn't care. I just wanted the answer she wasn't giving me. After a moment of us staring at each other, she backed up a step.

"I'll show you instead."

She left it at that and turned to walk off. This time, I didn't stop her. But now as I followed behind her like a child, she no longer threw long descriptions at me left and right. She just paced down the hall, with her focus on wherever she was heading to.

Soon we turned down another hallway, and I was greeted with yet another area that looked exactly like the first one. Oddly, this part of the hall was devoid of even the smallest of sounds. There was no patter of feet or muffle of voices. The doors were closed, and the blinds shut.

Walking up to a random door, she grabbed the handle and waited a moment. A scanner was built into it, and it lit up as she pressed against it. When the lock clicked, we entered a room twice the size of the other spaces we passed. It was brightly lit and the center of it held four tables. Each table was covered in tubes and tools, and everything looked as if it had been left in the middle of something. There were unidentifiable liquids all over the place, and a couple of them were smoking. Most of the items in the room were metal or glass.

As we entered, a slender guy with a short beard came out of a doorway on the other side. His skin was dark green, and the hair on his head was sparse. The folds of flesh on his face made him appear old, and he moved with elderly precision. He was lost in thought, and his eyes looked tired. So much so, he didn't seem to notice we'd been standing there.

As he walked to one of the tables, Alora called out to him. "Salesti."

With a single glance at us, he shook his head and sat.

"He shouldn't be in here and you know that."

His voice came from somewhere deep within, and he had an accent I'd never heard before. As I'd done since arriving, I teetered on the thought of questioning it but, as before, I decided against it.

Alora walked over and took a seat next to him.

"Surely you'd make an exception for the director's son."

He glanced at me, sighed, and gave in.

"What do you want?"

"He wants to see what's wrong with the director."

Salesti made a face. It was obvious he was about to do something he wasn't supposed to, but he didn't refuse. Instead, he leaned up and flipped a switch that was built into the table. It sat in front of a rack of test tubes, and it caused a burner underneath them to turn on. While the tubes were heating up, he started mumbling.

"Hope you're not looking for good news at the end."

There was another rack of tubes farther across the table, and he pulled them closer.

"The director is currently battling a virus that is rewriting her genetic code. We have a way of stopping it, but it isn't the best solution because it involves lowering her body temperature for a period of time that would kill her anyway."

He said it the same way you'd declare the sky is blue.

"We've managed to study the DNA of the virus, and even rewrite its genetic code but, currently, our treatment makes the infected cells behave erratically."

I watched as he slid a large magnifying glass from one end of the table to the other. He placed it directly in front of the test tube that was being held over the burner and, once the magnifying glass was steady, I got a clear look at a group of cells.

"This is what the director's cells look like when their around normal body temperature…"

They floated along peacefully and slightly sped up as the tube got warmer. At first, I didn't see anything unordinary. But a closer inspection revealed the cells themselves were the problem. Unlike normal blood cells, they weren't rounded and smooth. Most were quite lumpy, and none of them had identical shapes.

"…and this is what happens when we add our current treatment…"

He reached up and grabbed another tube. As he dripped a small amount into the first one, I held my breath. At first, nothing happened. But a second later, the cells started moving rapidly. He then slid the magnifying glass away, and I watched as the blood bubbled. It continued until it overflowed and poured across the table. When he finally turned off the burner, the flow continued for a moment longer before it stopped.

Salesti turned to face us.

"Exactly."

Getting up from where he sat, he signaled for us to follow him. He briskly walked into the doorway he'd come out of when we first saw him, and it turned out to just be a smaller room with a few supplies. A large board hung on one of the walls. It appeared to be more of a monitor, but the content on it was so smooth, it could've been written with an actual marker. As for the information itself, it consisted of a lot of symbols I'd never seen before. Some were interesting, but there were so many, I nearly got a headache just looking at them.

One of the symbols in the left corner of the board was circled, and Salesti rushed over to it.

"This number is the solution to this entire equation and it was probably the most unfortunate discovery we could've made."

"Why? What is it supposed to mean?"

"Well, this is never the solution when studying viruses that have evolved over time. I've redone this equation countless times and it always come back to the same thing."

He paused as if I were suddenly supposed to understand what he was talking about. When I didn't, he gave me a look that said I was likely an idiot.

"Because this isn't present in naturally occurring viruses, the director's illness isn't a naturally occurring illness…which means the virus was manufactured and purposely given to her."

For a moment, no one in the room said anything. Salesti stared at me, willing me to speak, but I didn't. When he realized he wasn't going to get a response, he clarified his declaration, as if I weren't smart enough to understand.

"Yes, someone is knowingly attempting to kill the director."

"But I saw her and she looked perfectly fine. In fact, she's better than I could have ever imagined."

Salesti shook his head.

"The effects aren't immediate. The condition of her cells is causing her body to age rapidly, but that doesn't necessarily mean she'll be 300 years old in half an hour. It'll be gradual. Relatively."

Even Alora was a little confused.

"What could Director Winor have done to warrant it? Few societies even know this planet exists."

Salesti's blank expression answered for him. He didn't know, and I could tell it wasn't something he was used to. Standing in a room and attacking a question he couldn't answer was something unusual for him. He could figure out that weird alien equation and even spend his time around bubbling tubes of blood. But when it came to what was supposed to be the simpler part of the equation, he didn't have an answer.

Interlude I

The directorial meeting room was lively with conversation. Back and forth, the other directors bounced ideas off each other, shared information, and made plans. I should've been involved. I was both the academy director and the only one who had been poisoned. But, to me, their voices were mere mumbles in the distance.

Allen was in the academy. It was a bittersweet reality that

repeatedly brought joy, only to follow it up with the infliction of pain. He looked so much like what I'd hoped for, but also nothing like it. On the outside, he was strong, and his words calculated. But, inside, he seemed void of most things that could define him as a person. Any less, and he'd be nothing more than an empty shell.

"Director?"

"...Yes? I'm sorry."

"Numan was just requesting your input..."

Riv was both annoyed and tired. For a moment, it was worrying because she was usually happier. But then I noticed the large planet hologram in front of us, and remembered it wasn't one of her favorite topics.

"I'm sorry, I've been processing a lot today. Have there been any new discoveries?"

"Yes, very good news with a very b-bad undercurrent..."

Numan tapped a control on the small monitor in front of him and stood up. The planet's hologram rotated and zoomed in, and Numan happily pointed to the area he was talking about.

"R-relative to the rest of the planet, this area is calm.

Which is quite fortunate for us because there are substantial reserves of fuel there. F-for communication purposes, the intelligence unit is calling it Prasolin, and the planet, Prasola. But those names are of course pending the approval of the other directors."

When I looked up, Riv nodded. I turned my gaze to Ruid, who put a single finger in the air. He also nodded, but it was nearly undetectable. With everyone in agreement, I turned my attention to Numan.

"Approved. Now, the bad?"

"Well director...I'd like to point out once again that this planet is in fact K-174d."

"And?"

"Given our history with this planet, I w-wanted to ensure once more that this remains the path you want to lead us down."

"Yes, and it is the path I would like my unit directors to support."

Surprisingly, Riv agreed.

"While studying your illness, the medical unit has

concluded that Prasolin could be a valuable element to your treatment…I must make it clear that I am still no fan of this project, but where the health of our director is concerned, I shall concede. Due to the timing constraints of your illness, I am in favor of a final mission to K-174d."

Ruid briefly waved a finger in the air.

"I am also in favor. Our previous officers were not provided with adequate means to protect themselves, which is a mistake we will not make a second time. Additional weaponry can be added to a T23, and continuous contact will be a must."

I nodded.

"Good, let's get started then."

Ruid stood.

"I'll start with preparations."

They all nodded and, within moments, they were rushing out the door. As it slid shut behind them, I found myself stuck in place, staring at nothing. Unsurprisingly, my thoughts ventured back to Allen. We'd been so far apart for so long, he had nearly become a wisp of my imagination. A victim of my failings or not, he was close, and I could see him at any moment.

Invigorated, I stood and rushed out the door. Initially, I moved with the authority I'd become so used to. The pace was calm and consistent. But every step came with an increase in speed and, before long, I was nearly running down the hall. A few of the passing officers seemed a bit alarmed. Some eyed me curiously, while others stopped and looked as if they were checking whether or not I were being chased. But what I was running from had already been left behind and was now well out of view.

My feet brought me back to the training room. Still rushing, I made it to the viewing window just as Allen's second training simulation was beginning. Behind me, the control captain counted down.

"Simulation commences in 3...2..."

Allen stood alone in the training room, and looked up just as the session began. A light vibration grew throughout the space around us, and it created a drum that continuously intensified. For a moment, Allen's eyes locked on mine. But the darkness of the simulation grew with every fraction of a second, and soon he was gone. Now, on the other side of the glass, there was nothing more than a black nothingness.

I stared into it briefly before turning to the officers at the control area.

"I suppose I'm a moment too late."

I smiled lightly, but was immediately met with complete seriousness by the control captain.

"Shall we take him out?"

I nearly said yes, but paused and changed my answer.

"No, no, don't worry. I can wait for him. I'm patient."

As I headed for the door, I gestured for Officer Yiani to follow me into the hall.

"Yes, director?"

When she appeared, she carried a look of confusion. As usual, officers marched up and down the hall, and a few acknowledged me with a nod. Not wanting to be overheard, I signaled for her to step closer.

"I was wondering how he did with you today? How is he adjusting?"

Nearly bursting, I tried to keep my voice low but, given the way Yiani's face briefly flexed into concern, I knew I'd given myself away.

"While he wasn't alarmed by all that is here, I'm not sure it is because he is adjusting. I believe he is failing to properly respond because either he can't, or he refuses to."

Guilt rushed over me. After living at the hands of whatever I'd left him to, he was broken, and the responsibility would always be mine. But so would the responsibility to help him grow from the state he'd been pushed into.

I hadn't noticed how quiet I'd grown until I looked up and met Yiani's eyes. Attempting to push away the moment, I gave a weak smile.

"I'm sure he'll come around. Officers always do."

seven

I awoke to the sound of the world falling apart. There was a beeping and ringing, so loud it entered my dreams and echoed in my chest. The room I'd been assigned was mostly dark. In it was a bed, a closet, a table, and me. Within the closet were a few combat suits. All fitted me perfectly as if they were made for me personally.

Across from the closet was a sliding glass door that led into the hall. The glass was opaque. With every person that passed, a shadow was cast into the room. Almost a second and a half apart, and all in the same direction, everyone was nearly running.

Dazed and confused, I pulled myself out of bed. The floor was cold to the touch. It was almost like walking barefoot across a glacier. The urge to get back in bed grew with every second, but curiosity got the best of me. Uncomfortable, I padded across the floor and over to the door. With a single tap, it slid open.

Outside was an endless stream of Academy officers. They moved uniformly, as if they were robots. Each step was taken in unison and each arm swing was identical. Their eyes were forward and focused, mind unwavering. It looked as though nothing could break them from their zombie-like state but, suddenly, one of the heads turned toward the open doorway.

She had dark hair, a couple scars, and eyes colder than the floor I stood on. In a single look, I was sized up. When her eyes finally met my own, they only remained a moment before they were snatched away. Again, she became robotic and zombified.

It was obvious what I was supposed to do. Behavior in the academy wasn't hard to guess. You simply do as you're told, and if you're not told, you do as you see and trust that those you are following are doing as they were told. Shutting the door, I rubbed my eyes and turned to grab a combat suit. Just as before, it suctioned itself to my skin.

When I opened the door again, there were still officers passing by, but the spaces between them had grown. A peek down the hall revealed the end of the line, and I claimed a spot just as it passed by. The march wasn't long and, soon, we were turning into a set of large doors that lead into the center of the building.

On the other side was an arena. It was the same arena I'd saw from Julie's office. The space was colossal and could probably seat an entire city. All over, officers bustled around the aisles and through the seats. Everything was laid out in a decagonal fashion, all the way down to the decagonal stage in the center of it all.

Four seats and a lone podium stood upon the stage, likely placed for the directors. Tapering away from this area was a walkway that disappeared through a large curtain. High up and in front of the curtain was a screen large enough for every eye to see. On it was the now familiar academy emblem against a white background.

As I stood in place and looked around, rushing officers nearly bumped into me. With everyone else moving with coordination and precision, I was a stone in an otherwise perfect stream. Every direction I turned, a moving wall of people blocked my path. None stopped to let me through, and none noticed I was even there until Alora appeared from within the crowd.

She acknowledged me with a nod, patted my arm, and signaled for me to follow her.

"Nice to see you. We'll be getting started soon, so just sit somewhere down there."

She pointed to an area of seats that were close to the stage, and then rushed off without bothering to check if I were following. Cutting through the other officers as best I could, I snagged a seat next to her just before someone else was about to take it.

All the officers in the bottom third of the arena −where we were seated −were combat officers. Above us was a third of white, and above them, a final third in blue. Unsure of what to do, I looked about, studying all that was happening. It all still felt like a dream that had lasted much longer than any other.

"Hey…"

Alora gestured for me to lean closer.

"In a moment, the directors will come out and be introduced. When they are finished, Director Winor will announce a mission, and YARA will choose the officers who are best fit for the assignment. If you are chosen, you will know, but I wouldn't worry. She won't choose an officer that has only just arrived."

"But why doesn't Julie choose?"

"Because YARA is our central system and holds all of the data present in the academy. If there is anyone, or anything, that can make an informed decision, it's her."

I nodded. Within minutes, the arena filled, and the commotion quieted. Most of the lights went out, and the ones that remained were the ones tasked with lighting the stage. As the room went dark, the crowd quieted to a silence.

A small group finally erupted from the curtain. Julie entered first, followed by three other directors. One was Director

Ruid, but the others I'd never met. One was a guy, taller than Julie but shorter than Ruid, with short, curly hair, and a demeanor that was unassuming. The other was more peculiar. She stood no taller than four feet, had dark green, leathery skin, and walked briskly to keep up with the other directors. Besides Julie, they were all dressed in combat suits. As they moved to the front of the stage, every officer in the arena stood and remained standing.

Each made their way to one of the four seats. When they had all claimed a spot, Julie stepped up to the podium. As she did, a large hologram materialized above the stage, allowing everyone to see her head and shoulders. It was nearly lifelike and, for a moment, it just peered across the arena. When it finally spoke, it used a tone that was nothing less than serious and purposeful.

"Thank you, please be seated. My name is Julie Winor, and I am your Director of Academy. Seated behind me is Nuet Numan, your Director of Intelligence, Freda Riv, your Director of Medicine, and Anais Ruid, your Director of Combat..."

As she said their names, each director gave a wave or a smile. All except for Ruid. Instead, he opted for a nod.

After a short pause, Julie continued.

"It is my pleasure to present to you mission number 9-7-8. The assignment is located on K-174d and-"

In the crowd, there were gasps. The room became tense, and a murmuring brewed. But Julie quieted it with a single hand. Before she spoke, she nodded in agreement with statements I hadn't heard.

"I know. This is the exact location of recent tragedies, but given the position that our academy has been placed in, it is important that we return once more. The fact remains that this particular planet is home to the largest supply of an element that could aid us in the production of our T46 aircrafts, and that very element could also aid the medical unit in-"

Midsentence, the room was plunged into silence, and Julie's hologram disappeared. Julie leaned in closer but, still, the mic ignored her. Confused, she turned to the directors behind her. The Intel director stood to help but, just as he took his second step toward Julie, the room went completely dark. The lights that had lit the stage were now nonexistent, and the screen hanging over the directors was blank.

Around the arena, a murmuring returned. With Julie unseen and unheard, it grew unbounded. But then the lights returned. One by one, they fulfilled their duty of lighting the stage. Beneath them, Julie and the other directors were revealed in the same spot our eyes had left them. Across the arena, the crowd quieted.

Leaning toward the mic once more, Julie tried again, and her hologram returned.

"It…It appears that there may be an issue with the YARA system. Surely, on-duty intel officers have resolved the issue, so we will press forward with our announcement. Following today's meeting, a thorough investigation will be completed. Now, as I was saying, the elements present on K-174d are expected to also aid in the production of a treatment for an illness that has recently gripped me."

It seemed like Julie's eyes found me amongst the crowd, but she looked away too fast for me to be sure.

"Obtaining these materials will be the objective of this

mission. We will now refer to the material as Prasolin, and the planet as Prasola. Its largest reservoir is located near a large volcano, and there appears to be little threat from local predators. Extra security measures will be taken, and additional defensive mechanisms have been added to the assigned T23."

She paused.

"Please know that officer safety will constantly be monitored, and defense and rescue teams will be waiting on standby...I do understand the pressure of this mission. However, I fully trust in the strength of this academy and there is no doubt in my mind that this assignment will end in success."

Again, her eyes traced over the crowd.

"With no objection, YARA, you may choose our officers."

She backed away from the podium. There were a couple robotic beeps, followed by a low hum. The emblem that had been shown on the screen was replaced by a single line going across the center. Staying within the middle, its position rapidly jumped higher and lower, until finally coming to a standstill with a final beep.

An odd, low vibration grew in my chest. At first, it was barely noticeable, but it grew stronger the longer I ignored it. Alora must have felt something similar, because she looked down at her own suit before standing to walk away. But with a glance, she read into my confusion and stopped.

She looked surprised.

"You were chosen."

"What do I do?"

She gestured toward the railing separating our section from a lower section below. There, two clear pods waited. They looked like rounded phonebooths, and part of them slid open. Walking away, Alora left me to decide whether I'd follow through. With legs that no longer felt like my own, I stood and began moving. Alora made it to her pod first, and was whisked away just as I made it to the other one.

As the pod rose, I gripped the handrail attached to its clear wall and, once in the air, I was able to see the entire arena in all its glory. The bars of the combat suits formed colored bars that cut through the darkness, and it created a sight that was oddly comforting.

Halfway to the stage, the entire room abruptly stood. Though it was impossible for every person in the room to see me well enough to know who was in the pod, it felt as though all eyes saw me clearly.

Three other officers made it before me and Alora. They stood just behind Julie, with their bodies perfectly upright, hands clasped behind their backs. They looked like lifeless statues. The first was a girl with silver-white hair, braided and in a bun. The other two were guys who were nearly replicas of each other. One was the bald and scarred officer I'd met when I first woke up in the medical unit. The other had no scar and long, wavy hair.

When Alora's pod landed at one end of the stage and she emerged, Julie greeted her with a nod. But as mine thumped to the ground, she froze. She didn't nod nor say anything. She just froze. Her face was a mix of surprise and something I couldn't quite place. Maybe it was worry. With her body unmoving, her eyes followed me away from the pod and all the way to the four other officers that were now waiting. Following unspoken directions, I stood as everyone else did.

After another second of staring, Julie awkwardly went back to the podium.

"I give you, team members 9-7-8."

The crowd erupted in cheers. It was a noise that was a stark contrast to the previous silence, and one that seemed to change everything in the room. From the number of people, to the air itself.

Julie turned back to us.

"Assignment's all yours officers."

One by one, everyone nodded before turning and walking away. But when it was my turn, I couldn't move as they did. The look on Julie's face wouldn't allow it. She looked worried, but she didn't say anything. After another moment, I turned and walked away without the sharp motions everyone else had.

The journey to the curtain felt as though it lasted an hour. The clamor of the crowd had died down, and now I was left with nothing but the drum of my own heart. Beyond the curtain, everything was darker. There wasn't much to be seen other than a door on the opposite side, which was just shutting as the last of the other officers passed through.

Halfway toward it, there came a tug at my arm.

"Allen…"

Julie stood behind me. Facing away from the light pouring over her head, her face was dim. Her eyes told few secrets, but worry was painted across everything else like a mask that couldn't be removed.

Her pause lasted longer than it should have.

"I…I don't know what to say, I…I don't know how you could've been chosen."

Her eyes searched mine for answers that were impossible to find.

"Maybe it was a mistake, it has to be."

"YARA makes no mistakes."

Ruid and the other directors emerged from the light behind Julie. Riv and Newman stopped about fifteen feet away, but Ruid came closer.

"This officer was chosen, Director. He must follow

through with what was decided. Otherwise, what will you tell everyone else? That you've not only broken our laws by bringing him here, but now you disregard that which we have trusted for nearly a millennium?"

Riv appeared on the other side.

"We must maintain integrity. Officer, will you stand to that which has been given to you?"

"I-I….I-"

"'Yes'. 'Yes' is the answer you are looking for."

Ruid's stare seized me. Behind us, the door I was supposed to pass through opened again. Alora appeared, but stopped when she saw the directors hovering over me. When Ruid noticed her, he gestured for me to leave, but Julie stopped me as soon as I turned.

"I'm calling for a review of this decision. I will not stand in the way of it but I do want to understand it. I have that right."

Julie and Ruid shared a moment only they could understand, before Ruid rolled his eyes and walked off. The other directors followed, leaving just me and Julie. Just as before, her eyes seemed to beg for something. But, as before, it wasn't something I was sure I could give.

She gave a small smile that quickly faded, nodded awkwardly, and walked off, gesturing for me to follow.

eight

We sat in a large room that held nothing but an expansive round table with an odd platform spread beneath it. Each seat featured a small screen in front, with a short row of switches just below that. Off to one side of the room was a glass wall overlooking the arena. Julie had taken a seat opposite the other directors, and everyone else filled in somewhere in between. Even with the four directors and five officers, the table was only about half full.

Director Numan tapped something near his seat, causing

the glass wall to become opaque. Instead of providing a window into the arena, it now donned photos of me and the other officers. Information about each of us was spread across each photo, but I wasn't sure what half of it meant. Even if I'd tried, I wouldn't have understood any of it because data points repeatedly appeared and disappeared.

Clearing his throat, Ruid started reading off whatever he saw on the tiny screen in front of him.

"Luna Ulmanh: Tier 7 Combat Officer, 5 years of duty, 23 successful assignments, 0 unsuccessful, discipline rating of 0, COT score of 117, an intel rating of 26, combat rating of 57, and medical 32. Notable assignment: Assignment 9-7-1 to the Yiani society. "

He glanced at Julie.

"Confirm or deny."

"Confirm."

Nodding, he tapped twice and moved on.

"Ravin Talmani: Tier 5 Medical Officer, 4 years of duty, 16 successful assignments, 0 unsuccessful, discipline rating of 0, COT score of 124, an intel rating of 22, combat rating of 37, and medical 62. Notable assignment: Assignment 9-5-7 to the Boram society. Confirm or deny."

"Confirm."

"Saav Talmani: Tier 7 Combat Officer, 4 years of duty, 26 successful assignments, 0 unsuccessful, discipline rat-"

He paused and eyed the officer with the wavy hair. Briefly put on the spot, he only gave an awkward, toothless smile and looked down.

"discipline rating of 5, COT score of 117, an intel rating of 18, combat rating of 59, and medical 27. Notable assignment: Assignment 9-5-7 to the Boram society. Confirm or deny."

"Confirm."

"Okay. Alora Yiani: Tier 2 Combat Officer, 2 years of duty, 5 successful assignments, 0 unsuccessful, discipline rating of 0, COT score of 115, an intel rating of 58, combat rating of 37, and medical 41. Notable assignment: Assignment 9-7-4 to the Errin society. Confirm or deny."

"Confirm."

"Allen Winor: Tier 1 Combat Officer, 0 years of duty, 0 successful assignments, 0 unsuccessful, discipline rating of 0, COT score of 67, an intel rating of 13, combat rating of 21, and medical 6. No notable assignment."

Challengingly, he looked to Julie.

"Confirm or deny."

Her mouth moved to answer, but then she hesitated.

"Then why was he chosen for a mission like this? He is a Tier 1 officer."

"Yiani is only Tier 2."

"Yiani has past assignments."

"We've all started somewhere. Confirm or deny."

"Deny."

Director Numan and Director Riv were surprised, but Ruid went unbothered.

"Director, I hate to do this, but the morale of our academy is at stake. Under Decree S17, a confirmation or denial may be overruled. I am hereby challenging your decision. Director Riv?"

Riv had been silent up until that point, but she responded

loud and clear.

"Confirm."

"Director Numan?"

Numan looked to Julie as if he were begging for forgiveness.

"Confirm."

"Then it is decided. These officers will complete the mission that has been given to them."

He turned to the rest of us.

"Follow me."

I watched Julie as we all followed behind Ruid, but she never looked back. She only watched Ruid. With cold eyes and tense posture, it seemed as if she were threatening him. But he never looked back, and it was obvious he was trying not to. Surprisingly, Julie never gave another objection, and we passed back into the hall without her even saying goodbye.

Ruid brought us to a dim room in the combat division that was filled with weapons. Ones I'd never seen before lined the walls, while others rested inside of lighted cases stretching across the floor. There were guns of all sizes, knives, and small packages of orbs that resembled the one I'd been attacked with.

Walking over to one of the cases, Ruid tapped on it and pointed to something.

"This R38 was approved recently. You're free to decide for yourselves, but something like this is a lot easier to handle in an escape."

"An escape from what?"

All eyes turned to me, but only Ruid spoke.

"An escape from anything or anyone that may want to capture you. Or kill you. Or torture. Take your pick, whatever you're afraid of, having this would help."

He moved to another case, which held some of the small orbs.

"But, of course, P98's are the easiest of the bunch. They're also the most ineffective."

He moved on, offering random information as he went, but I held back. With a lowered voice, I turned to Alora.

"Who would want to capture us?"

She shrugged.

"Probably the same group that killed the last team and poisoned the director."

"Killed?"

Noting my shock, she shook her head.

"We'll be fine. The last team wasn't prepared. We will be."

She walked off to catch up with Ruid. Attempting to shake off my new fear, I moved to follow but was stopped. Behind me, with eyes urging me to move quickly, was Julie. She moved back out toward the hallway, dragging me with her. Once we were back in the light of the hall, she nudged me out of view of the open doorway.

"I wanted to give you something."

She opened her palm to reveal what looked like a piece of black clay mashed into a piece of rubber.

"It'll let us have direct contact, so if you need help, I can-…here."

She paused and shoved the earpiece into my hand without finishing what she was going to say.

"Wear it in your ear and tap it if you need anything. I will come, I promise. I'll come alone if I have to."

I nodded. When it was obvious I didn't know what to say, she nodded back and turned to leave.

"Wait. How do you know you'd reach me in time?"

"Because I'd have to."

She moved toward the weapon's room, but stopped once more.

"I promise."

With that, she went back into the room, beckoning me after her. In the room, everyone else huddled at a table near the back wall. Light shined into their faces, and Ruid pointed and dragged his finger across it. When Julie and I neared, he looked up, eyeing Julie, but didn't stop what he was doing.

"Landing coordinates will place you here. Following your landing, you will travel 12 K units north. Though you can land in this area, it is not advised as you will not be able to properly survey the land from within the T23. Once there, mining barrels will only need to be rolled out and turned on. Any questions?"

Though I'd missed the beginning of the briefing, I said nothing. But it didn't seem as if Ruid was really open to any questions anyhow. Satisfied with the silence he received, he leaned away from the table.

"Well let's get the job done then."

Back in the hall, this time with everyone else, we passed sleeping cells like the one I had. Everything was mostly quiet, other than the mumble of words between Ruid and Julie a few steps back, and the chatter of the other officers a few steps ahead.

Though Alora walked alongside me, she didn't bother to say anything, so I broke the silence.

"Where are we going?"

"To Prasola, did you not hear?"

"Yes, but I don't understand what any of that will mean."

"It just means we've got work to do. Are you afraid?"

She stopped when I failed to answer.

"Avenurian officers are never to create families, but I'm a bit surprised the son of Director Winor is plagued by fear."

"Well where I'm from, we don't just leave the planet

whenever we want."

Glancing at Julie and forgoing a response, she started moving again. At the end of the hall, the elevator dropped us downward. In the elevator, I eyed Alora, but quickly looked away. But even without turning to meet the glance, she'd noticed.

"You'll be fine. Don't worry."

The elevator stopped once it's indicator read 'G1.' When the doors opened, we emerged into a hallway that wrapped around a large vertical chamber. It almost spanned the size of the overall building, with the center of it being completely open space.

The inner wall was glass. Lined with doors that resembled that of a garage, it provided unlimited entryways into the chamber. Each door bared an academy emblem, and jutting away were long platforms that held black aircrafts. They all had a large, curvy wingspan typical of bird drawings. Another emblem and a serial number was printed on one side. Other than the area that held passengers, they were relatively thin. Pebble-smooth in texture, they appeared dangerous and deadly in capability. As we walked, I peered through the glass in an attempt to see the bottom of the chamber. But covered in darkness, it was hidden from view.

Alora abruptly turned onto one of the platforms. Following her out, my throat tightened as we got nearer the aircraft at the end. With its ramp already lowered, it looked ready to devour me. Just before climbing the ramp, I threw a final glance over my shoulder, meeting the eyes of Julie. She stood quietly at the platform's entrance, with a face that was unreadable. Though she'd been openly worried before, she was now still as a statue, frozen and emotionless.

Inside, the rest of the team waited. The girl with the silver hair sat quietly, but the two guys bickered like children. The bald one sat at the front near an ocean of knobs and controls, while his brother sat behind him.

"You know, Ravi, YARA really could have picked a better pilot. You almost killed us last time."

Ravi shot his brother a look.

"But did I, Saav? Did I? What about the Henske situation? You know, the one that you caused. Have I ever complained about that?"

"That was your fault!"

They continued bickering as Alora and I joined them. The aircraft was compact, and only had seats for five people. The four in the back were against the wall, facing each other. The silver-haired girl and the childish twin sat on one side, so Alora and I took seats opposite them.

For a moment, I fumbled with the seatbelt, but stopped when I felt someone staring. In front of me was an outstretched hand.

"I am Luna."

"Allen."

"Yeah, we know."

The twin next to Luna had stopped bickering with his brother. Instead, he turned his attention to me.

"Did you think you were a secret?"

"Can't say I'm thinking much of anything at this point."

"Yeah, I understand."

His voice dropped.

"...Ravi's pretty dumb too."

"You know Saav, you're right."

His brother turned around.

"Guess that's why YARA chose me."

"You're chosen because you're the best for the mission, not the best overall. For all you know, it was a sacrificial choice."

Finally, my seatbelt clicked into place.

"Sacrificial?"

"Oh no, sorry. That's not really true."

He took a deep breath and rubbed his knees.

"Not true at all. People don't die on these missions, usually. I mean, the last team to Prasola were killed but that's not exactly normal…we're usually just crippled."

He smiled as if he'd done well at calming my fears. He hadn't. At the front, Ravi began slapping knobs and pressing buttons. A deep whirring churned within the aircraft, followed by the sensation of leaving the ground. Ravi hit a few more switches, and we moved forward. But with the end of the platform in clear view, I was struck with a realization. No exits were within view, and the top of the chamber was completely sealed. There was only one other direction.

We nosedived off the platform. The entire way down, I gripped the belts across my chest. With each second, we fell faster. Everything rocked violently. Through gritted teeth, fear escaped my lips. Any faster, and my skin would peel from my face.

The aircraft changed direction, finally slowing the fall. Now, we moved upward. But still, my eyes remained shut and my hands gripped the seatbelts. My heart beat so loudly, everyone else could probably hear it. Mentally, I was still falling.

"Are you okay?"

I opened my eyes to Luna. She looked concerned, but I hadn't the ability to answer her. Instead, I just dropped my head against my headrest, making sure to not let go of my belts. A glance out the windshield revealed a tunnel, wrapped in metal. Bright, white lights ran the length of it. At the end, an exit provided a small peek at an orange and blue sky.

After bursting through the exit, which sat within the ground, we climbed from a clearing that appeared to be the only one in a vast forest. An untouched blanket of trees, it stretched toward the horizon. Dipping and falling, it was graceful and, about a half-mile away, was the academy.

Sat just above the treetops, it looked like a disk floating atop an ocean. Perfectly circular, the building was wrapped in steel and glass, and the light of a rising sun lay over it. It was large, but its proportions became unclear as we conquered the sky faster and faster. Calm and peaceful, its world was perfect.

As we climbed toward the clouds, I uttered a single word.

"…wow."

160

nine

Outer space was quiet. Calm and peaceful, it was a darkness that made few promises. To my surprise, there wasn't much to see. It was even possible that the academy itself was more interesting. But as we barreled toward yet another place I'd never heard of, the planet it sat on was becoming nothing more than a dot in the distance. Green, blue, and white, it was a marble that grew bluer the further we traveled. Just over its shoulder was another dot, yellow, nearly white, with the blaze of a distant sun.

Beyond that, there was nothing. Specks of stars dotted the

background of the dark canvas, but they were far from plentiful. Small and faint, they were nothing like the drawings. Outer space was nothing like my expectations. It was plain, barren, and uninspiring.

"Alright Ravi, don't go too fast out here, you might hit something."

"Don't worry Saav, as long as you don't try to give directions this time, we'll all live."

Alora looked between them quizzically. As if she were trying to decipher whether or not they were serious, her head tilted. She even glanced out the window, as if to check for traffic. But with nothing for her eyes to find, she gave up and shook her head, as if she were clearing it.

She turned to Luna.

"How far do we have to go?"

"400 light years, give or take a few."

She glanced at Saav and Ravi, who were still arguing. When she turned, she lowered her voice.

"We won't make it."

Abruptly, Saav and Ravi's argument was cut short. Again, so Saav could turn his attention to me.

"How many trainings have you done?"

"Three."

He nodded, shifting his eyes awkwardly.

"How many do I need?"

"More than one, that's for sure…have you really never done this, ever? As in…ever?"

I shook my head.

"Not sure I believe I'm doing it now."

"Yeah, that's how I felt when I was brought here too."

"Brought?"

"Yeah. No one's born at the academy, or at least they shouldn't be."

"Why not?"

"Because rule stuff. We're supposed to protect societies, not start them, and babies expand populations and affect priorities and blow up suns and other bad things we don't want so…no births."

My eyes dropped for a moment.

"Well where were you brought from?"

Ravi jumped in.

"Talmani, but Saav was chosen last minute."

"What? There was a meteorite, Ravi, we were both chosen last minute."

"Yeah but you were chosen last, last minute. The last minute after my last minute."

"What does that even mean? There is no last after last, there's just last."

"So we agree that you alone were last? Good."

Saav's face scrunched from a mix of frustration and annoyance. He looked as though he were about to say something else, but I cut in.

"I've never seen another planet. Other than…that, of course."

With a thumb, I gestured toward where we'd left.

Saav nodded.

"Yeah, Avenur is pretty cool too. Couple of minutes we'll

be passing Andies Two. It's a beaut, but don't expect much. Everything in this part of town's a little hot."

He winked before turning back to Ravi and slapping him on the side of the head.

"Watch where you're going! You almost hit that."

He pointed to something that could have either been a rock in the distance or a speck on the glass. Surprisingly, Ravi didn't say anything back. He just tossed his brother a death glare.

Luna rolled her eyes at them both before turning to me.

"You will get used to them. I have…I think."

Just over her head, a light shined into the aircraft. It illuminated from a large planet, but the surface was nothing worth visiting. Most of it was wrapped in a layer of grey dust, but the parts that weren't glowed red and yellow like an ember. Near its north pole was a large swirl that slowly crawled across it.

"And that, my friend, is Andies Two. There's a third and fourth one, but they're not much to look at after you've seen that one."

"Well what about Andies One? Where's that?"

"We just left it…"

Ravi cut in.

"It doesn't look like the rest because it's terraformed. We like to cheat the system, if you haven't realized."

Saav put up a finger.

"It's not cheating if there's no one to catch you. Besides, we save lives."

Ravi shrugged.

"If you're lucky enough to complete your assignment. Otherwise, you end up at the Orweiian outpost with the other losers."

Saav turned.

"But we won't be losers. Not even you, trust me. The academy can break your joy, but it won't break your spine…Or maybe it can break your spine. But in that case, it won't break your joy."

Confused, I only answered with a stare, so he expanded.

"…Because you'd be dead. Dead people don't have joy."

Ravi sighed.

"Saav, please. Allen, excuse his lack of skillful communication. This isn't his first language after all."

"Don't make me sound stupid. I know what I meant. This language is so primitive, a Kozi could learn it. That's why Director Winor forces everyone to use it."

I turned to Alora.

"…what's a Kozi?"

She shrugged and looked at me as if I'd asked for the purpose of life. When she turned to Luna for an answer, she was zoned out. Catching on to the fact we were waiting for her to tell us what a Kozi was, she shrugged and gave the same look.

We passed what had to be Andies Three. It looked exactly like Andies Two, but it was slightly dimmer and there wasn't a large swirl on it. Instead, it was just equal parts red and gray. But still, it was magnificent.

For a few minutes, the aircraft was dead silent. Everyone was in their own world. Saav and Ravi had ceased their arguments for a while, but then Saav awkwardly looked around at everyone. Obviously uncomfortable from the silence, he started to tap his foot. Then, he patted his legs. Within seconds, he was beating his own little drumbeat.

Ravi sighed.

"Saav…I'm begging."

"How about you keep your eyes on the road?"

"How about you go to sleep?"

"I can't, since I have to be the eyes for both of us."

"Oh please, I crashed once, Saav. Once."

"You nearly killed us twice."

As they continued to argue, Alora whispered to me and Luna.

"…we are not going to make it."

Yet again, light shined into the aircraft. We were passing Andies Four, but this planet was much dimmer than the two before it. It was mostly gray and gassy, and it looked like a fishbowl with smoke blown into it. It was a lot closer to us than Andies Two and Three, and when Ravi saw how close it was, he tipped the steering.

"Fine, Saav. You wanna die, I'll let you die."

He tipped us even more, and now the planet was above our heads, rather than off to one side. As we neared it, a heavy pressure could be felt on the aircraft and, suddenly, there was a deep rumbling sound. Sparks flew off the edges of the windows, and a layer of fire peeled its way across the glass. As everything in the aircraft rumbled louder and louder, Saav became afraid.

"…what are you doing?"

"Stopping for gas!"

Everyone held on to their seats as we were pulled further and further into the atmosphere of the planet. Soon, we were enveloped in its gray air, and small rocks crashed against the windows. As more rocks ricocheted and the aircraft rumbled louder, Alora started talking to herself.

"I told you we wouldn't make it…"

Luna held on tight and gritted her teeth. She hadn't said anything, but as our world was violently rocked back and forth, she finally yelled at Ravi.

"Ravi, stop it!"

"If Saav wants to die, he'll die."

"Ravi, please!"

He finally reached up and hit a few switches. With a pressure stronger than any I'd felt so far, the aircraft accelerated away from whatever we'd been falling towards. Everything rocked and rumbled a moment longer but, finally, we broke away from the gray of the planet. As we tore back into space, Ravi taunted his brother.

"You're looking a little gray Saav, wonder why. You know, we barely broke the atmosphere."

Saav breathed hard and grabbed his chest. When he didn't respond, Alora did.

"We definitely broke the atmosphere."

"No we didn-"

"Ravi?"

Luna cut in.

"Do not do that again, okay?"

Her voice was more than serious. He nodded and eyed his brother, which made Saav look away. Feeling as though he'd won the battle, he grinned menacingly before looking back at the rest of us.

"Alright folks, time to crank things up because, at this speed, even Alora will be dead by the time we get there."

He started pressing buttons and pulling handles. At once, everything around us changed. Before, the planets silently sat in place, and the stars were distant and faint. But now, they all seemed to move while we stayed in place.

At first, it happened at a speed that allowed me to watch things come and go, but then it sped up. Space moved so fast, everything became small white specs flying past the window. This went on for a few moments, but then there was nothing. Nothing flew past and there were no longer any signs of stars or planets. There was just a black nothingness.

It was a nothingness that consumed everything and made me start to question whether or not I really existed. Whether or not I was still a person or...anything. It was odd to feel that way but, then again, the nothingness itself was odd too. A dark sea of black, space carried no proof that my life, or the academy, had ever really been anywhere. The only sign of existence was the aircraft itself. It shook and rattled, and the chaos of the inside paired with the tranquility of the outside nearly drove me insane. I felt trapped.

But then, things changed again, and the specs returned. At first, there were only a few. Ones that went by so fast, a blink would've hidden them. But then, their numbers grew. More and more zipped past, to the point where it felt as though we were back in the spot where we'd first started.

Everything slowed and the distant stars returned. But gone was the far away view of Andies Two, Three, and Four, and in their place was just a spatter of stars. There were more in view than there had been near the academy and, contrary to what we'd seen before, they were picture perfect.

Up ahead was a planet. Nearly the exact opposite of the Andies', it was large, and nothing on it was grey or red. It was mostly blue, but the closer we got, the more the blue gave way to other colors. There were large, nearly uninterrupted, stretches of green bordered by thin lines of brown. A few dark pools of blue were spread throughout, and some were much larger than others.

Just near the edge of what we could see was a range of mountains, and it briefly broke up the smoothness of the green ball. Other than that, everything appeared flat. It felt like looking at a painting.

The planet filled more and more of our view, until nothing else could be seen.

Just before we broke its atmosphere, Ravi started talking again.

"Intel's landing coordinates don't look the best to me, so I'll have to improvise…I can't promise a smooth ride."

Saav rolled his eyes.

"Surprise, surprise."

Just as we passed into the planet's atmosphere, the aircraft rumbled, loud and deep. Ravi had all but guaranteed a near-death experience, but no one panicked, so I didn't either. Outside the window, sparks began to fly, and fire once again raged across everything. The view of the world below was largely shielded behind the layer of fire but, still, bits and pieces could be seen through the flame.

The forest below us was dense and untamed, and seemed to go on forever. A few of the trees rose high above the rest, as if they were reaching for the sky. Views of the ground were few and far between. Contrary to what was seen on the outside, the ground was largely uneven, and it rose and dipped with the freedom of an ocean.

In the distance, birds flew from the trees. They were a dark, navy blue, and their sharp beaks were nearly half the length of the rest of their bodies. Initially, there were only a few. But then the group grew exponentially. It quickly became an entire flock, and they hurriedly flew away as we aimed for the very spot they would have been resting in.

"We're going too fast, Rav!"

Saav's voice was wrought with fear.

"I've got it, just hang on!"

The shaking and rattling died down but, still, we were moving too fast. The ground was getting closer and closer. The thought of crashing seemed to enter everyone's mind at once. Something at the bottom of the aircraft rattled and clanked. A force pushed against us harder as we fell. Soon, everything slowed down even further, but not enough to where we wouldn't crash. Just enough to where it probably wouldn't kill us.

The ground had gotten close enough to guarantee our fate. The tips of branches scraped against the bottom of the aircraft, and soon they were torn off completely. Horrifically, the top of the tree-line was splintered into a million pieces as we dropped below it.

I squeezed my eyes shut and waited. Everything in the aircraft was violently rocked. After a few bumps, there were a couple thuds, and everything stopped. Somewhere, there was the sound of a faint beeping. But gone were the sounds of things being torn apart. There was only the beeping, surrounded by an odd quietness.

ten

No one moved. Everyone just sat with their eyes wide as they took a moment to collect themselves. Something in the aircraft continued to beep, but no one tried to check it out. We all just sat and reveled in the fact that we were even alive.

The first to move was Saav and, unsurprisingly, he scolded Ravi.

"Good job on the deforestation, but I think you missed a few."

He got up and walked toward the back of the aircraft. Ravi

unbuckled and rushed after him.

"Well I'm sorry I didn't see any nice, soft, landing pads for you to sprawl across."

Everyone else unbuckled as Saav pressed something that caused the back door to drop open. He started to walk out, but Ravi grabbed him by the arm and tried to swing him around. He responded by snatching his arm away and shoving Ravi to the floor.

Ravi stood up and leapt from the top of the aircraft's ramp, landing on Saav. With Saav beneath him, he dealt a few blows before he was forced off. Taking the chance to flip the positions, Saav rolled on top of Ravi and returned the punches. Due to their equal strength, the upper hand was repeatedly switched, until Luna finally stepped in.

"Stop it! We have more important things to worry about."

They both froze mid-swing. Coming out of the aircraft, Alora backed her up with a shake of her head. As they pulled themselves from the ground, death stares were exchanged. It looked as if they'd start fighting again, but Luna distracted them.

"Ravi, that landing was too rough. What is the status of the aircraft?"

Ravi threw one last glance at his brother before turning back to everyone else.

"It took a beating, but we'll be able to fly it out. We'll just have to save what we have for when it's time to leave. Otherwise, we won't make it."

This riled Saav up again.

"Oh really? So how are we supposed to locate the Prasolin? ON FOOT?"

"We know we're in the right area, so if we have to find it on foot, that's what we'll do."

"And what about collecting it? I'm not sure I'll be able to hold a whole lot in my hands."

Alora turned to Luna, who responded for her.

"We will follow the original plan and leave the aircraft to search on foot. When we find it, we will summon the aircraft to where we are. We will use as few resources as possible, and will still be able to make it back to Avenur."

We all just looked at each other in silence. It was obvious that no one wanted to search on foot, so Luna tried to assure everyone.

"It'll work. Just activate the T23's beacon, and hopefully the academy will be alerted in time to ensure we do not perish while we search."

Ravi started trudging back toward the aircraft.

"If you say so..."

When he was out of earshot, Saav took another jab.

"Why is he acting like it's anyone's fault but his?"

He stared at us in disbelief, but no one took the bait. The matter had been settled and no one wanted to watch him and Ravi fight again. When Ravi returned, he was carrying three metal slabs in his hand. They were small and thin, and one side of each was mostly taken up by a monitor.

He walked over and gave one to Luna, and the other to Alora.

"It's a detector. Next best thing to a map."

They both nodded. Lightly, Alora tapped one side of it.

"Which direction should we go?"

As he turned a half circle and looked around, Ravi pointed in a random direction.

"That way."

Saav, still angry with his brother, jumped in.

"Why?"

"Because that's the way to go. Where do you think we should go?"

"Not that way."

"Why?"

"Because that's not the way to go."

Ravi eyed him, obviously contemplating another fight. Fortunately, Luna broke in.

"We're going that way."

She started walking in the direction Ravi had pointed, and Alora and I followed. Saav and Ravi took a moment longer to eye each other but, luckily, they started walking without exchanging fists.

The forest was even larger than it appeared. The trunks of

trees were nearly the size of buildings, and crossing a root meant climbing over it. Attempting to look to the top of a tree required a ninety-degree tip of the neck and, even then, they were cloaked in leaves and a blinding sunlight. Running up the sides were a plethora of branches, but the ones closest to the ground were mostly devoid of leaves.

The entire time we walked, it was oddly quiet. Scurrying could be heard every now and then, but nothing more. Surprisingly, Saav and Ravi were also quiet. Ravi walked with his head down as if he were lost in thought, and Saav walked with his eyes darting back and forth. He was obviously afraid, and when something scurried a little too close to us, he jumped.

It looked as though he were about to sprint away, but Alora stuck her arm out to stop him.

"Are you going to be okay?"

Saav started walking again without responding, so Ravi answered for him.

"He'll be fine...don't worry, there's no Henskie here."

Saav gave him the finger.

"Why don't you look at that? I found one after all."

The scurrying sound returned. This time, it was much louder than before. Everyone stopped moving and heads swiveled in all directions. Everything was dead quiet. From behind me, Alora tapped me on the shoulder and pointed up a tree. At first, whatever she was pointing at was well hidden amongst the branches and sunlight. But then, it scurried to the underside of a branch.

Its body was long like a weasel, and its white hair was puffy and untamed. It had large, green eyes that peered at us in wonder, and its tail would wave anytime it moved. Its ears were two large dishes that were nearly the size of its head, and a large, gray patch of hair was splattered across its face and left ear. Excitedly, it scurried to a different spot every time its eyes met our own. Giving up on any attempt to hide, it scurried down the tree and hopped to the ground. Saav backed up.

When it was about fifteen feet from us, it stopped and stared again. Eyes wide and ears perked, it looked back as if we were the oddity. Lifting off its short legs, it rested upright and tilted its head in curiosity.

Luna stuck her hand out, beckoning it over, but Saav swatted it.

"What are you doing?"

"If it wanted to kill us, it would have done so already."

"You don't know that."

Ravi jumped in.

"C'mon Saav, look at it. I'm sure we could take-"

When he turned to look again, the creature had moved and was now within two feet of us. Its eyes were still filled with curiosity but, even Alora became cautious.

"I agree with Saav. It's a bit too...quick."

Luna ignored the warning. Kneeling to the ground with her hand outstretched, she waited for the creature to get closer. It hesitated for a moment, but then it hopped the short distance and rubbed its nose across her hand and arm. It then stuck its head in her palm, before becoming restless and hopping across her forearm.

As Saav watched, his face twisted in disgust.

"You've gotta be kidding…"

The creature paused and looked up, staring Saav in the face. Its eyes grew wider and its ears twitched. To Saav's horror, it moved over to him and dashed around his legs. He dodged its every move, nearly falling over. Abruptly, the creature hopped from the ground. It landed at Saav's waist and ran across his body, stopping on his shoulder. Looking at the rest of us, it opened its mouth and let out a sound similar to a kitten.

Saav nearly fainted. Even with the creature behaving innocently, he wasn't fond of it. He stared at us with eyes that begged for help, but Ravi taunted him instead.

"It's not going to kill you, Saav. Look at it."

"I'd rather not."

Shrugging, Ravi walked off.

"Well I like him. You should name it."

"I think we should leave it where we found it."

After peeling the creature off, Saav tossed it to the ground. But within seconds, it jumped back. Annoyed, he sighed. Alora smirked and followed behind Ravi. Luna and I did the same, and

Saav stubbornly stood in place before giving up.

"The least one of you could do is take it from me. I don't need some forest cat within biting distance of my throat."

He side-eyed the animal again, which responded with a coo. From that point forward, he didn't attempt to take it off, and he didn't complain about it. He just let it be. With him finally quiet, conversation ceased and everyone walked with their minds elsewhere. In fact, the group had been quiet for so long, the animal wrapped around Saav's neck had fallen asleep.

Periodically, Luna would look at the detector she carried.

She stopped.

"Ravi, this has not changed at all."

As Ravi looked down at his, Saav shot him a look.

"Well that's because we're going in the wrong direction. Isn't that right, Rav?"

"No, we just haven't gotten close enough yet."

"Or, we're going in the wrong direction."

Ravi stared at his brother, challenging him to a dual. They probably would have fought but, from somewhere deep in the forest, there came a loud cracking sound. It was louder than anything we'd heard so far, and immediately everyone froze.

"…what was that?"

On his shoulder, Saav's 'forest cat' woke up, cooing lightly. Fearfully, he shushed it. Alora's eyes scanned the forest and, without looking at us, she pointed in a direction we hadn't been traveling.

"Go that way."

No one refused. In that moment, everyone was afraid. Especially Saav. I found myself staring at Luna as she walked with her eyes straight ahead, unwavering. She'd glanced at me a few times without saying anything, but then she grew annoyed.

"What?"

"Nothing, really. Just thinking…"

"About?"

"The fact that I'm even here…Just making my way through a forest. On an alien planet. With a purple lady."

Alora eyed me, but she quickly went back to scanning the forest. Luna's eyebrows raised for a moment, and she glanced as if she were trying to see if I were serious.

"That's not too crazy. There are lots of purple people in the universe, and everyone is alien to someone."

"True…but I'm not used to that I guess."

"Well you may want to get used to it."

Up ahead, light flooded into the shaded forest. Through the trees, a clear view of the clouds peeked in. At the sight of the sky, everyone moved faster, but when we pulled ourselves from the trees, we stopped.

We'd come out on top of a wide, large peak, and the forest below looked exactly the same in every direction. It seemed to go on forever. A few squawks and gawks could be heard, but everything was mostly calm. More than anything, there were just large trees that blended into each other.

Instead of a dead drop, the ground curved gradually. It looked as though a landslide had suddenly disrupted part of the forest, and we were standing just at the top of it. The dirt had settled, but it was obvious the landslide had been recent. Near the bottom of it, trees still poked out awkwardly from a wave of soil.

Saav whistled.

"Looks like we're going to be searching all day..."

Ravi took a step forward and peeked down at the landslide.

"Getting down shouldn't be a problem. But the drop looks a little steep at the top."

Saav smirked as he joined his brother near the edge.

"Well you'd know about steep drops, wouldn't you?"

"Keep it up and I'll teach you about one."

He jerked his head at the landslide. Saav took a step back. Surprisingly, when he turned to us, his question wasn't used as a jab at Ravi.

"So are we going down or no? Pretty sure this is going to take us well away from where we started, and getting back up doesn't look like an option without the T23 so..."

Luna walked over.

"Yeah...I think we should."

Behind us, another large cracking sound echoed throughout the forest. This time, there was a spate of squawks and gawks that followed it. Everyone's head swiveled, and I tentatively took a step back. When the noise came again, it was closer. There was a pause as we waited for the cracking to come a third time, but it didn't.

Saav threw his hands up.

"Well, guess it's decided. I'll be taking the landslide down. But if anyone wants to stay and deal with, whatever that is, be my guest."

Alora nodded.

"We should split up. We'll cover more space that way."

Saav stopped.

"Split up? Here? I'm not going alone."

Alora walked to the tip of the ledge and looked over before turning back to us.

"I'll go alone. It'll be fine."

Luna nodded.

"Saav and Ravi can take northwest, Allen and I will take north, and Alora can take northeast."

I peeked over my shoulder.

"What about everything else?"

"…we're not searching anymore of that area."

Alora walked back toward the forest. There was a bush near the edge of it that was so large, she probably could have climbed into it. Its leaves were nearly the size of a twin-sized mattress. Reaching into the bush, she tore a few of them from the root and handed one to each of us.

"These should help with the ride down."

The leaf felt tough. Its underside had tiny, fine hairs running the length of it. They were all soft to the touch, and the feeling of them drew a stark contrast to the hard, waxy shell of the other side. As I studied mine, Saav plopped his on the edge of the landslide and sat down.

His new friend was still wrapped around his neck, so he pulled it off and tossed it to the ground. But the tiny creature only looked at him quizzically and jumped back to the original spot.

Ravi smirked.

"You're not getting rid of him so give it up."

"I didn't ask for-"

Before he could finish, Ravi raised a foot and pushed him over the edge. In a split second, Saav's body had disappeared. The sound of him swooping across the dirt was loud, but it quickly faded to nothing. When Ravi turned back to Alora and Luna, they gave him scolding looks.

"What? Not like he's afraid of heights."

Without waiting for a response, he placed his own on the ground and followed after his brother. Once he could no longer be heard, Alora went after him, followed by me and Luna.

The free fall was longer than expected. The thud against the top of the curve hurt, but as the wind rushed past and the adrenaline rose, a smile slowly crept across my face. With the universe at my fingertips and my mother, relatively, within grasp, I relaxed into a state of content. In that moment, I somehow felt as though I were truly where I needed to be.

Interlude II

From the Desk of Julie Winor

The hall was silent, at least to my ears. The voices of the officers and the sounds of their feet were inaudible. Even as the directors walked near me, lost in conversation, I was alone.

"Director?"

One of the other directors called after me, but my mind was too preoccupied to figure out which one. Lost in thought, I'd outpaced them. Stopping, I turned and stared. Their faces were a mix of concern and bewilderment. Periodically shielding me from their gaze, officers crossed our view of each other. But after each cross, my comrades looked just as concerned as before.

Ruid stepped forward.

"How are you feeling?"

"I'm fine."

"Are you sure? You've been a bit distant, and I know that..."

His voice trailed off. He wanted to avoid voicing how I'd disobeyed the laws of the academy. He also wanted to avoid mentioning how he'd crossed me, but it didn't matter. Even by not mentioning what we all knew, he mentioned all of it.

"...you just don't seem well."

"I'm fine. Don't worry."

Above our head, the academy's intercom clicked to life. No words had been spoken yet, but none had to be. It had been turned on even though the only people who could use it were standing in the hallway. After noticing the impossible, nearby officers halted. Their faces searched ours for answers, but we had none. So, perplexed, the academy itself slowed to a stop.

Without words, Ruid signaled for a few officers to follow him. Others were sent in different directions, silently ordered to scan the building. But the instructions were pointless. Whoever could access the intercom was likely able to access the other systems as well. In fact, a single chuckle confirmed such.

"Oh, directors. Your aims are most unnecessary. I can see you. All of you. Within my reach is every bit of your technology, your plans…your safety."

Low and heavy, the voice was taunting. Almost childlike, it still managed to cause a chill. More officers joined those searching the academy, but the voice left an air of powerlessness. Somehow, the person it belonged to managed to feel as though they were everywhere, yet nowhere in the building.

"First, I must warn you: you will not find me. For ages I've waited for this day. This single building holds so much of who I despise, that I could never run in unprepared. But, unfortunately, you are. Your beloved directors have led you all down a path that carries a price all must share and, though I am most apologetic, I am not merciful."

The hall was nearly empty now. Some officers had remained, but only enough to form a detail around me, Riv, and Numan. Signaling to the other directors, I headed for our meeting room. The entire walk, the voice over the intercom wrapped itself around me. It owned me.

"Director Winor, where are you going? I am so excited that we could finally meet. Do you remember me? Last you knew of me, your academy was stealing from my people, later leaving us for dead. But how could you remember? This is a business you've ran many, many times."

Attempting to give updates, Numan spoke between the words of the intercom.

"The intelligence unit are unable to gain control of the intercom. Would you like for them to shut off the entire system?"

"No."

Shutting off the system would mean shutting off our only line of contact. We needed it. Though the voice was haunting, I couldn't stop listening. I didn't want to.

"Director, I will not waste your time. I will simply mention that your academy was given the chance to save my people. More than the ones you took in. But you didn't. Instead, you took from us and then came home to pat yourselves on the back. Well our strength is not perishable. We have prevailed, and now you must suffer for your crime. But, remember, I am most unmerciful. I will bleed this academy of all that it has, and then I will dispose of you."

He paused.

"Director, you will be unable to protect your officers and, in fact, if you intend to protect those who have only just deployed, the time to leave is now…See you soon."

I stopped. With the intercom finally turned off, the academy was draped in utter silence, but the words remained. I searched Numan's face for answers he didn't have. Unsatisfied, I quickened my pace, nearly running. Behind me, he continued giving updates, but I wasn't listening, and he didn't seem to notice.

Ruid was already in the meeting room. A few officers stood around him explaining whatever they discovered in their search. They were so invested in their work, no one in the room acknowledged the other directors that had entered. But it didn't matter.

A storm brewed in my chest and threatened to spill into the room. With my breathing harsh, I tried to force a calm.

"Leave."

A single word, and the room came to a standstill. Surprised, the officers froze for a moment. But then they all did as they were told. Nodding to each director as they passed, they left us to mend whatever wound the academy had just endured. Riv and Numan went to take their seats, but Ruid remained standing, studying me. He knew me too well to sit. Taking a step forward, he attempted to calm me before anyone else knew he even needed to.

"Director…"

"What was that?"

"We haven't figured it out yet, but we have-"

"Go get them."

"We will, we just need ti-"

"GO GET HIM!"

The room fell silent. In so short a time, I revealed myself. But even with my thoughts thrown out onto the floor, I stood my ground.

"Go get them. Now."

He nodded.

"Yes, we will. Right now."

He moved toward the door, but I rushed out of the room before him. Back in the hall, officers had resumed their marches around the building, but now they moved faster. Their movements were more precise and their minds more focused. We were officially under attack.

"Director!"

Ruid called after me, but I ignored him. When he caught up, he blocked my path. My path was never blocked but, in the moment, it didn't matter. Lowering his voice, he leaned in close enough to keep our conversation between us.

"Where are you going?"

"You already know."

"Director…"

"I'm going."

"Tell me, when was the last time you acted in a mission?"

Without responding, I bolted around him. But again, he came to block my path. This time, we argued with nothing but our eyes, but the exchange was brief and, again, I went around him. When he came to block my path a third time, he used his words once more.

"Director, please. Not only are you the head of this academy, but you're ill. Surely, this isn't the best way to enter a battlefield."

"I'm fine and whether you like it or not, I'm going. You can either come along or prepare the exit gates yourself."

When I went around him, he didn't try to stop me again. Instead, he followed just a single step behind. My pace was brisk, but my mind moved faster. Each moment lasted longer, and each pulled Allen further and further away from me. I was guilty. Allen was in danger because of my own selfish decision, and now my foolishness felt as though it were about to outrun me.

Down the hall, Talo appeared. She had the familiar

features of an old friend, and a build that was much stronger than I'd been at her age. Upon her head was short, curly hair, and a small scar at the center of her hairline. It was easy to miss, but if you saw it once, it became something you always noticed. As soon as she came into view, I mentally answered the question she was destined to ask.

With a nod, she stopped us.

"Directors."

"Officer."

She paused.

"I would like to offer my contributions to the team that is about to embark…I'm sure I have the training to be of assistance."

Ruid's eyes burned into the side of my cheek. Staring into Talo's face, I mulled the idea. But, even before she'd asked, I knew the answer.

"No."

She opened her mouth to say something, but then she stopped. Internally, she crumbled.

"Yes, ma'am."

She then moved to the side and allowed us to pass. She attempted to grip me with her eyes, but I refused them. The decision had been made. But instead of following my example, Ruid stopped.

"Do not think that there is doubt surrounding your training. However, our team is full and there are two less seats given that two directors will be active in this mission."

She nodded. Just before walking off, Ruid returned the gesture. From there, our walk was uninterrupted. We didn't speak but, periodically, he would glance over. His interrogative gaze was one I'd felt many times, but I never gave in. No matter how many times he tried, I maintained a wall that couldn't be passed or seen over.

In the aircraft chamber, officers were completing checks on a few T24's. They were nearly replicas of a T23, with the only difference being their size, speed, and proportions. Slightly larger, they would get us to Prasola in half the time, with room for more people and equipment. The officers surrounding them continued their work, but one walked out of an aircraft just as we were about to enter.

"Mechanical checks are almost complete, and Tier 11 defense has been outfitted. Everything inside the aircraft is fully prepared so, unless there is more you would like the team to complete, we'll be able to leave in just a few moments."

As I entered, Ruid stood at the foot of the entrance, watching me. Granting him a final response, I met his gaze. In so short a moment, he pleaded. But there was little to negotiate, so I didn't. I simply turned and found my seat, leaving him at the foot of the aircraft, staring beggingly.

eleven

The shadows chased me. With adrenaline high and fear in control, every direction appeared the same. Up ahead, Luna rushed alone, unconcerned with whether I lived or died. Cutting in and out of view, it was almost as if she were purposely leaving me. Undoubtedly, she'd felt this pressure before. She was familiar with it. Her movements were precise and calculated. She never even glanced over her shoulder, so it was obvious she didn't need any help, and especially not mine.

Like magic, she disappeared. I was alone. The shadows

grew larger and panic consumed me. The only sounds to be heard were those I made. Breathing heavy, I ran faster than I'd done in the training room. This time, the threat of death was real. It even polluted the air itself, thickening it into something nearly unbreathable.

But after thirty seconds of panic, Luna reappeared. Preoccupied, she stood in a clearing, studying something. She was still as a statue and went unfazed by my abrupt appearance. Rounding a tree, I almost ran into her. My breath caught and my muscles tightened. Without catching a good glimpse of her, I prepared to run in another direction, but then she spoke, bringing the world to a calm.

"You'll have to move faster."

I braced against a tree.

"Well if you keep disappearing we're gonna get separated for good."

She eyed me. Without saying anything, she decided my concerns weren't even worth her attention. She just went back to what she was doing. Two of her fingers were covered in a red powder. Rubbing them furiously, she was seemingly moments away from starting a fire in her palms. But then she dropped her hands and walked off.

"There's not enough here."

When she stepped away, a hole was revealed near her feet. Just below the surface, dirt turned into the powder she'd been rubbing. I kneeled to study it myself, but then remembered how'd I'd been left behind before. Abandoning my own lab work, I rushed to catch up.

With her eyes glued to the detector, she spoke without turning to me.

"Have you really never left your home?"

"Yeah, never. Is it really that unbelievable?"

"No, most people never leave their home. But you're the son of Director Winor so I just expected...more."

"Sorry to disappoint I guess."

She stopped.

"It was not meant to be hurtful, I am sorry."

I waved it off, so she responded with a nod and resumed

her trek.

"Just a warning: I understand this is new for you, but there is not enough time to study everything you see. Every minute brings us closer to failure so…just try to move faster."

"I'll try but I don't think I can help it. It's not something I get to see every day. Besides, I'll probably wake up soon anyway."

She side-eyed me.

"Do you still believe you are being deceived even when the truth is fully revealed?"

I shrugged.

"A shrug is not an answer. Tell me, what do you believe you are seeing? Dream or reality?"

"Maybe a bit of both. Only time will tell."

Her brows scrunched, but she let it go. When seconds passed in silence, I changed the subject.

"Mind if I ask questions of my own? It's only fair."

"I'm listening."

"Since you already know where I'm from, I wanted to know some stuff about you. Like where you're from and what your home is like. Is it like this?"

"Are you asking if I lived in a forest?"

Her voice rose, and her accent became thick on the word 'forest.'

"No, I'm asking if you're from another planet I haven't been to."

"Yes, I am from somewhere far from what you are used to. But your questioning is fruitless because I do not remember much of it."

She stopped and tapped the detector a few times. With nothing to do, I continued.

"So how long have you been at the academy then?"

"Nine years…no more questions."

"One more?"

"Fine."

"Why are we so secluded? We just blasted off a planet and through outer space, yet we don't seem to have any friends."

"The academy does not exist to make friends. We exist to help others avoid extinction."

She stuck out her hand, pointing to a large bug. Its shell was a dark, metallic green, and it carried a pincher that took up most of its head. If it had been the size of regular bugs, another step would've crushed it. But no. It was the size of my foot.

Stepping around it, Luna continued.

"...If we cannot, we bring some of the people to the academy. We all learn from each other, and each time we get better at protecting others."

"If you only bring some people, what happens to everyone else?"

"They die."

She said it casually. In fact, she didn't even bother to look away from the detector in her hands. It was disturbing and, for a second, we walked in silence. But it wasn't long before the silence was broken by her thumping me in the chest.

Just ahead was a large tree. Even as it lay on its side, it was nearly three times my height. Covered in the same powder as before, it was mostly red. Luna swiped her hand across it, studying the powder.

"We are getting closer."

She grabbed hold of the tree. Limbs out like a spider, she effortlessly scaled it and pulled herself over before I'd even left the ground. When I made my own attempt, I struggled. The powder made the climb slippery and, at one point, my foot failed to catch. Atop the tree, Luna chuckled and waited patiently. Once I was close enough, she graciously grabbed my hand and helped me over.

Making use of the view, she scanned the forest but, other than trees, there wasn't much to see. Oddly, there wasn't much to be heard either. Everything was quiet, nearly silent.

"Doesn't it freak you out how quiet it is? There's gotta be something else here other than us."

"There is a lot to be heard…Can't you hear it?"

"Nope. Nothing."

"Well when things get quieter, it means there is something trying to kill you."

She started her climb down the other side, moving as if her comment were not unsettling. Not wanting to be left standing in the open, I followed her to the ground. Fortunately, the climb down was a lot easier than the climb up. In fact, it was more of a slide down, slightly close to a fall.

Back on the ground, I jogged a few steps to catch up with Luna. But just as I did, there came a loud cracking sound. It was exactly like what had been heard at the top of the landslide, and it was much closer than any of the previous noises.

Luna's eyes scanned every spot in sight.

"Keep moving, but do not run. Just keep moving."

Repeatedly, the sound replayed in my head. Fear convinced me something would jump out at any second, but nothing did. Just as before, the forest was quiet. But with the silence growing louder and louder, I looked for ways to mentally occupy myself.

My mind wandered to the academy, back to Julie. She was so different from anything that could have been expected. In fact, she was better. But there was so much to her that was seemingly locked in a vault. The more I mulled it, the more I realized that the rest of the academy was that way too. They were all formal and robotically uniform. Without question, every person I'd met did exactly as they were told. It was odd considering how much of the world, or space, was available to them. Surely, the academy wasn't for everybody.

"Stop."

A few steps ahead, Luna was frozen in place. Yet, we were still alone. Even as I squinted, nothing revealed itself. With the tension growing, the feeling of uneasiness caused my palms to sweat.

"Luna..."

"Shh!"

Something moved in my peripheral. But when I turned, it was gone. Left in its place was a nothingness scarier than the thought of whatever had been there. The forest grew so quiet, I could almost hear our heartbeats. Seconds passed and, still, we didn't move. Again, something moved in the distance. But, unlike before, I caught sight of it just as it passed out of view.

It had the form of a large cat. Dark grey, it nearly blended with the distant forest. Hopping from tree to tree, it moved quickly. Though it was too far to be seen clearly, it had obviously turned to look at us. Its eyes were piercing, even at a distance. Frozen in shock, I waited for Luna to tell me what to do, but she didn't. Instead, she moved toward it.

Afraid, it rushed away.

"Turn around."

Her tone warned of death. Fearfully, I turned, but there was nothing there. The tension heightened.

"What am I looking for?"

"Shh!"

Luna had turned around too. The force of her voice told me so. At the sound of her turning back, I did the same. My breath caught in my throat and time slowed. Instead of being far off, the creature that had watched us from afar was now closer. It was close enough to where I could hop a few times and be within arm's length. Even worse, it could have probably jumped once to cover the same distance.

It was the size of a cheetah. Most of its hair lay smooth, but there was a short, spikey mane that circled its head and ran down its back. The spikiness relaxed near its hind legs and raised

once more down the length of its tail. It stared with large, black

eyes and, every couple of seconds, its nose twitched. A low

humming sound came from its mouth, but it never opened to

reveal any teeth.

After a moment, it tried to slowly step away. But the

movement was odd given the fact it would likely have the upper-

hand anyhow. Fortunately for us, it didn't seem to realize it.

When Luna signaled for it to stop, it did. Its stare was intense.

With eyes that looked permanently defensive, it willed us to make

the first move. But neither of us did and, instead, Luna knelt. Both

the creature and I watched as she got close to the ground. After

she signaled for me to do the same, I fearfully complied.

The creature stepped closer. The steps of the animal were

quiet. Even as it stepped across leaves and rocks, there was little

sound to be heard. Given the distance it crossed the first time, its

quietness was impressive, yet horrifying.

Knees to the dirt, we both just waited. Above us,

something rushed past. Leaves from the sky decorated the ground.

A glance revealed a few large silhouettes, dashing from tree to tree. Luna hadn't noticed. Looking into the eyes of the strange creature, she waved for me to do the same.

"Allen, do not look away. It is a distraction."

As more leaves fell, I came to a realization.

"But what if he's the distraction?"

A loud, breathy hiss erupted from the trees behind us. A moment after, we were knocked over. Attacked by a blur, I fought with something I couldn't see. But with a single swing, Luna forced it away. Fearfully, I jumped to my feet.

There was now a second creature standing next to the first. It was nearly identical, but its hair was a purple so dark, it was almost black. It stared at us just as innocently as the first but, after a moment, it stopped pretending. The trick had been revealed. Opening its mouth, it let out another hiss, and the first creature followed suit.

The hissing echoed throughout the forest. One by one, more of the animals revealed themselves. They encircled us, appearing from all directions. Within moments, there were at least twenty of them, and all were either grey or dark purple.

Unexpectedly, Luna hissed back. As loud as she could, she hissed and took a step forward. The creatures in front responded by taking a step back, but the others standing around moved in on us. Luna started hissing at them, turning in circles to ensure she eyed each one.

She snatched up a branch, holding it out defensively. Swinging and hissing, she jumped toward the creatures. They all responded by stepping back. Then, she turned to the one that had approached us and, in a voice that was demanding and intimidating enough to even shake me up, she spoke.

"BOW!"

None of them moved. I half expected the group to make animal laughter before mauling us to death, but they didn't. Instead, after a moment of thought, the creature bowed. With its eyes still watching us, it placed its nose to the dirt. Slowly, the others did the same.

She walked toward the one closest to us. A few of the heads raised, but then they fell back to the ground. Once she was close enough, the creature lifted its head and they both just stared at each other. Hesitantly, she rubbed the underside of the creature's mouth. To my surprise, it didn't snap it from her wrist.

There came yet another cracking sound. The creatures standing around all became tense, and each changed their stance to one that was combative. Their hissing started up again, but none was directed at me or Luna. When the sound came again, the creatures were brought to a silence.

Luna turned to me, fear in her eyes.

"We must move. Now."

She walked away from the circle and, as she moved, the creatures followed. Whatever direction she went, they maintained a barrier around her.

"Put on your mask, Allen."

Obediently, I detached the mask from my hip. Behind me, there was another cracking sound, followed by a yelp, and a glance revealed one of the creatures had disappeared. Specks of blood decorated a nearby tree but, other than that, there was nothing.

Luna picked up the pace. Leaping over stuff and doing our

best to follow a path that wasn't there, we ran. The entire time, the sound of yelps surrounded us as more and more of our new protectors disappeared. They became more frantic, and now only a few were left.

Soon, the forest thinned. Bursting out of the woods and into a clearing, we found ourselves near a large river. A rapid made it impossible to swim across. Not far off, was a waterfall. I stared at Luna in horror and, with mere seconds to decide, I grappled with our options. None were enticing. For a moment, Luna and I just stared at each other. But then she grabbed my arm and pulled me toward the fall. Near the edge, we peered over. The height was both unclear and unpromising. Encouragingly, what could be seen looked like the perfect height to only shatter a few bones. But everything below it was clouded in mist.

Behind us, the last of the creatures appeared at the edge of the forest. Limping, he moved forward a few steps. As if he were waiting for direction, he stopped and stared at us. He was both tired and worn. He dropped to the ground, but quickly brought himself back up.

Again, the dreadful cracking noise erupted from the trees, but our friend had given up. Exhausted and alone, he didn't even bother to turn around. He just stared at us.

A beast emerged from the forest. Dark grey, its head looked as if it were made of nothing but bone. In fact, so did the rest of it. There were scratches and scars going across it, but the damage was purely cosmetic. It had six legs, and two of them were smaller than the rest. As it landed on four of them, the two smallest ones never came close to the touching ground. Wherever there wasn't a tough shell, there was muscle, and it ripped in ways that made silent promises. As if he were trying to introduce himself, he opened his mouth to reveal teeth that could probably slice metal.

It launched itself toward our last protector, and a yelp echoed throughout the clearing. Within seconds, the creature was slung away, and its body landed in the water with a splash. The beast then turned its eyes on us, but Luna gave it no time to make a decision.

Without warning, she leapt, dragging me along for the

ride.

twelve

The water was warm. All the way down, it provided a glove that felt as though it were both there and not there. Breathing wasn't an option, just as adjusting our fate wasn't. The fall felt as though it lasted a full minute. My muscles tensed, and my mind braced for the impact. When it finally came, the light of the world was consumed by darkness, and we were forced into a lifeless void.

The force of the water was relentless. Fighting against it proved pointless, and giving in provided an end that promised nothing. Rapid bubbles made a swim impossible. Defenseless, tired, and confused, I remained at the mercy of the world. But soon the darkness rescinded, forcing me from the fall. Head above the water, I inhaled.

It hurt to breath. I wasn't injured, but I was sore. Battered, I'd been stretched to my limit. There was a slight ache in my wrist, and my stomach was full of an air that somehow bounced and danced around. Coughing, I attempted to clear both my throat and my head.

Below the surface, a shadow approached, gracefully ascending from the depths of the pool. My mind was clouded, so even as the creature drew nearer, I remained in place. But when something finally materialized next to me, I exhaled a sigh of relief. It was Luna.

She rolled her mask to her forehead.

"Are you okay?"

"Yeah, you?"

She nodded.

"I'm fine."

She averted her eyes and scanned for the edge of the pool. The grounds around it were uneven, and a large slope of dirt and torn trees led from the height of the waterfall to everything below it. The pool itself was large, forming a lake. Further away, the tops of trees cut through its surface. It looked as though part of the forest had just been forced underwater. They were just as green and lively as any of the other trees we passed, but their coverage was patchy. In some areas, they were abundant. But in others, there were none.

I turned to Luna, unsure of what to say, but she was no longer there. Instead, she had already swam halfway to the edge of the pool. As I followed, my ribcage ached. When the bank of the lake finally provided relief, I found myself crawling across it rather than walking. Luna sat away from the water, and I tiredly dropped myself next to her. With my cheek to the dirt, I closed my eyes and rested for a moment.

"We cannot sleep here. We must keep moving."

When she stood to leave, I rushed to move, but my head spun and my stomach followed. Defeated, I dropped back to the ground.

"Wait, wait. Just a few minutes."

Mouth partially blocked by dirt, my words were muddy. Luna stopped and stared as if she were trying to decide if she wanted to leave me. But then she just brushed a few strands of hair from her face and came back over to take a seat.

"I'm not sure how long it'll take us to get back up there."

"I'm not sure I want to."

"Why? Surely, you have faced worse."

I sat up, still sore.

"No…not really."

"The son of Winor is a man who has faced little challenges?"

"I've had challenges, but they were different. Nothing like anything here."

"Prasola itself is not a challenge. Finding Prasolin for the director is."

Her eyes dropped for a moment.

"I do not think I have ever wanted something so badly."

My eyebrows raised.

"Why is it even that important to you?"

"Is it not important to you?"

"I mean, I guess but…I don't know."

"Allen, make up your mind."

She stared intensely, forcing an answer.

"Yes…it's important to me."

"Okay, why?"

"She's my mother."

"But you have only just met her."

I shrugged.

"Maybe that doesn't matter."

"Why not?"

I paused.

"I don't know. I've never had that before, so I guess I want to protect her now because of it."

"Even if you do not fully believe you are here?"

I nodded. When Luna finally spoke again, she kept her eyes focused on the trees on the other side of the lake.

"Well in my case, she listened even when I didn't know all of the things I should say. It was an invaluable gift, and now I want to give her something in return."

She stood up and brushed herself off.

"Time to move."

Again, thick trees and large leaves covered our path but, unlike before, everything was brighter. The trees were fewer, and more sunlight made it to the ground. The path was flatter, and the sound of small animals echoed as they moved above us from branch to branch.

As we walked, Luna stared at the detector in her hand. Periodically, she would suddenly point and change directions, and I'd follow. The process worked. But every view of the forest looked the same, and I grew bored. I was tired. With the forest providing a comfortable mix of light and shade, my mind was cloudy. I needed sleep.

Luna stopped. We stood near the center of an odd clearing, and the surrounding trees formed a nearly perfect circle. The area was large and looked as though it'd been cleared on purpose. Across the inward-facing side of each tree, was a light red stain. Its spread was uneven, and it looked as though it'd been sloppily spray-painted on. A lot of the branches were bare, and they drew a stark contrast to everything around them.

It was Prasolin. The detector in Luna's hand beeped incessantly. Excitedly, Luna turned a few circles before looking up. Her eyes traced over the trees, and she paused as if she were intrigued. Approaching one of them, she stared at it a moment before sliding her hand across. The Prasolin rubbed off into her palm but, almost immediately, it evaporated to nothing.

When she turned, her expression was one of disappointment.

"This is not enough, but maybe more is close by."

"Who do you think made the circle?"

She shrugged.

"The intelligence unit has not had enough time to study the life on this planet."

She walked away, but I stayed behind. Walking over to the same tree that she had brushed her hand across, I brought my face close to the Prasolin. The smell of it was odd, but it wasn't

repugnant. Curiously, I swiped a finger across it and brought it

close to my nose.

I inhaled too much. My nose tingled and my eyes watered.

The tingling traveled down my throat and into my chest, before

briefly spreading across my limbs. It was cough inducing. The

world became blurry, and everything slid around. But it didn't last

long. After coughing a few times more, the sensation disappeared,

and I was only left with the odd smell of the Prasolin.

Rushing after Luna, I feared she'd gotten too far. But when

I caught up, it was as if I'd been there the whole time. She still

carried the detector, studying it closely. Unaware of my absence,

she was in the middle of talking about something.

"Without it, we will all suffer...do you agree?"

She turned, waiting for a response, but I had none. We

just looked at each other briefly before I idiotically nodded.

"Uh huh."

"...are you okay?"

"Yeahhh uh...whydoyouask?"

I was out of breath. Luna studied me, but then gave up and went back to the detector. Momentarily, my eyes would water, and everything would become blurry again. But then, it would all clear up. I squinted to see better but, each time, it only made things worse. At one point, while I was preoccupied with trying to see clearly, I bumped into Luna. Crashing any harder would have knocked her over.

She was startled, but her face turned to one of concern.

"Are you sure you are okay?"

"Yeah…"

I shook my head with a confidence I didn't feel.

"I just, sniffed a bit of the Prasolin and…it just has me feeling a little weird."

Leaning in to get a better look at my eyes, she got so close I could feel her breath brushing against my cheek. When she didn't see whatever she was looking for, she nodded.

"It is foreign, so your body may need a moment to adjust."

She went back to walking and studying the detector. Again, the world became blurry. I took a moment to rest against a tree, but pulled myself together before Luna could turn around. I'd only rested a moment, yet she was now a lot farther away than expected. My vision became useless. Blurry and bright, every part of the forest became one. When I blinked a few times to clear it, Luna was nowhere in sight.

The sounds of the forest dwindled to nothing. I was alone. My breath quickened, and my palms sweated. Suddenly more tired than before, I braced against my knees to catch my breath, but it didn't help.

"LUNA!"

My voice echoed throughout the forest. As the seconds ticked by, I felt hotter. No response came, so I tried again.

"LUNA!"

I braced against my knees again, but quickly brought myself back up.

"Allen? Allen?"

From somewhere far away, a voice called out to me, but it wasn't Luna. It was Julie. After a pause, she called again, this time raising her voice a bit.

"Allen!"

"Yes…Julie? Where are you? I don't. See you."

There came a deep breath before she spoke again.

"I am close by, I-I'm on my way. Like I promised. Are you okay?"

With my head still spinning, I turned in circles in search of either Luna or Julie. I stumbled, but quickly got back up.

"Allen? Are you okay?"

"Yes…I just need to find…Luna."

Heavy breathing interrupted my words. Julie attempted to ask more questions, but her voice got lower and lower until it was unclear whether or not I'd even really spoken to her. While I tried to convince myself I'd be alright, something moved in my peripheral. A tiny creature stood near a tree that wasn't too far off, staring. It was nearly a replica of the 'forest cat' that had attached itself to Saav. The only difference was the fact that this one was a deep, dark red.

For a moment, it was still. But then it bared its teeth and let out a low, defensive growl. Afraid, I froze and, again, the world slid. A rub of the eyes cleared it, but now the creature was gone. But standing a little farther away was a person. His stare created an unease that was arresting, and he stood in silence. Too far to see clearly, he was almost nothing but a silhouette. He was dressed in a combat suit, and stood with his legs apart and his arms at his sides. His face was covered in a mask, and his fists were balled. His suit resembled my own but, instead of the deep black I'd grown used to, it was dark gray.

There came the sound of a growl. When I turned, I was met with the face of the red creature as it leapt from a branch above me. Roughly tossing it against a tree, I searched for a weapon, and picked up a fallen branch just as the creature took another leap. Just before it reached my face, I swung, and it was once again thrown to the ground. It yelped. I stumbled backward and fell, causing me to feel wobblier than before.

Standing to my feet, I looked around for the guy who had been watching me, but he was gone. I panicked. Next to the creature I'd knocked down, were two others and, quietly, they analyzed their friend. As it lie motionless, they nudged it with their noses.

They turned to me. Angrily, they bared their teeth, and I dashed in the first direction my feet led me. The bushes were more abundant than I remembered, and they grew thicker the farther I went. Every few seconds, I'd hear a growl. With every glance over my shoulder, I caught a glimpse of the tiny creatures, and more appeared with every second that passed.

I tripped over something and landed face first. When I raised my head, I was once again in the clearing that Luna and I had walked away from. Standing to my feet, I attempted to clear my head again, but the sound of growling surrounded me. Everywhere, bushes shook erratically.

I backed into the center of the clearing, turning circles. The forest was alive. Every bush shook, and growls grew more threatening. There was a moment of calm, but then the bushes burst with the growling, red creatures.

They circled me. When I locked eyes with one, he lunged, and the rest followed suit. It felt as though I was wrestling a pack of dogs. Every time I tossed one away, another took his place. My head spun, my eyes watered, and the ground slid. More rushed from the forest, and I found myself nearly flat on the ground. With my senses impaired, the fight left me, and I breathed hard as I willed it all to end.

"ALLEN!"

The wrestle of the creatures disappeared. Instead, they were replaced by Luna. She kneeled over me with eyes full of fear. Across one cheek, she sported a large scratch. I looked around for all that had attacked me, but nothing was there. There was only Luna.

She got up and walked over to one of the trees. She studied the Prasolin it was covered in, but she made sure to keep her face away from it. After walking back over, she kneeled again and examined my face once more.

"It is a hallucinogen."

She gently touched my arm as I stood, but I moved it away.

"How do you feel?"

I gently rubbed my fingers on the sides of my head, and pressed against my temples. To my dismay, the movement revealed I'd lost the earpiece Julie gave me.

"Slight headache…Did you pass a guy at any point? I saw someone watching me, but he disappeared."

"No, no one."

The detector beeped loudly. Luna glanced at it before looking over my shoulder. Saying nothing, she cut between the trees, away from the path we'd taken before. Fearful of another episode, I jumped to follow behind her.

There was another clearing hidden behind some bushes and a few trees. It wasn't as large as the last one, but it sat at the mouth of a cave and, as Luna walked toward it, I froze.

"It's a cave."

"It has Prasolin, and probably much more than what we found back there."

She looked at the detector again. The cave's entrance was covered in a thin film of Prasolin, and her eyes briefly traced across it all. There was a low, echoing moan coming from it, but Luna didn't seem to care. She paused, took one last glance at me, and walked inside.

For a moment, I remained where I was, but then something scurried in the bushes, reminding me of my episode. With anxiety high, I dragged across the clearing and into the cave. Though I eyed the Prasolin, I didn't stop and, within moments, most of the sunlight was gone. Once again, I was at the mercy of a world I couldn't see.

Interlude III

From the Desk of Julie Winor

I raised my voice again.

"Allen!"

No response came, leaving me to stare at the communicator in my hands. According to the signal strength, I'd lost connection. My hands began to tremble, but I took a deep breath and fixed my posture. The T24 was silent. Ruid hadn't turned to me since he sat down, and he never bothered to say anything. When I eyed him, he ignored me. The officers at the front quietly manned the controls, tapping across random things as we went. Outside of the aircraft was Andies Two. Even from far way, the swirl of its large eye was unsettling. It moved across the planet as if it were attempting to consume the light below it, but it never succeeded. Instead, a glow peeked through the cracks of its cloudy shield, and its inner self was revealed.

"A1, this is T24-A111, in a few minutes we will move into HyperG, please confirm."

Our pilot called back to the academy, requesting the final authorization. There was a short pause before it finally came.

"T24-A111, you are cleared for departure."

I breathed deeply. Usually, the speed increase made me nauseous. Closing my eyes, I tried to preoccupy myself with something other than the thought of Allen being killed, but another glance at Ruid brought a memory that was only marginally better than what it was supposed to replace.

I'd been nineteen years old. On my way to the grand arena, I walked amongst the other officers. Most of them walked alongside the new family they'd made at the academy, but I walked alone. I'd grown up here but, even in all those years, I built few bonds with the people around me. Other than my parents and Anais, officers avoided me.

I kept my eyes focused ahead, but every so often they'd wander into the faces of the people I passed. Most would look away, but some would scowl until I looked away first. It was an experience that had become just as common as the act of breathing. It was never unexpected or startling, and I did my best to ignore it.

It was against the rules of the academy for officers to bear children, yet I was born to two academy officers. My birth was something everyone was aware of, but no one ever faced. They just treated my family as though we carried a plague that would consume them if they even thought about extending a hand of friendship. But I'd endured the scowls of officers so many times, I stopped being hurt by them.

I moved as if I were perfectly unaware of those nearest me. When I made it to the arena, I took my seat and waited. Back then, there were fewer officers. Though there were enough to nearly fill the arena, many seats went unclaimed and, unsurprisingly, most surrounded me.

The voices of the other officers obnoxiously broke into my secluded world, but I ignored them. To my ears, the sounds just blurred together and became a single ball of noise. Even in a room of so many people, I was alone. The curse of my birth had called for it.

Once everyone was seated, the lights were dimmed, and every voice fell to a silence. The stage remained lit, lighting a path as the director came out. There was only a single director, Sagenti Ilo. She reigned in a manner that could incite terror, and her tone was usually one of disdain. In fact, she was possibly the reason so much warmth had been sucked from the academy. In the days of my parents, officers were more carefree, patient, and imperfect. But Ilo changed that. With her leadership, she taught the academy to fear its directors. Whether it be through the assigning of missions that officers never returned from, or the outright banishing of personnel.

Her briefing was taut, and her voice was cloaked in its usual style of disinterest. Language separated us, and I nearly fell asleep listening to her. The academy was filled with so many languages, communication was a never-ending endeavor. But even my thirst for new skills couldn't entice me to listen. With her speech rough, almost hateful, she wasn't someone I wanted to learn from and, given the chance, I'd have willingly left her and the academy behind. But, with my parents dedicated to Avenur, I was stuck.

I knew she spoke of a planet with an infant society on the verge of self-inflicted extinction. But that was typical, and I failed to understand any of the details she gave. When she finally stopped talking and stepped away, I waited for YARA to make her choice. When she did, time slowed.

She'd chosen me.

I was never expected to take a mission. There were rumors that any I took would be sabotaged, and my family believed it. In every way they could, they ensured I learned few skills that would get me chosen. Living under a veil of fear, I was forbidden. But

YARA was not obedient.

Making my way to the stage, I walked through a sea of silent bodies and watchful eyes. Sagenti waited near the podium, her glare reducing me to nothing. When I crossed the stage, I expected more officers to join, but that didn't happen.

Instead, I was presented to the room in the director's native language. She then turned and used words I couldn't understand, but I knew what she wanted. With a slender finger, she ordered me to embark. Alone. Fear suffocated me. Again, she gestured for me to leave, so I did. Typically, the arena stands and applauds officers that are embarking on a mission but, unsurprisingly, no one applauded me.

My parents were waiting behind the stage. Overwhelmed and scared, I grew angry.

"Ik na tosas yu."

'They didn't stand.'

Unlike myself and my father, my mother was an optimist.

'You alone were deemed better than everyone else. They were shocked.'

I shook my head.

'No one applauds the illegal born.'

Guiltily, my parents eyed each other. With saddened expressions, neither of them said anything. When we made it to the aircraft chamber, Anais was waiting for me near a platform entrance. The sight of him always made me smile. He was an odd boy with a peculiar personality, but he was nice, and genuinely so. Much like my parents.

His eyes studied me. Though he said nothing, he read my thoughts with little effort. Silently, he waited while my parents hugged me and gave well wishes. Once the farewells were exchanged, he accompanied me to a T23 and, out of earshot of my parents, he tried to cheer me up.

'You're brave for this.'

'YARA gives no choices.'

'And YARA makes no mistakes.'

Inside the aircraft, I strapped myself down. The voice system spoke, but I ignored it. Instead, I focused on a map that had appeared across the windshield. It was covered in stars and constellations, and it zoomed until a single planet was focused in the middle of it. The planet was mostly water. Its surface was mostly even, and everything looked calm and stable. I sighed in relief.

While I stared, Anais checked the various parts of the aircraft for me, but I interrupted him.

What am I supposed to do once I get there?

He'd been setting specifications on the aircraft's internal system, but he finished up as he answered my question.

Stop them from killing each other.

With that, he leaned over, kissed my forehead, and walked away. I watched him exit from the back of the aircraft before shutting the door. As I hovered, I turned and looked out the back window. Anais stood at the entrance of the platform. For a second, we both watched each other. A part of me felt as though I were leaving him forever.

The aircraft's internal system had already started preparing my language skills, and it kept repeating itself as it waited for me to respond.

"Thann ek yu dit mlac, 'Hello.'"

I turned away from Anais. Attempting to focus, I repeated the greeting. My pronunciation was off, but the system continued anyway.

"Bon-jour."

"Bunjoo."

"Nǐ hǎo."

Before diving over the edge of the platform, I turned once more. Anais was still there, and he looked even sadder than he had mere seconds before. His eyes had watered slightly, but he didn't cry. He just silently watched me.

Realizing I daydreamed too deeply, I suddenly found myself back in the aircraft, rushing to Prasola. Everything was just as it was before. The only difference was that we were in HyperG, and the light of distant stars now stretched in all directions. Next to me, Ruid sat with his eyes forward, ignoring me.

He was no longer Anais. At least not on the outside. He'd discarded that shell a long time ago, and in its place was someone who'd been hardened. Probably more so than the rest of us.

Glimpses of his old self sometimes slipped out, but as I stared at the side of his face and studied the look in his eyes, I realized Anais wasn't there. In fact, he hadn't been for longer than I could even measure.

With a need to focus, I turned away. Instead, my attention was brought back to the mission at hand. Back to Allen. Soon, my strength would be tested. The consequences of failure were unbearable, so I'd succeed. Though our enemies had yet to reveal themselves, I'd have to. If I didn't, I'd once again lose Allen, and this time it would be permanent. Again, it would be my fault. So with my mind back in the place it'd been before I daydreamed, my thoughts were once again brought back to Allen. Back to my oldest born.

thirteen

The cave was dark and the air was cold. The light of day slowly dwindled away behind us, while the path in front seemed to go on forever. The smell was a mix of soil and chemicals. The farther we went, the more uneasy I became but, unsurprisingly, Luna was fine. We'd walked so far, the entrance had become a dot in the distance, yet she hadn't turned around once.

The uneven ground provided a path that was unpredictable. It sloped downward, gradually leading us deeper. For minutes, it threatened to give way, before finally becoming hard and jagged. With it, the air became colder. A peek over the shoulder revealed the cave's entrance was now not only a mere dot, but also quite a bit higher than we were.

The detector beeped every few seconds. It quickly became the only sound we heard, other than our own breathing.

"We don't know how far this even goes. How far are you willing to walk?"

"As far as it takes to discover the Prasolin..."

Luna stopped and turned to me.

"The director needs it."

Her face was half hidden, and the only thing clearly visible were her eyes. Everything else was covered by the darkness, her black combat suit, or both. As she continued ahead, she picked up the pace and, soon, I was following with nothing to guide me but the sound of her feet and the faint light of the detector. It felt as though we were the only things in existence.

"I'm pretty sure we're going to get lost in here..."

"We won't."

"So how far away is the entrance?"

She stopped again, causing me to nearly crash into her. Even in the dark, I could feel her searching for the distant dot of light. As expected, she couldn't find it. We'd gone too far.

"I do not know, but we will be okay. There is only one way out."

As she resumed her march, she peered down at the detector.

"We are getting close enough anyway."

The walls of the cave widened. More space was made for all of its unknowns, and its echoes grew louder. The ground became less jagged, and switched to a soft, moist clay that became wetter with every step.

A small glint could be seen every so often. It happened even as there was little light to cause it. Initially, they were faint, nearly undetectable. But then, the amount and luminosity grew. Luna was so focused on the detector, she didn't even notice, but curiosity got the best of me, and I slowed my pace.

I crossed over to where the wall should have been. Made of clay, it was porous. Its surface was cold to the touch and weathered looking. Markings covered it in a way that appeared

purposeful. They were hand-written. As I got closer, they glinted

more rapidly and part of me wanted to stop for fear of what

curiosity would reveal.

Luna hadn't stopped. Only marked by the faint glow of the

detector, she was now just a spot in the distance. My mouth

opened to call out to her, but I stopped. Yelling down a dark,

empty tunnel wasn't something I wanted to do so, instead, I just

rushed to catch up.

I kept my hand near the wall. Strangely, each of the

markings glinted when my fingers passed over. Character after

character, line by line. At one point, I became entranced by their

glint, and attempted to trace one of them. It was cold and

unexpectedly hard, like marble.

I walked away, but the glinting didn't stop when my hand

was removed. In fact, it did the opposite. It glinted more, and it

did so faster. Beautiful and alluring, the markings sparkled in a

multitude of colors.

A few at a time, they all sparkled and twinkled, and their

light began to spread. It started down the cave's path and ran until it caught up with Luna and passed her completely. When she realized what was happening, she stopped. She looked confused but didn't say anything. Her eyes just scanned the markings around her, and she finally turned to me just as I neared her.

"What did you do?"

"I just touched it…"

She walked over to the wall and touched some of the markings herself, but nothing changed. They all just continued to sparkle.

"What does it say?"

"I do not know."

She looked at me strangely before turning back. Her eyes traveled faster than her hands and, when they stopped, I followed her line of sight and saw she was staring to the end of the tunnel. Given the light of the markings, we could see it wasn't that far off. I followed her toward it. The whole time we walked, the markings continued to glint.

Near the end of the tunnel, the sound of music bounced

against the walls. It was so quiet, we could have imagined it. Echoing from a place that couldn't be seen, it was soothing. There were the sound of flutes and a light bell, but none of it was distinct. Somehow, the noises managed to clash against each other while still forming a harmonious whole.

The tunnel opened into a large room. The chemical smell was replaced with something lighter and, strangely, it was airy for a space stuffed beneath the ground. The ceiling was much higher than the tunnel, and lots of large, uneven columns stretched toward it. At the very center, it became pocketed. It looked as if the throw of a stone could bring the whole thing crashing down.

The lower third of the wall was round and smooth, and the markings that had led us there ran across both sides and converged on the opposite end. At this point, they ran vertically before coming to more markings that formed a circle near the ceiling. In the center of the circle was a single character, and it was much larger than the rest of them.

A few of the columns were labeled with the odd symbols, and they too glinted as we walked past. Other than the markings, they were also infused with shards of gold, and near the top of each was a ring of metals that glowed from deep within.

"Who do you think built this?"

Luna and I had split up to explore opposite ends of the room. My voice echoed as I spoke, and it made me feel as though I were talking much louder than I was. When Luna responded, her voice was even louder.

"A group of people that are likely dead."

"Why dead?"

"Because it seems important. They would have killed us already if they were around."

"Comforting...what do you think they used it for?"

"I do not know, maybe a temple."

As we continued exploring the room, I realized parts of it were splattered in Prasolin. The tint of it was light, and it spread in a way that lead me to believe something, or somethings, had exploded there. I kneeled to get a closer look but, with my earlier episode fresh in my mind, I kept a safe distance.

"The entire thing is covered in this stuff..."

"I know, but it may not be enough."

We crossed the room toward each other, and stopped when we met in the middle. We were just in front of the circle with the large symbol in the center of it, and its light rained upon us in a way that looked as though we stood in the faint light of a foggy window.

We started crossing toward it, but our feet struck something. It was a pile of gunk covered in a thick layer of dust and Prasolin. Nothing about it was distinct, and we both stared at it, willing it to explain itself. Some parts were hard and straight, while others were sunken and weak. Breathing too hard on it might have caused it to collapse in on itself.

Luna glanced at the detector.

"I believe we found what we were looking for but-"

"It's not enough."

She nodded.

The detector beeped crazily. Luna brought it closer to the pile, and the closer she got, the louder it beeped. She mistakenly got too close, and the dust caused her to sneeze. Along with the

Prasolin, a lot of it was blown into the air. To my dismay, it caused a stinging sensation in my nose.

Quickly wiping her nose, Luna reached out to feel the pile itself.

"GO!"

A voice echoed throughout the dome. Terrified, we both jumped, and were brought face to face with a strange creature. He'd appeared out of nowhere, and he stood a few feet away on the opposite side of the pile. Just over four feet tall, he angrily balanced himself on a staff in his hand. He was covered in dark brown fur, and stood on two feet. His features were small and flat, and the rise of his nose was barely noticeable. His head was elongated with long, thin hair falling just off the back of it. Wrapping around his jaw and chin, it formed a beard.

"GO!"

Luna took a step forward, which caused the creature to do the same. He grew agitated, so Luna stopped moving and instead used her words alone.

"I am sorry. We are looking for-"

"No. You leave Coer's temple."

With every word, his voice rocked.

"You be here before, and now you go."

We all just stared at each other. Surprisingly, I was the first to break the silence.

"…What's your name?"

"I am called Coer. I have called you sky devils, but what do you call you?"

"We are Avenur, but I think you are mistaken. We have never been here before."

When Luna answered, he shook his head.

"No. You be here long, long…"

He placed his staff against the ground.

"…and you take everything. Now I am nothing."

A tiny sound came from my wrist. Luna must have heard it too, because she looked down and responded by pulling her mask over her head. When she did, I realized it wasn't my wrist making the noise. It was my mask. As I pulled mine on, the small creature stood frozen, staring at us. But by the time the mask was secured in place, he'd disappeared.

"Wha…"

"Luuuna! Somebody, please!"

Saav's voice echoed throughout my head. When Luna responded, her words came from both her mouth and my mask.

"Yes, Saav, what is the matter?"

"Rav and I found the stash. We can stop looking because I'm sure there's enough to go around."

Ravi added,

"We've already called the T23, so we'll come around to get everyone."

Part of me was relieved, but part of me was also disappointed I'd have to leave the temple. As I took another look around, I wondered where the small creature had disappeared to. Oddly, his voice alone filled the dome.

"You are not welcome, and now you go."

With a gust of wind, the markings faded and flickered one by one. In the same fashion they had become lit, they fell to darkness. The circle near the ceiling was the first to go.

Threateningly, the darkness crawled down the wall and surrounded us. Within a second, it had made its way down the tunnel, until we were once again standing in utter darkness.

Neither I nor Luna had the answers to anything we wanted to ask, so we said nothing. Instead, we rushed back toward the tunnel and made our way out of the cave. The walk back passed a lot quicker than the walk to the dome. But when we made it back to the mouth of the cave, we burst back into the light and immediately froze.

Standing just outside the clearing, was the guy I'd seen earlier. Completely covered in a combat suit, his head was hidden. A rod was attached to his back, crossing through a hump that sat just between his shoulder blades. Partially hidden amongst the trees, he failed to notice us even as we stared. Instead, his head was turned, studying the forest in the opposite direction. In the distance, the cracking sound of a beast cut through the air. Seemingly, this was what he was waiting for.

His head swiveled, landing on us. For a moment, we all just stared at each other. Slowly, he turned the rest of his body.

Stepping into the clearing, his movements were cautious, as if he were afraid we'd run away. When he finally entered the clearing, he stopped. Reaching behind him, he gracefully pulled the rod from his back and, with one swift motion, the rod was split into two. Moving his feet apart and raising his hands, he switched into a fighting stance.

Next to me, Luna sighed.

fourteen

Even through a mask, his stare was lifeless. His body was positioned for offense, and he appeared merciless, robotic even. When seconds passed and neither me nor Luna made a move, he did. Swinging his arms as far back as possible, he launched one of his rods. The throw was strong, causing it to shoot across faster than expected. It missed my skull by barely an inch, creating a whizzing sound. Stretching his arm out, he then opened his palm as if he were requesting a hand.

I turned to Luna, but she didn't look back. Instead, she

kept her eyes on the man. Behind me, something moved and, a moment later, the rod shot back in the opposite direction. As if it were under his command, it returned to his open hand. Fear brought my heartrate to a drum.

"Woah…"

Luna took a deep breath and tried to rush over. But after two steps, she was stopped. Coming from the other side of her, another person in gray appeared, gripping Luna by the throat. They were the same height, but this new person was stronger. With a single hand, she lifted Luna from the ground. She stared her in the face with a coldness that threatened a tighter grip. But instead, struggling to breath, Luna was dropped.

I rushed to help, but was put in a chokehold by someone who came from behind. Their arm was nearly as beefy as that of Director Ruid. Its grip increased until it had filled every space around my neck. As Luna was sprawled across the ground, choking, I fought to free myself but, locked in a chokehold and unable to breathe, there was little I could do.

With my neck nearly wrung, I was freed with a twist that

threw me to the ground. My chokes for air joined those of Luna. Even as my eyes watered and my throat ached, I attempted to get to my feet. But with the strength of a horse, I was kicked in the stomach and brought back down.

All three of the masked, gray faces stood over us. The woman in the middle kneeled and reached for my face. Defiantly, I tried to move away, but my head was snapped back. With one hand holding my head in place, her other hand removed my mask. As she dropped it on the ground beside us, her gripped tightened and pulled me closer. For a moment, she studied me some more.

Turning to the others, she nodded. Whatever it was she'd found in my face, the others understood. She then turned to Luna, who watched everything with bated breath. The hand was finally removed from my throat, but it was immediately replaced by another. I was pulled from the ground and to my feet. It seemed as if I were about to be thrown over a shoulder, but all movement stopped.

As if serving as an introduction, there came a familiar crack and growl. Just beyond the clearing, the beast that had chased me and Luna over a waterfall stood, preying. From the shadow of the trees, his stare was menacing. So much so, it seemingly drew us physically closer to each other. Slowly, and with a low growl, his back raised, ready for attack. I was let go, and all attention shifted to him instead. For the briefest of moments, there were no longer sides because, unbiasedly, the beast stalked all five of us.

Luna dashed for the trees. Briefly, she dragged me along until I was smart enough to grab my mask and move my feet. Every step felt like a gamble, but my back was never met with the grasp of claws or the throw of a rod. The forest felt as though it stood much taller than before, and shadows looked as though they stretched much farther. Bushes were larger, and the rustle of the leaves felt like a warning of impending death. There was no map and no plan. Just an unbeaten path and a never-ending forest.

I looked over to Luna to see how she was faring, but her mask hid everything I was searching for. In that moment, her movements were as robotic as those of the people we'd left behind. Everything was precise and quick. Where I'd nearly stumbled a few times, she hopped over things with ease. I wanted

to say something, but I wasn't given the chance. Behind us, the

rustle of leaves and the beating of paws grew louder.

I peeked over my shoulder. The beast had easily covered

the distance we'd run. In so short a time, it had gotten so close, the

noise of its pants sounded as though it was just behind my ear.

The group that had attacked us was nowhere in sight, and there

were no signs of anything being left of them. Somehow, that

brought both joy and fear.

I tripped. I'd been moving so fast that, even after falling to

the ground, my body continued moving. Rolling and crashing

through the brush, I felt scratches and the stings of wounds I knew

wouldn't amount to what was to come.

I tried to jump to my feet, but the beast had gotten too

close. The sounds of growls and the beating of the ground

approached like a parade of death. I stared in horror. In a moment

that was nearly Shakespearean, it lunged from the cover of a

nearby bush.

Everything happened in slow motion, and the moment felt

like the longest thing I'd ever experienced. But its lunge was violently interrupted. Masked, Luna had appeared, and she'd made a weapon out of a large branch.

"Get up!"

The beast rolled across the ground, catching its bearings. Angrily, it growled and rubbed at its face. Hurriedly, Luna helped me to my feet. We ran again and, this time, no time was wasted on shoulder glances.

Abruptly, Luna snatched my arm in another direction. When she slung me around, she pressed herself against a nearby tree, and I obediently followed suit. For a moment, we both just stood there, panting. Not far off, the noise of the beast grew louder. It slowed to a stop just as it neared the area we were standing in. From where he stood, we were out of view. But a quick look around would easily reveal our hiding spot.

As paws thumped back and forth, sweat formed a waterfall down my face. I pressed closer to the tree. If I'd pressed any harder, I would have become a part of the bark itself. Luna was pressed just as closely. Balanced atop a single root, one wrong move would send us both stumbling to the ground.

As the sound of claws came around, we moved in the opposite direction, making sure to stay as close to the trunk as possible. A low rumble came from the throat of the beast. He knew we were there. When I turned to Luna, she was gone. For a moment, there was an internal panic, but then I looked lower and there she was. A part of the tree was hollowed out, and she was in the middle of sliding herself into it.

A loud gawking sound came from somewhere in the forest. It resembled a calling of some sort. When it came a second time, it almost sounded like the remnants of a chant. Distracted, the beast stopped its search.

Luna had slid as far into the hollow as she could, so I did the same. The act of bending down meant pulling myself away from the tree, and I held my breath as I did. Once inside, I allowed myself to breathe again, but only in short bouts.

"Where are you guys?"

Saav's voice filled my mask and, in that moment, it was probably the loudest thing I'd ever heard.

"The last place the T23 tracked you was near a cave so, feel free to give us directions…"

When neither of us responded, he continued.

"But! No worries, we've got all day. No rush. Take your time."

He sighed as if he were annoyed. Outside, a branch snapped. The large claws of the beast waited just a few feet away, but he didn't seem to know where we'd gone. Angrily, he beat the ground a couple of times, and let out a sound that was soul-shattering. It was a rumble that seemed to fill the entire forest, including the hollow we were stuffed inside.

The sound of the strange chant echoed again. It was almost as if it were a response to the beast. Mulling a decision, it took a few steps away from the tree and turned in a few quick circles. Giving up on us, it finally took off in the direction of the yelling.

Luna and I both pulled ourselves from the hollow. Far off, the beast was still searching for the source of the chant. Not wanting to attract any attention, we lightly stepped away from the tree. Next to me, Luna whispered with an obvious ting of fear.

"Ravi…Saav…"

"Ahh, so we're not chasing ghosts after all! Tell us where you're at so we can come and get you. There's no time for a search seeing as there aren't a lot of gas stations in this part of town."

It sounded like he was eating something, and the thought made me envious. Luna and I were both on the ground, afraid to move faster than a brisk walk, yet Saav was sitting in the aircraft, eating. It was as if he hadn't even considered the possibility that we were in danger.

My anger got the best of me.

"We're in a forest, I don't know where we are!"

He crunched on something and gulped loudly.

"Well tell me what you're near."

"TREES!"

I'd spoken too loudly. I knew it, and Luna did too. Slowly, we both stopped. Before turning around, we knew what to expect. Even though the beast was still far off, reality had a sense of humor. Through all the trees, we watched him stop and look in our direction. It was as if there was a single sliver of a distant view, and he stood right in the middle of it. Which meant we were also standing in the middle of his.

We broke into a run.

"Are you guys running? What's wrong?"

"Predator. Get ready to pick us up."

Shockingly, Luna didn't sound as angry as I felt.

"From wher-, Wait, ohhh I see you."

Saav shuffled a little as he put his food down.

"Holy-...Hope you're wearing your wrangling boots boys and girls!"

The forest was ruffled and blown around as a thick gust of air passed over. The T23 was right above us, but there was no way we could get to it from where we were. The trees were in the way and climbing wasn't an option.

Luna grew irritated.

"You can't get us from here!"

This time, Ravi responded.

"Up ahead, forest flattens out. We'll get you there."

There was a point where the trees broke off and then there was…nothing. It just looked as if the sky covered everything that was above and below where we were. As if we were running toward a cliff. But then I got a better look.

We were approaching a lake that was so calm, the top of it looked like a mirror. It reflected the sky and stretched until there was nothing more to see. As we neared it, the beast growled, bounding after us faster and faster.

We stopped just at the edge of the water, but the sound of death forced our feet again. Hesitantly, we stepped out. The lake only rose halfway to the knee. As soon as we touched it, the T23 roared over us. Just up ahead, its entrance opened, and it started to lower to the water. The only thing we had to do was cross over to it.

My heart pounded in my ears as we ran the stretch. Behind us, there came a large splash.

Saav appeared at the opened door.

"No worries, sir, this is only going to tickle."

He started firing a weapon I'd never seen before. The

sound of bullets rang out loudly, creating a line of splashes behind us. Once we were close enough to the aircraft's ramp, Luna and I both took a single leap.

We thudded across the edge of the ramp, and the T23 began to rise. A loud snarl and growl called after us, and a claw appeared at the foot of the aircraft. Saav began shooting again. The sound of bullets, growling, scraping, and thumping filled my head until I thought it'd burst.

But then, the beast let go. It hit the water below and, finally, I allowed myself to breathe. Oddly, the act of inhaling and exhaling felt new to me.

Saav slapped my shoulder as he went back this seat.

"Good job, officer."

Luna and I tiredly pulled ourselves to our seats. When Luna pulled her mask off, she revealed a layer of sweat almost as heavy as mine. There was so much, it dripped, yet still managed to leave a pool across the skin. Within seconds, the air of the T23, paired with the sweat, made it feel as though we'd been submerged in ice water.

We sat quietly, panting. Saav sat nearby, giving us a moment, while Ravi was piloting at the front. Everything was peaceful. But as we allowed our limbs to relax and our minds to wander, content to take in nothing but the sky around us, Luna leaned forward. With a tilt of her head, she looked confused.

"...where is Alora?"

fifteen

Saav's brows furrowed. He paused as if he were trying hard to come up with an answer. Next to his foot was the tiny creature that had found a home around his neck, and it jumped to his shoulders as he stared at us, bewildered. When the creature's tail brushed into his face, he swatted it.

"Twoh, c'mon..."

Ravi flipped a switch on the dash and turned around.

"...we haven't heard from her since we split up."

Saav side-eyed Twoh, sighed, and spoke under his breath.

"This is why *I* didn't want to be the one to go alone."

He lightly rubbed Twoh, which made my and Luna's eyebrows raise. Compared to the last time we'd seen them, Saav had done a 180. It was as if he wasn't merely content with Twoh's presence, but fond of it.

Ravi turned back to the controls.

"We should be able to pinpoint the location of her suit..."

Saav tore his attention away from his new friend.

"And if we can't?"

"We keep looking."

I sunk in my seat.

"Well we might want to find her fast because some other people have definitely found us."

"What do you mean?"

Both Saav and Ravi turned at once. I'd obviously become too overwhelmed, so Luna answered.

"We were attacked. I am not sure why, but they wore combat suits. It was almost as if they were the academy's shadow."

Ravi turned back to his controls.

"Well that makes things a bit more urgent."

I sat up.

"Where's the backup? Never in my life have I run from something the size of a car, just after being choked off the ground with a single hand."

Saav chuckled, but stopped when I eyed him.

"Sorry."

Ravi jumped in.

"They responded to our beacon, so a squadron should be coming in pretty soon. We just have to make it until then."

Luna nodded.

"And find Alora."

"Yes, and find Alora."

Resuming what he'd started, Ravi went back to his controls to find Alora, while everyone else waited quietly. The whole time we did, Luna and I just sat and watched Saav. He'd become so comfortable with Twoh, he allowed it to jump all over him without giving much of a fuss. He even returned some of the playfulness by lightly poking and rubbing the small creature.

Just as he rubbed the sides of Twoh's face, he caught us staring and he froze.

"…What?"

"So, you named it…"

"No, Ravi named it."

"No I didn't."

"Okay, I named it. BUT, he earned it."

My brows raised.

"…How?"

Ravi jumped in again.

"He saved Saav's life."

"I wouldn't say he saved my life. He merely provided a helping hand."

Ravi turned with a look that easily called Saav's bluff.

"He saved Saav's life."

Saav waved our attention away from his brother.

"Okay, okay…he saved my life. BUT, I could have done it myself."

Ravi disagreed with a side-eye.

"Anyway, we have Alora's last location, but it was logged too long ago to mean anything."

Saav tossed Twoh to the floor.

"She could be dead by now."

"Don't say that."

"Well sorry I'm not one to beat around the bush, Ravi."

Luna cut in.

"How long will it take us to get there?"

Ravi shrugged.

"Not too long."

He pulled back on a handle, and the aircraft accelerated. Everyone buckled up, but Saav did so with a quip.

"Don't get too happy with the acceleration. Remember what happened last time."

We tore through the sky at a speed that nearly broke the sound barrier. Disregarding Saav's warning, Ravi flew in a way that made me fear for my life. Everything lightly rattled and, for once, I considered taking Saav's words seriously.

Up ahead was an expansive rocky field, where large stones

formed hills and pillars. Many of them were large enough to climb across *and* fall from. Part of me wondered what it would take to make the entire area tumble to the ground. Natural bridges connected a few of them, but many looked as though they were within seconds of a collapse. The ground below it all was jagged with more stones and covered in gravel.

Slowing to a hover just above a clearing in the rocky field, Ravi landed. The large pillars looming over us seemingly became taller and taller, casting shadows that covered the aircraft. With a slight bounce, the T23 rested against the rough terrain, and the landing was rendered complete with an appreciative sigh from Saav.

The aircraft quieted, and the back entrance was opened for everyone to file outside. The air was hot and humid. Nearly suffocating, it was heavy against the skin. There was an odd smell wavering past, and it was a mix of decomposition and eggs. With every footstep, foreheads wrinkled and noses drew in further.

The ground was crunchy. Many of the stones shifted as they were stepped upon, and small clouds of dust were easily kicked up. Once, Ravi almost fell, but Saav stuck his arms out to catch him. When he did, Twoh hopped from his neck to explore on his own. Curiously, he sniffed around the stones until his body disappeared around a large hill. As Saav stared after him, Ravi lightly slapped him on the head.

"He'll come back. Calm down."

Saav turned to the rest of us.

"Is it just me or does something smell really…weird."

"Yeah, smells like death honestly."

I responded as I stared at one of the pillars. Standing at its base, my eyes traced the height of it in wonder over what had kept it so structurally sound. Certain areas of it rested on stones that were much smaller than everything placed on top of them, yet nothing about the pillar was top-heavy.

When Saav caught me staring at it, he walked over. His eyes followed the same path mine had. When he got to the top, he nodded approvingly.

"Nice…"

Ravi and Luna were still searching the area behind us. As

we studied the work of art, Luna called out to everyone.

"Guys…"

She stood next to a large pile of stone, staring at the ground. She didn't move to pick up whatever was in front of her, and she stared down as if it were something that would bite her if she got too close.

As we came up behind her, we got a closer look at what she was staring at. Immediately, we all understood why she'd been so hesitant to pick it up. It was a black cloth, texturized like reptilian skin, and had a transparent, but dark, portion on the front of it.

Luna finally reached down to pick it up. Everyone's reaction was a mix of horror and wonder. Thoughts of the worst-case scenario spread, and Ravi nervously started to make up excuses.

"Maybe she dropped it."

"So why is it torn."

"I don't know, Saav. Maybe it caught onto something and then she dropped it?"

Saav responded with a questioning hum. Taking the mask from Luna, he turned it over in his hand and rubbed across the fabric. After he was satisfied with his observation, he handed it to Ravi.

"I don't think she dropped it."

Luna attempted to steer predictions in another direction.

"Then where is she? There is only a mask and nothing else."

Saav shrugged.

"I don't know. If she dropped it, she would have come back for it...what do you think?"

All eyes were averted to me. Luna's and Ravi's begged me to hop on the optimism train, but I couldn't. Shaking my head, I sided with Saav.

"I don't think she dropped it."

"Boom. The heir of Winor has spoken."

Ravi walked off.

"Whatever, Saav."

Everyone followed suit and continued looking, but it was

obvious what we all thought. We wouldn't find her. Somehow, Saav and I ended up in the same area. Nearby was a large pile of stones that were so large, we couldn't even see the rest of the team. He was initially quiet, but with Ravi and Luna out of earshot, he voiced his predictions.

"We're probably not going to find her. She disappeared on a planet this big, and we find a tattered mask in a stone field that reeks of decomposition."

"Who knows, maybe we will."

I feigned optimism, but it wasn't too convincing. Saav was right, we likely wouldn't find her in such a place. But a small part of me also sided with Ravi and Luna. A small chance was still a chance. Besides, I found Julie, and she'd been dead for two decades.

"I don't even know what we're looking for. We're digging though *rocks.*"

Saav stopped and stood upright. When I didn't voice an agreement, he sighed and bent down to pick up an oddly shaped stone. Tossing it in the air a few times, he looked around for something to throw it at. When his eyes landed on one of the pillars that was just beyond the other side of the pile, he skipped forward a step and launched it.

The stone arched through the air and hit the pillar just above its middle. Bouncing off, it made a clicking sound and fell to the ground. Initially, the throw didn't have much of an effect, but then parts of the pillar slid. A few stones fell away, one by one, but then the whole thing tipped over at once.

It crashed into the one closest to it, which also caused another collapse. Dirt and dust was kicked up, and I feared one of the larger pillars would fall just at the right angle to land on someone. Fortunately, none did.

Ravi and Luna were still out of sight on the other side of the pile. But as the dirt settled, Ravi sighed.

"Saav…"

"…what?"

"Why? You could have killed one of us, including your forest cat."

Twoh appeared around the pile. He ran to Saav and settled comfortably around his neck. Dirt covered his short body, but there were no signs he'd been hurt. Still, Saav rubbed him apologetically.

When we emerged around the pile, Ravi and Luna were just standing there, waiting to scold Saav. Their expressions were equally annoyed, and Saav picked up on it.

"Sorry..."

We walked over to the fallen pillars. At first, everything looked as expected. There were large, broken stones, and dirt. But a closer inspection revealed that the top of the pillar had caused part of the ground to cave in. As we got closer to get a better look, more dirt and stones fell inward.

The hole grew bigger and bigger. Soon, it destabilized the few remaining pillars. Everything came crashing down, kicking up cough-inducing amounts of dirt. When it all settled, the hole revealed a wide room that had been just below the ground.

Most of it was covered in dirt and stone, but the edges were visible. The wall looked as though it'd once been circular, but had since become jagged, uneven, and unsound. Strange markings covered all the parts we could see, and they closely resembled the ones Luna and I had seen in the cave.

Everyone climbed inside. Luna was the first to reach the wall, and gently brushed a hand across it.

"This looks like what we found early."

Confused, Ravi turned to her.

"You found a wall of markings and didn't tell anyone?"

"Well they were running from death, Rav..."

Ravi rubbed his own hand across it.

"Wonder what it means."

"Probably nothing nice."

Luna shook her head, countering Saav.

"We saw someone who was different from those that chased us. I believe his people made these."

Ravi stopped again.

"You saw TWO intelligent species?"

I nodded.

"Yeah, but neither were all that welcoming."

Saav walked along the wall as he brushed his hand across the markings. Unlike the ones in the cave, they were indented.

None of them sparkled. As he continued to stare as if he would suddenly start translating, Luna backed up and brushed her hands off.

"I wonder what this was used for."

I withdrew my own hand.

"Probably a graveyard. Sure smells like it."

Saav turned.

"So where are the bodies?"

I shrugged.

"Just a theory…"

Luna cut in, but Saav countered her.

"Probably buried elsewhere. This could have been a ritual ground of some sort."

"Okay, but they'd likely be close. So where are they?"

Ravi turned to his brother.

"Is it possible for anything to exist without you seeing it?"

"I'm just asking a question, Ravi."

"Well this planet is 9x the size of Avenur. They could be anywhere."

Ravi took another look around.

"This was underground, so maybe that's where they live."

"So where's the door to get out?"

We all looked for an opening, but there were none. End to end, the space was sealed. With a shrug of his shoulders, Ravi gave up.

"…I don't know."

Luna began her climb out of the hole.

"Well there's no time to map the structure of an unknown species. We still need to find Alora."

Everyone followed, but Saav was the only one to respond.

"Where should we look now?"

"Everywhere if we have to."

"And if we run out of fuel?"

"The academy is sending help."

Ravi scowled.

"Stop being so pessimistic."

Saav didn't ask any more questions, and we began crossing the field in silence. The edge of the field was far off, bordered by a short span of less rocky dirt, and then a forest. As we walked, birds flew from the trees, and most of the leaves shook. But no one paid attention to it. We all just trekked toward the aircraft with our thoughts on Alora.

The disturbance in the trees grew, prompting more squawks. As the noise intensified, we all stopped. The sun had lowered and was now just above the tops of the trees. As we watched, a section of the forest came alive. Its movements indicated something was coming toward the clearing but, already tired out from the day, we all just stood, more curious than fearful.

A shadow moved through the branches. Slowly, it waved in and out of view, before whatever it was began to pour down the side of a tree. It was thick, and its width was nearly a third of the tree it slid down. Initially, no eyes could be seen. But once it's black, slimy body slid across the ground, parts of it rolled back, revealing large, shiny eyes.

It was long like a snake, but slimy like a slug, and there was a low rumble as it slid across the ground. As we stared, the front of its body split to reveal a fine-toothed mouth. It then picked up speed but, casually, Saav dismissed it.

"Nope."

Ravi sighed.

"That's gross."

He resumed his walk to the aircraft, and everyone else followed. We walked more briskly than before, and soon we were rushing into the T23's entrance. In sync, everyone went to their seats and buckled up. Ravi turned everything on, and we rose. As we did, the slimy creature moved faster, now causing a small cloud of dirt and rocks to rise around it.

We accelerated forward, but the creature closed in on where we were. No one knew how high it could rise.

"Alright Rav, don't let us down this time."

The acceleration picked up just as the head of the creature rose to chase after us. Its body stretched further than I was comfortable with but, fortunately, it was only met with the heat of the aircraft's exhaust. So with the open air in front of us, and the creature behind us, everyone's mind once again reverted to Alora.

Interlude IV

From the Desk of Julie Winor

The lights of the universe shrank back to their normal speckled form as we slowed out of HyperG. Directly in our path, but still far off, was Prasola. It was a bright ball that beckoned us onward, daring us to face what it held.

"Are you sure you are ready for this, director?"

Ruid had finally turned to me. Half of his face was lit from the light of a distant sun, while the other was hidden alongside the worry he refused to fully reveal.

"Yes, I am. What about you, are you sure you're ready for this task?"

I turned away, rejecting his gaze.

"After all, there are rumors you've grown a bit rusty with age."

Even without seeing him, I felt the raise of his eyebrows and the tilt of his head. We both knew I was only taunting, so he refused to let it get to him. Instead, he chuckled.

"Officers do not carry rumors, director. But yes, I'm sure of my fitness and can assure you that your combat director will display nothing less than peak performance."

"Even to those you'd rather not bring back?"

As I turned to look him in the eye, he hesitated.

"…yes, even those whose presence is quite the liability for the morale of the academy."

"Morale. Fortunately, values change. I was once a liability for the morale of the academy…but look at me now."

I smiled and looked away, before turning back.

"You know, you may or may not be aware, but there's actually an exceptional officer on Avenur right now who carries that same label of liability. But, oddly, in today's environment, she doesn't face the same reception I did. If that's not proof of the value of change, I'm not sure what is."

"Are you telling me or yourself? Besides, what is the cost of that change? How long does the challenge last? When making these types of decisions, how much are you willing to forfeit?"

For a moment, we had a standoff. I gave in and looked away first because, despite what was on display on the outside, the exchange had caused me a bit of anxiety. In so short a moment, my heartrate had sped up, threatening to break free of my ribcage. But my words had been honest and steady, and that is what I held with the highest regard.

I relaxed in my seat. I hadn't noticed before, but my body had become tense, and my posture rigid. A pressure had built and was moments away from consuming me. As intended, his words had reminded me of things I didn't want to remember. So easily, I'd let my guard down, and he always knew when to strike. My mind wandered back to a version of myself that was so distant, I sometimes questioned whether she had actually existed.

I'd just completed a mission, but it was to the dissatisfaction of the academy director. It was a fact that hadn't been stated, but I'd known what to expect. I'd caused it, purposely. My parents walked on either side of me, and both lent an arm of support. Other than the three of us, the academy's main hall was empty. It was almost as if we were the only ones in the building.

I was brought to the academy court. It was a midsize room with no seating. One wall held a high window, and behind it was where the academy director sat. Other than a blank wall, there was nothing else there.

The court was nearly dark, with the only lighting being that which fell from the window. When we entered, Sagenti Ilo had already been waiting, and she watched us with eyes that cast darkness over her lower face. It had been caused by the lighting above her, yet it didn't seem entirely accidental either.

My parents stopped near the door, but I continued until I was just within the light of the window, looking up into the eyes of someone who could have been a manifestation of pain itself. When our gaze met, her presence tightened its grip around me once more, and she spoke. From within the box, her words were translated from her native language before being dumped out of a speaker just below the window.

"Ak rever kom."

You know why.

Her tone alone delivered a lashing. Enduring it, I nodded.

Then you must also know what the laws of the academy require. You were given a mission and ultimately refused its objective. Fortunately, it went as planned. It prevailed. But you will not.

My parents stepped forward. Stopping just behind me, they caused a low, drumming tension to build further, preparing me for what I knew.

For your transgression, you are sentenced to the Orweiian outpost, where you will live out your days...however long they may be.

Quickly, my mother entered the light of the window.

Director, if your will allow it, we will serve her sentence.

My heartrate leapt. When I attempted to object, my father cut me off.

No! You will not-

She is our creation. Her existence is our transgression, and so it is our debt to her.

As my head swiveled between them, I spat commands, but no one listened.

No! Get back!

The entire time, Sagenti Ilo watched, calculating and, when our eyes met once again, it was obvious what she had decided.

Very well, officers. You will serve in her place, as you wish.

Broken, I froze. For the first time, my hate for Ilo eclipsed my fear and, silently, I stepped forward. I eyed her threateningly, but she appeared more amused than offended. Without breaking our stare, she waved her hand.

And so it is done.

sixteen

There were still no signs of where she was. She hadn't answered any messages or requested help. It was as if she didn't care to be found. Maybe she was dead. But that was the case everyone avoided bringing up. Instead, the team made excuses. Even going so far as to say she was probably unconscious, but alive. Realistically, she was unconscious, but for good.

I resorted to just scanning the ground. My eyes searched for signs of something tall, purple, and hopefully alive. But everywhere we flew, there were just weird birds and random creatures. They avoided the T23, moving frantically as soon as they noticed it. Periodically, they would look over their shoulders as they sprinted away. The small cave animal said we'd taken everything so, despite how true or untrue that was, maybe he wasn't alone in his sentiments.

"Alora, if you can hear this, we're searching for ya, bud."

No response came, and the ride continued in silence. Gradually, the world below us died off. Trees became scarce, and their branches barren. Gone were any signs of animal life. What was left of this part of the forest amounted to no more than dead leaves and brittle trees. So quickly, everything below the T23 went from something that was lively and colorful, yet terrifying, to something more depressing than the tension in the aircraft.

Up ahead, there was a crater. Massive, it sloped deep into the ground. It was darker than the brown land around it, and it swallowed any remaining signs of life or hope. Initially, we all just stared. But Saav was discontent with the silence and broke it, speaking under his breath.

"What do you think caused it?"

Ravi shrugged.

"Meteor maybe."

Spotting something in the distance, he squinted.

"…Alora!"

He pointed out the windshield, his finger aimed near the far edges of the crater. There, a tiny figure moved amongst the trees. Slender and purple, she walked with signs of exhaustion. Her suit was in tatters, exposing her back. She looked lost, as if she were only wandering.

Aggressively, Saav patted Ravi's shoulder.

"Land this thing!"

Just beyond the edge of the crater, we landed but, even as we got closer, Alora went unaware of the T23. She just trudged with her head down. Dark dirt was blown upward, creating a cloud that we settled inside of. As the world calmed around the aircraft, Alora came into view, still wandering. Even with us coming to a stop within 40 yards of her, she just ignored us. We might as well have not been there.

Outside, the air was dry. When the aircraft's door lowered,

all the moisture inside of it was nearly sucked out, but nothing left the aircraft faster than the other team members. In single movements, belts were unbuckled and feet moved. Luna was the first to make it outside.

"Alora!"

She stopped. Frozen, she stared at us as if she were trying to decide if we were really there. She stepped forward but stopped again. Confused, she said something too low to hear. When no one responded, she came toward us, still mouthing indecipherable words. Everyone rushed to meet her in the middle. After a glance over her shoulder, she moved faster, but then stopped again. Fear across her face, she mouthed to herself and pointed.

Saav turned to the rest of us.

"Why is she acting so weird?"

Behind us, a spray of bullets littered the ground. Some ricocheted off the T23, but all created a path leading up to the team. Shocked, no one moved. Everyone just watched as an aircraft took a few more shots before landing near the edge of the crater.

It was almost a replica of the T23. Matte black, it kept both its abilities and its passengers hidden. It landed near the edge of the crater, not far from our own and, when its door dropped open, four people emerged from it. They looked just like the group that had attacked me and Luna. All wore masks, and all moved in the same uniform, robotic fashion. Detaching medal rods from their back, they approached us aggressively.

Saav stretched his neck.

"Guess that means they're not a part of the rescue team."

He started toward them, arms outstretched.

"Ah, family! We've been waiting for the help to arrive."

No response came. Instead, one of the newcomers rushed forward. He took a swing at Saav, which was dodged, but immediately followed it up with a second. With a blow that could shatter bones, Saav was knocked to the ground. Clutching his stomach, he fought to regain his breath. Unimpressed with him, his attacker continued toward the rest of us.

Luna turned to me, gesturing toward Alora.

"Get her inside the T23!"

Saav rolled over and pulled himself to his feet. Moving quickly, he dodged the swings of the other attackers. Given what he'd experienced moments before, he now moved with precision. Blow after blow, he held his own. Those he fought had moves of their own, but Saav was better. The only thing giving them an upper hand was the fact that there were three of them, but only one of Saav.

As Ravi and Luna ran to join the fight, I rushed to Alora. Her body lay across the ground, unresponsive to her name being called. Tiny puffs of air disturbed the dirt around her mouth. After rolling her over and ensuring she was still breathing, I helped her up. Her weight felt like triple my own. Weakly, her feet attempted to help, but they were ineffective, and she grew heavier by the second.

Through gritted teeth and short breaths, I motived her.

"C'mon…we've got a long way to go."

The fight raged on. Outnumbered, the rest of the team stood firm, but they weren't perfect. With all having been trained under the academy, their fight was coordinated. Watching them felt like watching a single machine with multiple parts.

Alternating between protecting themselves and protecting each other, they were a billboard for what academy officers were capable of.

"Allen!"

Just in time, I dodged a fist, dropping Alora in the process. Backing up, I dodged one after the other. Coming to the rescue, Saav appeared with a tackle. In between punches, he wrestled for the upper hand.

"Go!"

Making it back to Alora, I moved faster than before.

"Almost there, just a bit more to go."

We were only halfway to the aircraft's door. Like a portal to safety, it beckoned us forward. Alora became heavier, and her feet dragged. Her eyes were closed, but she was still breathing. Exhausted under her weight, I pushed forward. I stopped, caught my breath. Then I pushed forward again. Stop. Go. Stop. Go.

Once we were at the aircraft, the ramp became a challenge of its own. It felt like climbing a mountain while dragging a truck.

When it ended and our feet touched the inside of the aircraft, I dropped. Sweat fell from my forehead, creating a small puddle on the floor. My legs ached. My blood pumped so aggressively, it created a pressure that repeatedly squeezed my head. But the fight wasn't over and I needed to help.

I looked for a weapon. Near the door, the weapon Saav had used earlier was buckled to the wall. Undoing the buckles, I rushed outside. Now spread out, the rest of the team had also grown tired. They had not lost the fight, but their swings were not as quick and their hits not as hard. They were nearing defeat.

Raising a weapon for which I had no experience, I aimed and shot. Barely missing Ravi, I hit one of the attackers. For a moment, the fight froze. All eyes turned to me. But then the fight returned. Each attacker dealt a few more punches, but their new target was obvious. They wanted me.

With three shots, they were all knocked down. As they rolled around, the rest of the team rushed over. Luna pointed inside the aircraft.

"In!"

I took another shot and ran. Everyone dashed past, making me the last to make it back inside. Saav and Ravi reached for Alora and, after lifting her into a seat, Saav buckled her in while Ravi started the T23. As Luna, Saav, and I fumbled with seatbelts, the aircraft roared to life. A black cloud was blown up, briefly shielding the world from our eyes.

Our attackers had moved back inside their own aircraft and, just as we sped away, they emerged from a dark cloud of their own. Everybody breathed heavily. Next to me, Alora was slumped over. Her eyes remained closed, but her lips moved, fighting to be heard. Bringing my ear closer to her, I finally understood.

"I am…sorry. I am sorry."

"Nothing to be sorry for."

Saav nodded.

"That's right, Alora. Don't worry. The only thing that can hurt us at this point is Ravi's flying."

Loosening his grip on the controls, Ravi turned his head.

"This isn't the time, Saav! Do you wanna fly?"

"Yes!"

He reached for his belts, but Luna stopped him.

"Stop it! Can you two wait? Do you not see what is happening?"

Letting go of his belts, Saav dropped his hands. Ravi turned around and flipped a few switches, thrusting the aircraft forward. Behind us, shots rang out. Bullets peppered the outside of the aircraft. Discontent with sitting still, Saav reached for his belts again.

"I'm sure you got this Ravi, or, well, Luna is sure you got this, but I can't just sit here."

He stood and reached for the handles lining the ceiling. Handle after handle, he made his way toward the door of the aircraft. He pulled a knob on the ceiling, extending something that looked like a hose. After maneuvering it to his lower back, the hose was attached. Safely attached to the aircraft, he pressed a control near the door. As the door lowered, air rushed inside alongside the sound of ricocheting bullets.

Luna turned to me.

"Mask."

At the front, Ravi sighed.

"Don't mess this up, Saav."

"You know, Ravi, there are ways that we're not alike."

With the door nearly fully opened, he grabbed a weapon that was latched into the wall. It was bigger than the one I'd wielded only minutes before. Just below eye level, the dark windshield of the other aircraft stared back at us. As Saav brought the weapon to his shoulders, the aircraft raised.

Its guns locked into place, but it was too late. Aiming quickly, Saav took two shots. Each of the guns were partially ripped off, rendering them useless.

Saav readjusted the weapon.

"Up!"

Ravi followed instructions and, rapidly, we rose higher. Saav took shots at the other aircrafts windshield, cracking it. Just before it banked out of view, the glass shattered. For a moment, things became much quieter than before.

Saav shook his head.

"Don't see it."

Ravi responded with a shout.

"Keep looking!"

"There's not a lot to se-"

The aircraft quickly passed into view. It flew diagonally from top to bottom. With no guns left, it had attempted to collide instead. It had missed, but the force of its movement knocked Saav down. The weapon he held was dropped. Scrambling, he reached for it, but his fingers were too late. The weapon slid down the ramp and dropped to the world below, leaving Saav empty-handed.

"Well that's just great!"

He moved back to where the other weapons were latched. As he chose one, Luna unbuckled and came to join him. Locking herself in place with a line of her own, she grabbed a weapon. They both positioned themselves, ready to take their shot. In the distance, the aircraft circled up and around. Together, Saav and Luna took their aims.

Some shots landed, but few had an effect. As the aircraft got closer, Luna shouted over her shoulder.

"Allen, below your seat-"

She took more shots, temporarily covering the sound of her voice.

"Grab the orbs."

My heart rate doubled. Unsure of myself, I felt around the area below my seat. Just between my feet was a small handle and, after unbuckling my belts for better reach, I pulled it, revealing a drawer. Inside were three orbs. All were metal with glassy, red, rings going around their center. The rings pulsed as I picked them up.

With them held against my chest with a single hand, I moved toward Luna and Saav. Maintaining balance proved harder than intended, and twice I almost fell. Just as I reached them, I wobbled. One of the orbs was dropped, causing it to pulse brighter. At the sound of the clink, Saav looked down and his eyes widened.

The orb pulsed faster. Quickly bringing his foot back, Saav kicked it. Flying out into the open air, it exploded just in front of the other aircraft. It created a ball of fire whose light was temporarily blinding, but it had exploded a moment too soon. Shots emerged from the black cloud that was left behind, followed by the other aircraft.

Luna tossed her weapon aside. She replaced it with a slightly larger one on the wall next to her. Loading it with the last two orbs, she aimed. The first shot exploded just beneath the belly of the other aircraft. The force of the explosion only knocked it off balance. Taking aim again, Luna shot the last orb just before the other aircraft attempted to bank, but it had moved too late. The orb shot through the open windshield. A second after it disappeared inside the aircraft, the explosion came. It ripped the aircraft apart, shielding the destruction in fire and smoke.

The aircraft had managed to get closer than before, so the explosion was close enough to rock our own T23. It sent a wave through the aircraft, rattling anything that wasn't tightly held in place. So, only secured by a single hand holding onto a ceiling handle, I lost my balance. I fell hard against the ramp. My hands searched for something to latch onto, but there was nothing. In a blink, my body slid down the ramp toward the world below.

I felt the aircraft disappear from beneath me faster than I could process it. As my fingers cleared the edge of the ramp last, Saav's masked face appeared. He'd jumped. Hand outstretched, he fell toward the ground, reaching for me and, just as his fingers wrapped around my wrist, his line tugged and refused to extend any further.

With my safety dependent upon a single grip, I grasped his wrist with my other hand. Below us, the world was far away, yet too close all the same. In my mind, everything above and below us faded away. The only thing that mattered was ensuring our grip never loosened. Staring through the dark of our masks, I pleaded for such and, as if making a promise, his grip tightened. When I tightened my own, I got a verbal response.

"Nobody gets left behind, officer."

seventeen

A light rain fell. We'd landed in a large, uneven clearing so Ravi could check everything in the T23. The side of a hill that rose and abruptly broke off on one side provided us with a landing pad. Below the jagged side of the hill, a small creek cut through and disappeared into the forest. Smoke rose from the T23, but not much.

While pressing buttons and reading reports, Ravi muttered and cursed under his breath.

"Looks like we used more than half our resources in that

little scuffle."

He stopped and turned, eyeing me and Luna.

"We should be able to make it to the Prasolin, maybe even off the planet. But I can't promise much more than that."

Luna stood to look at the reports he was reading.

"How far is rescue?"

"Edge of the system. Not far."

"We will be fine. Just get us to what we were sent to pick up."

Ravi nodded.

"We'll be good to leave in a few minutes...where's Alora?"

"She went to clean herself up at the lake. I'll go get her."

I stood.

"I'll go with you."

Saav was leaned against the wall at the end of the aircraft, just out of reach of the rain. He was lost in thought, but his eyes followed Twoh's every move. Outside, the small creature ran about, unbothered by the fact that he was getting drenched. When Luna and I made it to the aircraft's entryway, he perked up, ready to follow.

Saav broke from his trance.

"Where are you two going?"

Tired, my voice came out flat.

"To grab Alora."

"Why is she even out there?"

"She said she needed a moment."

He stood up straight and followed us down the ramp.

"What? We literally just got her back. Doesn't she- wait. RAVI? LET'S GO BUDDY."

Surprisingly, Ravi appeared at the entryway and walked out into the rain without a fuss.

"Yeah, I probably shouldn't stay back even if it means time away from Saav."

Everyone moved in silence. We walked to the beat of the rain, accompanied by the sounds of gawks and scurrying. We'd all become so unconcerned with the things around us, we no longer feared its possibilities. Seemingly, its possibilities also no longer feared us. Everything just existed in an odd harmony.

"Does it scare you?"

With my thoughts interrupted, I turned. Saav, Ravi, and Twoh walked a few steps ahead, but Luna trudged just beside me. Patiently waiting for an answer, she glanced over. Her silver hair was tied back, and soaked bits of it fell across her face. The rainwater gave her a sort of glow. For a moment, I saw her differently than before, but then the realization quickly faded.

"Does what scare me?"

"Seeing things so far from what you've ever known."

I shrugged.

"Not really…or maybe just not a lot, or not anymore. I don't know. Mentally, I just keep reliving the realization of the academy and Julie and…everything. The shock of it all doesn't leave room for much else."

"I've never heard anyone refer to Director Winor by that name."

Unsure of a response, I kept quiet, and a silence fell over us. But then Luna spoke again.

"When I woke up in the academy, I was horrified. I cried

for days, because I could not remember much before that point. The people I met knew little themselves. I was told I had been found alone in a capsule, floating through the dark of space. But anything beyond that, there were no answers."

Her brows furrowed, but relaxed almost immediately. When she glanced over and our eyes met, she quickly looked away.

"Sometimes I get bits of a memory, but they're never complete. So for me, it was scary."

Her voice dropped a bit at the end. As she stomped through the rain, something about her was different. Maybe she trusted me more, or maybe she was tired. Maybe everyone was in a state of vulnerability. Either way, her demeanor was no longer robotic. Her strides were the same, and she still traced the forest with an accusatory eye but, still, she was different.

Up ahead, the trees stood fewer and the sight of a lake peeked through. It sat well below the height of the land around it, creating a comfortable slope to rest upon. Tiny ripples danced across its surface as the rain pattered it. Oddly, it was calming, and the noise it made, paired with the sounds of the forest, created a place that dared you to never leave.

"Alora?"

With no one in sight, Luna's call went unanswered. Near the lake's center, ripples formed, bigger than those created by the rain. At first, they were barely noticeable. But they grew quickly. Unlike normal ripples, they grew and became more distinct as they spread further. By the time one broke at the edge of the lake, near our feet, it had become a small wave. Splattering over the edge, it hit the ground with a force that was evident of something other than regular water.

Something emerged from the lake's surface. It was smooth, round, and purple. Covered in glowing markings, it became the head of Alora. With her bare back to us, the markings were on full display. Their light made them more distinct than before, and they were unending as more of Alora was pulled from the water.

She rose so smoothly, it looked as if she were mere seconds from floating out of it completely. But just as her waist reached the surface, she stopped. With her face to the sky, she held her hands up, as if she were praying. No words came from her mouth.

Hesitantly, Luna stepped forward.

"Alora?"

The markings faded as her hands came to rest at her side. Turning around cautiously, she stared. Her eyes were a little glassy. She didn't say anything, and she didn't look angry. She just looked as though she'd been in middle of something that we'd broken off a moment too soon.

Her voice came out low as she moved forward a bit, creating more ripples.

"...Hi."

She waded toward the edge of the water. Reaching into the water, she pulled the rest of her tattered combat suit up and over her head. Even with the collar around her neck and the arms over her shoulders, most of her back was still exposed. But, though she'd looked hurt when we found her, she was now free of wounds.

She exited the lake and took a seat on its edge. Awkwardly,

everyone else did the same. With her knees to her chest, she rested her chin on her hands. The entire time, the only thing to be heard in the forest were the sounds of the forest itself.

Somewhat more reserved than usual, Saav broke the silence.

"So, are you ever going to tell us what happened or...?"

"I was captured."

She glanced over her shoulder before turning back to the water.

"It was brief, but it happened."

"How did you get away?"

"I downed the aircraft they put me in. I'm not sure where it was going, but I don't think it was somewhere worth seeing. At least not alone."

She paused.

"During the flight, I longed to be back home, but-"

She looked back.

"Where is it? Where is home for us?"

She turned away again.

"So much of this forest reminds me of a place that no longer exists. While exploring, I started to question myself. I questioned the academy and its presence on this planet. I questioned the life I now have. Why is it that I am so content to live longer than the very place that created me?"

She paused again.

"Without my home, who am I to be in a world that will always feel foreign?"

So quickly, a tension had slithered from the lake. It wrapped itself around us, thinning the air. Luna had already told me the academy only takes in people who are remnants of places that once existed, and even uncaringly mentioned that everyone else is simply left to die. But, unaccustomed to it all, I had no answer to offer Alora.

When a voice finally spoke, it was Ravi's.

"At some point you have to realize that you are now as much of your home as you are yourself. Everything that you are and everything that it was now exists within a single person, or even a couple of people...But either way, if you give up on yourself, you've given up on it as well."

We all stared out into the lake. When Alora did speak again, it sounded as if she were talking to herself as much as she was talking to us.

"I can hear them sometime. I've even spoken with them, but I don't know how much of it is real. Whether or not I'm really able to contact them, or if I'm simply playing mind games with myself."

Luna grew curious.

"Hear who?"

"My people. But mainly my father. He tells me I must continue and that I am not to worry of their whereabouts, because they are always with me. But, again, I don't know how much of that is real. He was always the mouth of my people anyway."

When no one could think of something to say back, Alora stood up.

"We must continue. The director is waiting."

As we walked, I kept taking peeks at her. Everyone I was surrounded by was different from myself, but Alora was the most striking in appearance. Now, I also knew there was a lot she didn't talk about. I didn't want to pry, but I found myself tugging at the thought of asking her questions. Luckily, I didn't have to because she called me out.

"You're curious but my story isn't fascinating. Quite the opposite actually."

"I'm sorry. Didn't mean to make you uncomfortable. I was just thinking about everything you said…"

She glanced over for a second before turning to swat a branch out of the way.

"Well it's all true, but none of it is anything of fascination. I never had true parents. At least not in the sense you'd think of a parent. My mother and father were the mother and father of many. But still, they noticed me. In a sea of more than 10,000, I was truly their one…But it doesn't matter, because now they are gone."

She paused.

"And I must learn to accept it."

"What happened? If you don't mind."

"My home was weak. It was no longer strong enough to keep us, and we were not strong enough to believe it. I thought I could stop everything from happening but, in a show of nature, I failed. I would have been left to die with everyone else, but the academy showed up and gave me an opportunity I selfishly took. Now I'm here, serving the needs of another society while my own ceases to exist."

She fell silent. Formally ending the conversation, she separated us by picking up her pace. The rest of the walk continued in silence. Once we were back in the aircraft, everyone strapped down and Ravi lifted us from the ground. This time, startup was calm, even comforting. As we once again rose into the air, Saav took a deep breath.

"Rav?"

"Yes?"

"The Henske thing was my fault, and I'm sorry for criticizing your flying. I know you can't help it."

Sarcastically, Ravi sniffed.

"Stop it Saav, you're gonna make me cry."

Behind him, Luna stared into her hands. She looked lost, as if she were so far in thought, she was no longer with us. She was somewhere else. Somewhere far away. I wondered what that place could be like but, considering her earlier revelation, she probably did too.

Alora was sitting straight up, looking at nothing in particular as well. She was frozen, nearly like a statue, but she couldn't be observing much because there wasn't much to see inside the aircraft. So maybe she was somewhere else too. Somewhere that was possibly even farther away.

With everyone in their own worlds, I attempted to fall into my own. I thought about Julie. It was odd to think that there were now things that I found more shocking than her even being alive. But there were. In so short a time, the universe had dumped a chest's worth of information, daring me to buckle under the weight but, somehow, I hadn't. At least not yet.

When I looked up again, we were losing altitude. Initially, we passed the clouds slowly, but things sped up. As Ravi tipped us forward a bit, a large volcano came into view. Its peak was capped in snow, and its mouth soothingly exhaled a bit of smoke. Beneath the smoke, it emitted a red color.

In a voice that was slightly nonchalant, Ravi introduced us.

"Welcome to mother Prasola."

eighteen

We landed near the base of the volcano, not far from the forest bordering it. The aircraft shook as it rested, and the world became quiet as it powered down. The exit ramp was lowered. No one spoke as we dragged ourselves out. Outside, the ground was soft, almost spongy. Every footstep sank at least an inch into the ground, and there was a slight suction as every foot was lifted. Other than me, no one seemed to be bothered by it.

The air was heavy. Breathing felt like lifting weights in the chest. Thick with the smell of chemicals, it was almost painful. But no one else was bothered by that either. They all just stretched and breathed without the slightest of worries. It was odd. Paired with the red smoke wafting about, it wouldn't have been surprising if we were all unconscious within two minutes of standing around.

Luna scanned the area.

"So…where is it?"

Ravi gestured toward the ground.

"You're standing on it."

While he and Saav went back into the aircraft for something, everyone else inspected the ground. The soil was warm. Though it was spongy, small clumps of it easily crumbled in the palm. Thin, white fibers stuck out of it, and tiny pods of something was scattered within. Dropping a clump, I dug a bit deeper and, sure enough, Prasolin was revealed underneath. The layer of it was deep and, no matter how much we dug with our hands, it never gave way to anything else.

Something rumbled inside the aircraft. At the top of its ramp, Saav and Ravi appeared with two large objects. They were made of a dark metal, and mostly round like cylinders. Their bases tapered to a large, rounded point, and their top was flat. A single ring sat on a flat slope near the top edge. Other than that, there were no markings. Laying on their side, they rose just above knee height.

Saav and Ravi rolled them outside and, once they were out of the way, Alora and Luna took their place. Inside the aircraft, the floor had been opened, revealing several compartments. There were four large pockets, two of them empty. The two that weren't held more of the objects that had just been rolled out.

Alora and Luna pulled the first out together. But, steadying it, Alora rolled it down the ramp alone. As Luna moved to remove the last one, I rushed over to help. A button in the compartment caused the floor of it to raise, but not as much as needed. The bullet-shaped object inside had to be lifted the rest of the way, using a few handle cutouts on its top and sides.

Moving it was a chore. Luna squatted on one side, grasping it by a handle on each end. I did the same on the other side, but my stance was a bit more unsure than hers. I gritted my teeth from the task. It was heavier than expected, and getting it out felt like removing a tank. For a second, it didn't even budge

but, when it finally did, my legs nearly buckled under the weight.

After it clanked onto the floor, Luna smiled. Embarrassed,

I looked away and started rolling the machine outside. At the

bottom of the ramp, Luna thanked me and positioned it near the

other three. Each of them rested at the end of a deep trail,

revealing the path they'd been rolled.

Alora and Luna walked around them, pressing the single

button on each. One by one, they hovered about ten feet in the air.

Positioning themselves vertically, they slammed into the ground,

which drove them halfway under. Their rings lit up blue,

flickering, and they emitted a low, humming sound. After about

three seconds of humming, the noise rose dramatically. It

drowned out most things near it and echoed down into the nearby

forest.

"WHERE ARE YOU GOING?"

Over the noise, Luna's voice struggled to be heard. Saav

and Ravi had left us and were now nearing the forest. At the

sound of Luna yelling, they both slowed to a stop.

Ravi called back.

"That's going to take a while."

"So? We are not coming to find you!"

They had already started walking again. This time, neither of them stopped. Instead, Saav mockingly yelled over his shoulder.

"HUH?"

Followed by Ravi.

"WHAT?"

When they finally disappeared amongst the trees, Alora turned to Luna. Annoyed, she sighed. As Alora started to follow them, her voice was just as low and calm as it had been at the lake.

"We shouldn't split up anymore. They are in danger even if they believe they are safe in a pair."

She didn't bother waiting for a response. Luna turned to me with a stare I couldn't read. With an obvious annoyance, she jerked her head after them, and we both rushed toward the trees. The suction of the ground made every step awkward, and running back into the cover of the forest yet again was a drain on the spirit.

Joining Alora, we quickly caught up to Saav and Ravi.

They wandered with no obvious destination, because they were too focused on whatever they were talking about. Unsurprisingly, they were too preoccupied to notice we'd even arrived. A disagreement had started, and the conversation seemed moments away from a fight.

Ravi was the angriest.

"Yeah well, you tell me…"

He shoved Saav into a thicket so large, his brother disappeared inside of it. But when Luna attempted to say something, Saav cut her off from behind a few large leaves.

"Ravi-"

"I'm fine."

He climbed out, rubbing his eyes. It looked as though he were about to say more, but he didn't. Instead, he froze, fear strewn across his face. Ravi had already walked off, but he turned when he realized Saav still hadn't caught up. When he did, he froze also.

Behind us, Alora had taken a moment to kneel to the ground, but it looked as though she'd done it out of pain. Her markings glowed, lighting paths across her skin. She grunted, fighting through whatever she was feeling. Veins bulged, and muscles flexed.

Slowly, she raised her head, looking as if she were moments away from a scream. Her eyes glowed like her markings, staring through us rather than at us. The pupil and everything surrounding it was a single light, seemingly seconds away from bursting out of her face. It looked as though the light had swallowed all the life behind it. When she finally spoke, she breathed hard.

"I can see them."

Everyone waited for more, but nothing came. She grunted and clenched her fists. As if kneeling required too much, she fell flat on the ground. She rested against one hand, while the other clenched and unclenched. But then she inhaled deeply, lifted her head, and became calm.

Her markings still glowed, but she no longer looked as though she were in pain. Slowly, she just pushed herself backward until she came to rest against a tree.

"They want us to leave...we're in more danger than we thought."

Luna walked over and knelt in front of her. When she spoke, her voice was barely audible.

"Danger of what?"

Alora didn't respond. It looked as though she hadn't even heard Luna. She also didn't seem to notice she was in front of her, staring into her face. It was as if Luna no longer existed. For a moment, everything was quiet. Giving up, Luna rose from the ground.

"We should-"

The sounds of an explosion rocked through the forest. It shook the trees, causing a flurry of scurrying. Around us, the world became louder. Everyone backed towards each other, searching for the source. A second explosion came, causing a ringing in my ear. The sound separated me from the world, leaving me only aware of the things that could be seen in any single direction.

A column of smoke rose into the air just above where we'd

left the T23. It was dense and black, rising like a warning that had come too late. Against the beauty of the Prasolin sky, it created a dark crack that threatened to reveal an ugliness none of us were prepared for.

The sounds of the world returned just as Alora's glow faded away. She looked around as if she were lost but, quickly composing herself, she stood and rushed away.

"We must leave. Now."

We sprinted. The forest whizzed by in a blur, masking everything inside of it. Smoke filled the trees. It grew thicker as we approached the base of the volcano, nearly choking us. Just before the edge of the forest, Luna's voice cut through it.

"MASKS!"

Reminded of the one magnetized to my hip, I pulled it on. Protectively, it suctioned itself to my head, and the air in my lungs became cleaner. The world became clearer. Though the smoke remained, the mask revealed signs of everything it hid.

Two of the mining machines were destroyed. Each carried a blaze that enveloped them and danced from their heads. The metal that could be seen had blackened. Surprisingly, the other

two machines looked just as good as they had before we left.

"Why only two of them?"

Smoke blew away. Nearby, an aircraft was rising in the air.

As it rose higher, the matte black machine looked as though it'd

been made from the smoke itself. Just like the other we'd seen, it

closely resembled an academy T23, but more weapons lined the

bottom of its wings.

Luna stepped forward, but stopped when bays on the belly

of the aircraft dropped open. The edges of the view through my

mask began to glow red. As the weapons locked in place, we were

stuck. There was nowhere to run and nowhere to hide. Lured by

the explosions, we were trapped.

I inhaled sharply and held my breath. Time slowed,

moving at a speed that was barely noticeable. There came the

sound of the weapon hammers preparing themselves and, a

moment later, the ground was torn apart.

Bullets cut through the dirt. The noise was murderous but,

oddly, none of them seemed to reach me. Confused, I looked

down at my combat suit. Sparks flickered off it, creating stars

amongst the smoke and soot, but I felt nothing.

"ALLEN!"

Luna yanked at my arm. The whizzing of bullets and

commotion of dirt muddled my thoughts. Luna had already run

toward the T23, so I rushed after her. I arrived as the aircraft's

ramp was closing but, just as my feet touched it, Luna yelled my

name again, pointing toward the sky.

I turned and was met with the sight of a shadow dropping

from the dark smoke. It closed in on me within a moment, and I

felt the squeeze of beefy arms. Just as quickly as the shadow had

appeared, it was pulled back, and I was dragged along with it.

The ramp of the T23 closed as I watched the aircraft get

smaller. The team was attempting to come after me, but the

aircraft that had shot at us made it difficult. As a battle ensued and

the T23 was forced away, I was pulled toward a larger aircraft

hovering high above the mining machines.

Whoever grabbed me was attached to a line that pulled us

back into the opening of the aircraft. More hands grabbed at my arms as the first let me go, and I was forced backwards. With no time to think, I was shoved into a cage and the door was shut.

I slid toward the ground, but was thrown against the wall of the cage as the aircraft accelerated. Across from me, someone covered in one of the dark gray combat suits eyed me, but decided I wasn't that interesting after all.

The inside of the aircraft featured more controls than what could be found in the T23. Monitors and buttons covered a lot of the wall space. There were so many, everything was draped in a bluish tint from the light. With the aircraft's movements becoming more consistent, I stood to get a better look.

There were two seats at the main controls, with two inward-facing seats just behind each of those. Other than the person standing across from me, there were only three other people. A pilot kept everything moving smoothly, while another person sat behind him, and another stood just over his shoulder. The one standing turned and watched me for a moment, but ultimately decided I wasn't a threat. But when she glanced over again and saw that I'd stepped too close to the cage wall, my fingers resting in a few openings, she rushed over.

"Do not touch. Back away."

Her accent was heavy, but her pronunciation was precise. Fearfully, now that I was alone, I backed away and, with a nod, she moved back to where she'd been. Outside the windshield, we flew through a blanket of clouds. The light of the sun shone in, mixing with the blue tint of the monitors, and it left a tone that contrasted with what was actually happening.

For the second time in my life, I'd been kidnapped. But this time would likely be different, as it was obvious I wasn't being taken to Julie. I peeked over the shoulders of those standing near the front, but the monitors in front of them remained out of view. With no way out and no plan to conjure, I backed toward the wall and slid to the ground.

We flew for a while longer, before slowing to a hover. As the aircraft landed, I nervously stood to my feet. Though the tension was high inside my cage, it didn't reach much farther than that because everyone else was nonthreateningly calm. When the cage door opened, a hand beckoned me forward. My arms were forced behind my back, followed by the cuffing of my wrists, and I was nudged toward the aircraft's exit.

I'd been brought back to the large crater where Alora had trudged alone. We'd landed on another side of it, and a large, nearly transparent shell covered us. The shell obscured the world on the other side, blurring most of the crater and everything lying beyond it. It was an odd thing to see, but it paled in comparison to what to lie within the bubble.

Amongst a few other aircrafts, we'd landed in front of a round tower. It had not been there when we first discovered Alora, but now, hidden within the large shell, it jutted from the ground just outside the crater. It had a peculiar design, which started wide and tapered to a point on the front side of the building. Few windows covered it. Near the point at the top, an 'x' was deeply engraved. The top two 'arms' of the x extended much farther than the bottom two, and they ran until they disappeared off the edge of the building.

There was a walkway that only lead to a blank wall, but it moved as we got closer. Sliding apart, it revealed a slope that pointed us toward an underground opening into the building. More gray combat suits stood guard near the entrance. One eyed me as we passed, and watched until I was in the building and the wall slid shut behind us.

The inside of the building was large and brightly lit from a few windows, but the things inside were mostly dark. There were dark floors, dark walls, a few dark aircrafts resting in random spots, and a dark mood. The atrium stood a few floors tall and was topped with a high ceiling. A large, silver geometric symbol covered the middle of the floor, and parts of it glowed as we walked over it.

Opposite the entrance into the building was an elevator sitting next to a spiral staircase. The staircase only connected the first and second level, but the glass wall of the elevator shaft climbed until it disappeared into the ceiling of the atrium.

I was brought to the elevator and, inside, one of the gray suits pressed a few buttons, placed his palm on a scanner, and the doors closed. We rose from the ground and, due to the transparent wall of the elevator shaft, were given a clear view of the room we'd just left. Around it, everyone seemed to be busy with something. It was a lot like the academy, but the difference was that there were far fewer people.

Within moments, the sight disappeared and was replaced with the dark of a solid wall. I looked into the masks of the people surrounding me, but no one cared to look back. I turned my attention back to the wall, but jumped when I felt a sudden sting. Behind me, a grey suit officer held a thin tool that had just been retracted from my neck. The outside of it was dark but transparent and, holding it up to his face, the officer inspected what was left inside. Unbothered by my shock, his eyes moved from the tool to my face, and he nodded, satisfied. When the elevator doors finally opened, I exited first while still giving him a dirty look.

Directly across was a large room with a glass wall. A few control centers were spread around it, and a planet hologram hovered above each. The floor beneath each of the control centers sat lower than the walkways separating them, and the main walkway led to a control area that was three times the size of the smaller ones. A large dashboard ran the length of it, with a team of monitors towering over it. Beyond that, there was only a large window that gave a clear view into the calm of outside.

We stopped at the end of the main walkway. The dim room towered over us, only lit by the holograms and the light shining through the window. Initially, it appeared empty, but a person revealed himself when one of my kidnappers called out to him.

"Aywan, ru est yi."

Whoever he'd called out to had been staring at the monitors, which appeared to show camera feeds from around the building. Given the distance we were apart, it almost looked like feeds of the academy.

As I was being uncuffed, the silhouette of the man backed away from the monitors and turned to us.

"Most honored guest."

His voice was deep, and his accent heavy. Though he'd greeted me with a compliment, his tone was one of disinterest. It sounded as if I were just another task for him to check off a list, rather than a full person that had been brought to him.

A short stack of stairs brought him atop the walkway, and every step he took caused a chilling clank to echo around the room. With the light of outside shining through behind him, he remained a silhouette for most of his journey.

"I must admit you were not my first choice, but you are honored nonetheless."

Just as he began to reach us, his features came into view. He looked a bit older than anyone else I'd encountered since arriving at the academy, but he also seemed to be in good health. His back was strong, and his arms flexed with little effort. He wore a suit like that of everyone else, but his was bulkier, with a few extra pockets and some controls going down one of his arms.

Part of his face had been horrifically burned, to the point where one of his eyelids looked to have been melted over. The large mark covered about half his face, starting just after the edge of his platinum hairline, and ending at the corner of his lips.

He stopped. For a moment, he just stared. He studied me, and he continued to do so even when he finally spoke again.

"Welcome. I am Commander Gol."

nineteen

I only stared. Partly in awe and partly in fear, I found it hard to speak. Fortunately, it didn't seem to bother him. For a moment, he only stared back, seemingly picking apart my existence.

With a nonchalant wave of the hand, he dismissed his officers and turned to walk away. The clank of his feet returned, and he appeared unworried about the fact that he had just turned his back to an outsider.

"I'm sorry it was you that was brought. I would have preferred your director, but she is running a bit late."

He stopped halfway down the walkway and turned.

"I would have waited longer, but time has stretched too far."

My stomach tightened. The feeling of nausea began to brew, and I briefly felt lightheaded. When I attempted to take a step forward, the movement was weak and I almost fell. Though I caught myself before the fall, standing became too great a task. Tiredly, I sank to the ground and moved backwards until my back came to rest against the glass wall separating the room from the hall.

Unbothered, Gol only watched. Once it looked as though I'd found a position against the wall that was more comfortable than standing, he continued.

"For too long, my people have grown weary...they can wait no longer."

Breathing heavily, I failed to muster a response. Gol took note of the state I was in, and the realization made him smile.

"I apologize for the serum you've been given. It was supposed to have only been used on an unruly captive. But given the trouble your purple comrade caused, I suppose my officers didn't want to take the chance again."

His eyes wandered to the planet hologram hovering

nearest him.

"You know, the people of this world were also quite unruly. But those that are unruly and act too quickly typically fall the fastest."

His eyes briefly found me again, and he began to walk over. As he moved, he looked to each of the planet holograms he passed.

"It is a shame really. How unfair that those who have the strongest passions to maintain what they have are also those who can lose so much so quickly…but all is never lost. With proper leadership and guidance, the things we love can be reborn. They can be improved."

He stopped, staring coldly.

"Because even in the face of failure and absence, the love and longing we feel for certain places, people, things, and ideas, does not falter. And with calculated action, that is enough. We are an example of such."

My stomach finally granted me a moment of calm, and I spoke while still holding my stomach.

"What does that have to do with me? Why bring me or anyone else here?"

"Because that is what I wanted. Does it not suit you?"

I shrugged.

"Guess I don't see what there is to win. There's not much I can tell about the academy."

"Win? Sounds like a term that should be reserved for mythical heroes."

He shook his head.

"There are no real heroes here, for everyone is the hero of the story one chooses to tell. But I don't seek such a title. I seek equilibrium and balance. In the case of my people, you may call it revenge, but I am not a man of terror. I do not believe in distributing punishment before a people have been read of their crimes. That is why you are here."

He moved closer.

"You are merely an ambassador."

He stopped just in front of my feet. His silhouette towered over me, but then he knelt. When he spoke, his voice was lower.

"Are you aware of your mission number 9-3-7? I am told you're the result of a more recent looting, but I suppose anything is possible."

I responded with nothing more than a headshake, which satisfied him.

"Very well then."

The room began to dissipate. Starting at the window, it peeled away and passed over us, revealing a world we hadn't just been in. Faster than could be processed, I went from laying against the wall in the dim room, to standing upon a small mountain, overlooking a lively city below it.

The land surrounding it was covered in desert sand, though the city itself had lots of trees and greenery. Near the far end of it were a lot of glassy, oddly-shaped towers. Lights lined some of them, creating a colorful image that blinked in some spots while repeatedly disappearing and redrawing itself in others. It looked to be late afternoon, and clouds were rolling in from one direction, threatening a light rain.

Oddly, I could feel vibrations and hear sounds coming from the city. Through the flickering of visions and echoing of sounds, there were sights of people walking around, hugging, running, sleeping, eating, and partying. All these things mixed harmoniously to form a vibration that was calming. In so many ways, the world I looked down upon felt as though it had reached a point of existence that was just and proper.

Gol stared into the side of my face.

"Do you like it?"

When I nodded, he sighed.

"Well you are looking at something that no longer exists."

"How'd we get here?"

His eyebrows rose.

"I was told you had already made use of our technology. Much like your training room, the tower you're in manipulates the threading of time and space."

He stepped toward the city below.

"It is the only way we are able to visit a place this beautiful."

"Why is that?"

His eyes briefly dropped to the ground. Turning away, he pointed toward the sky. At first, it was unclear what he was pointing at, but the fate of the city eventually revealed itself. Fighting to stand out in the light of a setting sun, a few of the 'stars' in the sky were moving. With each passing second, they grew both bigger and brighter.

"Soon, all that you see will be destroyed…"

After a pause, he spoke again with a tone much lower than before.

"But not before a few guests arrive to steal all that we have."

Stepping forward, I squinted to get a better look at the city, but my attention was broken by the sound of commotion behind me. Fear gripped me, and I turned to find that I was no longer on the mountain. Instead, I was standing on a large walkway within the city. The buildings bordering the walkway were mostly metal and glass, and the walkway ran for as far as I could see, forming intersections with other walkways. They all cut through the buildings like roads, even though there appeared to be no cars.

Far off in the distance, the lights of the towers rose toward the clouds. The tallest building was topped with a spire, and it pointed directly at the approaching meteoroids. There were more than could be counted, and deep, ground-rumbling booms could be heard as they began to rain upon the horizon. As the crowd grew bigger and everyone's attention was given to the approaching danger, rain began to fall and an alarm sounded. Contrasting the previous stillness, the crowd moved quickly and Gol's voice entered my head.

"Our satellites were knocked out first, and as hundreds of bodies plummeted our planet, our leaders were too distracted to focus on the aircrafts arriving alongside them. We didn't know what they wanted, and many of us assumed they had come to help. For a while, that is also what it seemed."

Cutting through the light of the horizon, columns of dirt, smoke, and fire viciously jutted from the ground. Even at a far distance, they rose quickly, forming a row like the bars of a prison cell. Chunks of rock began to rain upon us, and they smashed through buildings and punched holes in the lights of the towers. Bit by bit, they dismantled the beauty of the city.

Someone bumped into me, nearly knocking me over. It turned out to be a child carrying a large, rounded bag. It was so full, she could barely see over it and her tiny arms looked as though they would give out any second. She'd nearly dropped it when she ran into me, but she quickly adjusted her grip and rushed away.

When I turned to see where she had run to, I found that I was no longer on the walkway. I now stood at the edge of the city about a mile away from the towers, which were now falling apart. Three large, boxy aircrafts were parked nearby, and each was being filled by people rushing from the buildings. Painted large across their entryways were the familiar three bars of the academy.

The people approaching them formed lines, and a masked academy officer waited for each at the door. The combat suits they wore were different from the ones worn now. With no reflective reptile-like skins, the suits were mostly smooth. They all had a utility belt, and their faces were hidden behind bulky helmets. As each person came up to them, they would tip their neck and the officer would press a pen tool into it. After a quick flash at the point of contact, the person would grimace or yelp, and then be ushered onto the aircraft. Inside, everyone was strapped into rows of seats that nearly required them to stand.

"Our people were tagged like animals of a farm."

Gol had appeared next to me, and he looked on at what

was happening as if it were the first time he was seeing it. He moved closer to the line, inspecting people as they passed. With each step, the desert ground crunched beneath his feet. No one in the line acknowledged his presence. At one point, he reached for someone, but quickly withdrew his hand. Mumbling in a language I couldn't understand, he spoke in a voice that was so low, it could have blended with the wind and rain that grew heavier with each moment.

Looking toward the city, he sighed.

"I was the head of our defense. I should've protected them from such things...but I failed."

When he turned to me, his face was stony and his eyes cold.

"But I will fail no longer. I've worked hard to avenge them and, this time, I will succeed."

I moved toward him, shaking my head as the rain fell harder and his expression tightened.

"But...they're helping them?"

"This was not help. All but a few of these people will die

during your genocidal trainings."

Behind him, the lines became unruly. The aircrafts had reached capacity, and officers were now forcing people away from the doors. Those that were being turned away started to panic, and a few began to cry. Two of the academy aircrafts were lifting off, and the last was about to follow. But just as an officer was pulling the door closed, someone rushed forward, screaming in a language I couldn't understand.

She had two small children with her. They both had long, dark hair that nearly covered their faces in the rain. She carried both in her arms, and they clung to her as she ran to catch the aircraft. When she made it to the door, her words grew more frantic.

She was begging, not for herself, but for her children. She had placed them on the ground, and repeatedly pushed them forward while pleading with the officer at the door. As rain muddied her words, the people next to her began to call out to the officer. They too began to plead for the children, and multiple hands either beckoned the children forward, or pushed them closer to the door.

As the officer stood quietly, another appeared, rushing her. When the two children finally made it to where she stood, she knelt and cupped their faces. Looking back to the mother, she stared silently for a moment, before nodding and grabbing them. Initially, the other officer attempted to stop her, but quickly gave up.

The crowd watched in silence as the door to the aircraft was shut and the mother fell to her knees, crying. Her hands trembled, and her wails danced with the noise of the rain. Plastered to her face, the ends of her hair fell into her mouth. The aircraft powered up, blowing raindrops in all directions, and the mother sank further, wailing into the wet ground.

As we watched the aircraft disappear into the sky, the crowd gathered closer and comforted her. Calmer than before, Gol turned to me once again.

"Other ships landed near military facilities and government buildings, and they used the commotion of the moment to steal our technologies. With personnel scattered and our leadership coordinating an evacuation of our own, many were left defenseless."

He stepped closer, coming so close his breath broke through the rainfall and brushed against my face.

"But they will be avenged. I will enjoy every moment of it, and when I grow bored of you, the universe's opportunistic thieves will feel what we did."

He stared a moment before adding,

"I will make sure of it."

In a blink, the world went dark. I was no longer in the doomed city. Instead, I found myself lying on the ground inside a cell with white walls. Thick glass stood in place of prison bars, and it allowed a view into a hall that was empty. Across from me was another cell, which was also empty.

My head hurt. For a moment, the room spun. Given the grogginess I felt, it was possible I'd been unconscious for ages. But my mind offered no explanation. It was almost as if everything I'd just saw were merely a dream, even if I were sure it had been real. Even in the quiet of a cell, I could still hear the wailing of the mother and feel the rumble of the ground being torn apart.

Overwhelmed, I sat up and backed against the wall behind me. Though I was confined to a cell, likely destined for death or torture, the silence provided an enticing comfort. With so much happening, I'd lost track of who I was only a week ago. So quickly, I'd been consumed by the academy. Reality had reached a point where the believable and unbelievable had blended, and I'd been left feeling more lost than I had while sleeping on a sidewalk. But the sudden silence changed that for me, even if only for a moment.

Relaxed, I closed my eyes, but doing so only brought me back to the sight of the doomed city. Stuck within my new cell, I could almost feel the patter of the rain and the rumble of the meteorites.

I wondered what had become of the people taken by the academy. It was a place that seemed to force a choice between being an officer and being whatever you were before. Luckily for me, I hadn't left much behind. The only mother I'd ever known wasn't really mine, and the father I'd been taken from was too old and frail to do much of anything. So, in a way, I'd always been a prime candidate for their way of life.

twenty

Stuck against my hip, my mask emitted tiny vibrations. A voice accompanied it but, initially, I ignored it. But when the voice came again, I nonchalantly pulled the mask over my head.

"Psshh, Officer Winor, please respond. Psshh, Officer Winor, if you're alive, say, 'Saav is the best officer ever.'"

I sighed. When I tried to speak, I was reminded of my headache, and groaned.

"Where are you? I'm in a cell and don't know how long I'll be here. I think they're waiting on Ju- the director."

No response came.

"Hello? Saav, where are you?"

"Psshh, I'm sorry, I believe you have the wrong frequency because Officer Winor was instructed to say, 'Saav is the best officer ever."

"Stop wasting time and come get me! I don't know when they're going to show up again."

"Psshh, I'm sorry, but-"

"Saav! Stop and co-"

Outside my cell, one of Gol's officers appeared. He was obviously supposed to be standing guard, and wore their usual suit with a large gun strapped to his chest. Knowing I'd been caught doing something I shouldn't, I froze. But it was too late.

Reaching over and placing a palm on a scanner I couldn't see, he opened the cell and rushed inside. My mask was snatched off my head and tossed across the room. Causing my head to spin, I was pulled from the ground and roughly pushed against the wall.

"I-I-"

Angrily, he pulled me from the wall and tossed me to the

other side of the cell. As I caught my footing, he raised his gun, aiming for my chest. Taking a deep breath, I froze and prepared for the worst, but the gun was suddenly dropped. Contrasting the previous aggression, the guard laughed, resting against his knees for a moment. When he rose again, he snatched off his mask.

Saav.

"You really should have repeated the secret message. I didn't recognize you for a second."

While I stared, partly in shock and partly in anger, he laughed a moment longer.

"Okay."

He took a deep breath.

"We've probably got about two minutes before they realize I'm here so we may need to move things along."

He pulled his mask on and turned to leave, but stopped when he saw I was still staring at him, unmoving.

"No, seriously, we don't have a lot of time. Also, here."

Moving just out of view of the cell, he grabbed a uniform like the one he was wearing, came back into the cell, and offered it to me. I snatched it from him, still angry, and he flashed an innocent smile, which only annoyed me further. But with time running out, I started pulling my combat suit off.

As I changed, Saav waited near the entryway. I moved quickly, and he glanced over his shoulder just as I was pulling my new mask over my head. He nodded approvingly when I exited, but I ignored him. As we walked down a cell-lined hall, there were no attempts to shake off my anger. Instead, I basked in it and, unbeknownst to Saav, I toyed with the thought of pushing him out of the T23.

He led the way through a maze of halls that were mostly empty. He talked the entire time, and only stopped whenever we passed one of Gol's officers. We'd only passed a few, and they all seemed to be too busy to suspect anything. Most didn't even glance in our direction. It was surprising, but we were also helped by the fact that everyone in the building wore their masks.

"-That, and this tower is pretty much a ghost palace. Felt like I was walking around for ages before I found you. Wasn't stopped once. Which is disappointing considering I kind of wanted to run fast, jump high, dodge a few bullets. But nope. Walked around this place like I was the janitor. I'd be dead by now if this were the academy. You'd have to be a god to sneak in there unnoticed. Plus there's the At-"

"Saav?"

"Yeah?"

"You've said a lot, but you haven't said how you got here or how we're getting out."

"Oh, sorry. Well, our T23 took too much heat after you were taken, so we had to land. The landing was rough, but you can't ask for much with Ravi at the handle anyhow."

We reached an elevator, which opened after scanning the palm of Saav's suit. It turned out to be the main elevator I'd been in earlier. As we ascended, there was nothing but a solid wall on the other side of the concrete. Given the number of floors we passed, it appeared I'd been locked deep underground.

"And then we had a little fire fight. You know, ran fast, jumped high, dodged a few bullets, that sort of stuff. We took the aircraft the idiots had brought, which is designed almost like a 23, so obviously they're not afraid of stealing stuff. My guess is they took the design back when they killed off the first team that came here. Which wasn't too long ago so they must be moving things along at holy speeds. Can you imagine having to-"

"Saav?"

"Yeah?"

"How are we leaving?"

"Oh, everyone's waiting in the aircraft. Ravi thought it was a stupid idea but whose going to find them? There are like ten people here, they're busy."

"Why send one person?"

He shrugged.

"Only had one suit. The others were a little...tattered."

Above our head, an alarm sounded. It echoed and vibrated from each of the floors we passed, and soon the elevator was surrounded by the noise. Excitedly, Saav snatched his mask off.

"Finally."

"...what is that?"

He smiled and lightly tapped his mask against my chest.

"That would be my new theme music. Means it's time to run fast, jump high, and dodge some bullets."

He studied the elevator's keypad.

"They'll probably be expecting us on the main floor, so we'll go to the one above it. Make 'em work a little."

He tapped a button and placed his mask back on his head. Just before his face disappeared inside of it, he caught sight of my worried face, and grinned alongside a quick eyebrow raise. Tired, I only sighed. When the elevator door opened, the noise rushed inside. There was no one waiting for us but, even so, the noise brought a tension that almost made me wish for the quiet comfort of a cell.

We came out onto the second floor of the atrium. There was a walkway, bordered by a railing, and each faraway end of it only gave the option of a hall leading back toward the center of the building.

Peeking over the railing, we caught sight of a few of Gol's officers just as they caught sight of us. Saav leaned away, adjusted the weapon strapped to his chest, and used it to gesture toward the main door I'd been brought through.

"Remember, we need to get through there. Doing a flew flips may be fun, but soon they'll realize Ravi is parked out fr-."

"Hey!"

At the end of the walkway, a gray suit appeared. He froze a moment, as if he were surprised to see us, but he quickly raised the weapon he was holding. Fortunately, Saav was quicker. Taking aim, he knocked the weapon out of his hand. When a few more gray suits appeared, he unstrapped his gun and gave it to me.

"You'll probably need this more than me. It won't penetrate the suits, but it can buy you time. Just aim for the head."

He dashed toward the gray suits. I went to follow, but stopped at the sound of feet behind me. Another of Gol's officers had appeared, so I raised the weapon I'd been given and started pulling the trigger. A couple of the shots were a direct hit, but the officer didn't stay down.

When he got too close, I aimed for his head. Dazed, he staggered. I then used the weapon like a baton, and he fell against the railing. He attempted a few swings of his own, but was too disoriented to land anything. Given the momentum, I quickly swooped underneath him and forced him over the railing. When I rushed to help Saav, the officers he'd been fighting were already unconscious. Two were unmasked, and so was Saav.

Frozen, Saav stared at me, and the silence was only broken by the sound of a thud on the bottom floor. Awkwardly, he nodded.

"I mean…okay."

Breathing hard and feeling proud, I pulled off my mask, tossed it to the ground, and slapped his shoulder as I passed.

"Let's go, officer."

At the end of the walkway, two more of Gol's officers appeared. I began to shoot, but Saav grabbed my arm and dragged me toward a spiral staircase near the elevator. Feet clanked down the steps above us just as we neared the bottom, and a few gray suits waited just at the landing. Taking aim, I cleared the way for us.

We started to run for the main entrance, which was still tightly sealed, but the gray suits caught up and a fight ensued. Saav proved to be more useful than I was, even without a weapon of his own. The floor of the atrium became a spatter of movement, and I lost sight of who was who.

At one point, I mistakenly clubbed Saav across the back. He turned, ready for a fight, but sighed when he saw me.

"Thanks. I definitely needed a pat on the back."

When another of Gol's officers took a swing, the fight resumed.

"AZAH!"

Everyone froze. Cutting through the crowd was Gol, and his officers spread apart as he came nearer. I raised my weapon, which caused a few of Gol's officers to do the same. But with a raise of his hand, he calmed them and they dropped their aim. As he got nearer, he remained unbothered by my weapon, which was still raised. Instead, he looked past me and at Saav. I moved out of his way, but Saav remained, still holding a defensive stance. Staring with a look that was hard to read, partly because of his scarred face, Gol stopped about five feet from Saav.

"…son."

Dropping his arms, Saav relaxed.

"Oooh you must be using your bad eye."

Behind him, there came a deep rumble. It was heaviest just on the other side of the main entrance, but it rocked throughout the entire building. I and Gol's officers seemed to be the only ones who had noticed. Both Gol and Saav went unbothered.

Gol took a step closer but stopped when there came another rumble. This time, the noise was louder, and the building shook harder. Slowly, Saav began to move away. When Gol attempted to step toward him again, Saav raised his hands.

"No worries, I'm just…trying to get in front of your good side."

For a moment, Gol stood frozen with the same dumbfounded look on his face. Just as he started to move again, mumbling something indecipherable, another rumble came, and the main entrance was blown open.

Debris, dirt, and smoke blew into the room. Most of the people standing around were far enough from the door to have not been hit, but Gol had been standing right in front of it. His body landed near his officers, and they all rushed to his aid. But the entire time they inspected him and pulled at his arms to help him stand, his dirt covered face only looked to Saav.

It was an unsettling gaze, but the moment was broken by Saav yanking at my arm. Tearing my attention from Gol and his officers, I chased after him, dashing through the gaping hole that used to be a carefully placed entrance.

The covers that had been over the incline leading outside were blown open, and pieces of them littered our path. When we finally emerged from the debris, one of Gol's dark aircrafts hovered in the smoke, waiting. But instead of shooting, it rotated and came to rest on the ground. When its entryway was dropped, Luna appeared.

"Is he okay?"

Referencing me, she looked to Saav for an answer.

"He's moving isn't he?"

He dashed past her and, when I came up just after him, Luna stuck out her arm, stopping me. She grabbed my shoulders to steady me, and checked around my head. Inside the aircraft,

Saav grew annoyed.

"You may want to hurry up unless you're in the mood to have to check the rest of us too."

She nodded, and we moved inside. Ravi was seated at the front, and Alora sat just behind him. Saav was buckling up in one of the inward-facing seats behind Ravi, but stopped as Luna passed him on her way to the empty seat at the controls.

"What about me? You let me run right past."

She glanced over.

"You are fine."

"How do you know?"

"Because you are still talking."

Saav reached down and felt around the floor near his seat. When his hand emerged, he held a slightly torn mask.

"So, I'm always talking."

As he pulled on the mask, Ravi turned around for the first time.

"Exactly."

Outside, a few of Gol's officers appeared just as the

aircraft's entrance was shutting. I buckled in next to Alora, who offered me a partially torn grey mask.

As I nodded and accepted it, Ravi brought us into the air. The smoke rising from the building was blown about as we rose but, even in the cloud, a spray of bullets found us. Maneuvering carefully, we broke free of it all, only to be brought face to face with another aircraft rising from the ground. Its windshield was nearly as dark as its body and, behind it, Gol's officers remained hidden.

Neither aircraft made a move. Across from me, Luna grew nervous.

"Ravi..."

"No worries."

He pressed buttons and flipped switches. Below our feet, weapons in the aircraft moved into place. He maneuvered us backward, all the while firing on the other aircraft. The bullets rained down just as abundant as the ones we'd been greeted with. Gol's officers responded with gunfire of their own and, momentarily, the sound of clashing metal was the only thing that could be heard.

Ravi slapped two switches above his head, abruptly shutting the aircraft off. As we fell backwards, my heart felt as though it would reach the ground before the aircraft but, after a second, everything turned back on and we were thrusted forward. As we sped away, the aircraft shuddered violently.

We aimed for the sky, but the sound of bullets threatened to pull us back down. At the controls, Ravi grew more apprehensive.

"We're not losing them any time soon."

He curved the aircraft back in the other direction. Every bullet felt twice as powerful as the one before it. A missile was fired, coming at us head-on. Banking sharply, we barely dodged it, and the other aircraft banked to follow, effortlessly keeping up.

The journey to the ground felt longer than the path to the clouds. Once we made it, leveling just above the trees, the forest was violently shaken awake. Leaves were torn from branches, and blurs of animals dashed around as they ran from the chaos of wind and bullets.

Up ahead, the trees dropped away and were replaced by a stretch of blue blobs. As we neared, they rose, and shrieks of fear cut through the air. They became a field of large birds, and turned out to be the same we'd seen before we crash landed on Prasola.

Plenty got away, but they rose in a never-ending stream. Ravi diverted, but it was too late. As bullets cut through their wall of blue, they rained from the sky in a shower of despair. Those that weren't shot were knocked down by those that were, and the entire group was brought back to the ground.

We approached a lake that ended halfway to the horizon. It lay calmly, unconcerned with all that was happening just above it. Trees lined the distant edges of it, barely peeking through the light of a setting sun.

At the front of the aircraft, the radio crackled to life.

"T-t-tea-team members nine…ni-nine…nine, seven, eight…."

The voice was broken, repeating itself or skipping words entirely.

"AC…four…forty-seven… AC47…"

Saav grew excited.

"A beacon!"

Ravi nodded.

"They've got to be close…"

"There!"

A group of T23s broke from the clouds and fired their weapons, forming a path on the water's surface just behind us. The battering was harsh. Oddly, Gol's officers didn't attempt to defend themselves against the onslaught. Instead, it kept its focus on us.

Halfway across the lake, a shot ripped off the tip of our wing. The area was tattered and busted, and wispy smoke flowed from it. Something pierced the underbelly of the aircraft and, slowly, things begin to shut off. Screens flickered, fighting to remain but, one by one, they all failed.

Ravi fought to stay calm.

"Fuel is dropping rapidly…Landing's gonna be rough."

Saav sighed.

We began to lose altitude, losing more of the aircraft with

every moment. As we descended too quickly, the world felt as though it wasn't really there. The aircraft didn't exist and neither did the academy. I was dreaming again. Disconnected from everything, I found my mind somewhere in a safer reality. In a place where sleeping on the street provided more peace and comfort.

As we dived into the forest lining the lake, I squeezed my eyes shut. The scrape of metal clashed with the breaking of trees, and heat and fire surrounded us on all sides. Still feeling as though I were moments away from waking up, I opened my eyes. The world around us existed in a passing blur of black, grey, green, orange, and yellow. Somehow, even so close, it was all so far away and, after another moment of commotion, everything stopped.

I opened my eyes, unaware I'd closed them again. Strapped to my seat, I could feel the force of gravity attempting to pull me closer to the ground. But it failed. Everything at eye-level was blurry and indistinguishable. A cool breeze blew past, comforting me. Far above, silhouettes sped through the sky and, somewhere in the distance, someone screamed my name. But I had no time to wait for them. With the feeling of tiredness falling over me, I

closed my eyes and allowed myself to rest.

twenty-one

Everything was dark. A wave of low mumbling came and went, but the words were indecipherable. A deep, distant groan encased me, and it repeatedly stopped and started again. It felt as though I were simply sleeping. But I was not. Large hands tugged at my shoulders and, when they finally stopped, a chill rushed over me.

The voices continued to muffle their way into my head, until I felt someone pat me. The noise became unbearable. So, surrounded by the commotion of a circus, I panicked. It felt as though I were under attack and, no matter how much I tried, my eyes wouldn't open.

As the noise continued, bits of it became actual words.

"Don't be afraid. There's no reason to be afraid, Allen…Allen…"

With every call of my name, the voice faded away until, finally, I was alone again. But the silence lasted only a fleeting moment, before the mumble of voices started all over again. This time, they weren't as garbled. Some even provided comfort and a sense of safety.

One was urgent, even slight angry. But the other was tepid. The urgency and anger in the first voice grew as a direct result of the tepidness of the second. Their words were unclear, but their tones rose and fell. It was as if they were in a competition to see which could force the other to give into their own attitude.

As I became more aware of my body, I realized how exhausted I felt. The simple act of opening my eyes required a fight. At first, the lids only fluttered, begging for another moment of rest. But when they gave up the battle, I was met with a sight more confusing than the mumbling I'd heard.

I'd been placed in a container. It was laid horizontally, and the lower half of it was padded like a mattress. But it didn't matter much because my body didn't lay flat against it anyway. Instead, I hovered about five inches above it. The air was foggy and light, and breathing felt like not breathing at all. But, oddly enough, it wasn't painful. It just made the world feel empty and void of purpose.

My limbs were weak. I wanted to push against the glass or call out to someone, but I couldn't. my eyes were dazed, and the lack of power made me feel as though I were trapped in a dream. It was as if my mind were fully awake, but my body wasn't. Internally, I yelled out, but the words never made it to my mouth.

I attempted a turn of the neck. It happened so slow, I thought I hadn't moved. But a blink of the eyes shifted time itself. Suddenly, I was looking in the direction of the voices. They had sounded as if they'd been standing across the room, but they had actually been right next to the container.

There was little light, so they only appeared as silhouettes, but their gestures and body language betrayed them. It was Julie and Director Ruid. Julie spoke with urgency, while Ruid remained just as nonchalant as he'd been during the introductions in the grand arena.

They moved slower than normal. It felt as though I'd been watching them for a full thirty seconds, but their movements only indicated half of that. For what felt like years, they argued. But when Julie caught sight of me in her peripheral, she stopped. Surprised by her abrupt quietness, Ruid followed her eyes. Nervously, she reached over and pressed a button on the side of the container.

The fog was sucked away and, slowly, my body came to rest against the padding. Sweat formed a sheen across my skin. Ruid lifted the lid, allowing cold air to rush inside, and air filled my lungs, once again giving the world a sense of weight.

A thin shirt and a pair of shorts clung to me, glued down by the layer of sweat. Whatever was in the fog had left a light blue residue behind, and it became powdery as the air struck it. I must have looked like a clown, but the faces of the directors didn't show it. At least Julie's didn't. She looked at me with concern, while Ruid remained uncaring.

As I processed more of the world, I tensed up. Julie no longer looked like the Julie I'd seen the first time I woke up in the academy. She looked worn. Her eyes still shone with authority, but now they were accompanied by lines that would've taken years to form. Her hair still hugged her scalp like a fitted crown, but it was longer and there were strands of gray scattered throughout. Most shocking of all, she could no longer stand. Instead, she sat in a chair that hovered off the ground.

She reached over, pressing her hand against my forehead. She then stood up, balancing against the container, and stared directly into one of my eyes. After a few seconds, she switched to the other. When she sat back down, she cleared her throat.

"How are you feeling?"

"Exhausted."

My throat was dry, and I was overcome with thirst. But, seemingly satisfied, Julie nodded.

"I was afraid your body would reject our medicines, and things would become...unfixable."

Her eyes fluttered for a moment, but she quickly became composed again. With the calm returning to her face, she took a deep breath, and relaxed in her seat. As if her volume had bothered me before, she lowered her voice.

"I'm sorry I sent you on that mission..."

Her voice broke, but no tears fell. Ruid eyed her, but he didn't say anything.

"It was too early for you, and it was obvious that something had gone wrong with YARA but...anyhow, I've ordered the suspension of any foreign missions until further notice."

She glanced at Ruid, and brought her eyes back to me.

"So you won't have to leave again...to go anywhere."

She grabbed my arm, squeezing it lightly.

"As soon as you're well enough to leave this room, I'm going to attach you to my hip."

I nodded, and turned my gaze back to the ceiling. Part of

me still yearned for sleep. It was odd given the fact I'd been comatose. But even in those few short moments, the tiredness had grown too strong to ignore.

Julie turned to buzz out of the room. But just before she moved, I reached for her arm.

"And everyone else?"

She patted my hand.

"They're all fine. We came to pick up and finish the job, so don't worry about it."

She gently pulled away, pressed another button on the container, and buzzed out of the room. Just as she and Ruid passed through the door, a medical officer came in. He began asking questions, but I ignored him. Instead, I stared at Julie.

She'd stopped as if she weren't ready to leave. She stared blankly down the hall before turning to meet my gaze. Giving me an even clearer view of her aging as she sat in the light of the hallway, she just stared. Her eyes were mysterious, and her gaze arresting but, still, she looked unbelievably tired. After a couple seconds passed, she finally buzzed away.

The medical officer quietly examined a few monitors that hung over my head. The angle protected their content from my eyes, and I only had the effort for a single attempt. But the look on the officer's face indicated something complicated. As if he still felt Julie's presence, he glanced at the door and then down to me.

"It's hard to look, isn't it?"

His accent was heavy, and every word sounded calculated. I turned to him, feigning ignorance of what he was referring to. But he knew better, and we were both aware of what he'd meant.

"Her progression. So fast, she does not believe it. But she is tired, and now her soul withers."

He'd turned to the door, staring as if Julie were still there. He turned back to me, pausing as if he were expecting me to add a comment of my own, but I had no words, so I said nothing. Instead, I turned back to the plain, white ceiling.

Giving up, he went back to the monitors and tapped one of them.

"I'm happy to say you will be well."

He started to say something else, but stopped when

another person appeared at the door. With perfect posture and a lean build, the person had wavy hair and smooth skin. His face was that of a new friend. He stood in silence for a moment, awkwardly, before deciding my gaze was enough of an invitation to enter.

As Saav walked over, we were both unsure of who should speak. At first, he was tense. But then he braced against my container, sighed, and made a face.

"You look disgusting."

I laughed, which revealed that laughing was painful. But he was right. With parts of my body dry and powdery, while others were wet and sweaty, I was sure I was disgusting.

Leaning away from the container, he switched his attention to whatever was on the monitor, and I grew curious.

"What does it say?"

"That you're gonna die. Painfully as a matter of fact."

The medical officer was still examining whatever was on them, and he reached down and tapped a couple buttons on my container before continuing his examination. Unburdened with the thought of telling me what he really saw, Saav rested against the container.

"It took you the longest to wake up, so we feared the worst."

"What's been happening while I was out?"

"Just rest and training. Director Winor won't allow anything else."

I dropped my eyes for a second. When I brought them back up, Saav was standing patiently with his arms crossed. Still tired, I sat up, struggling the whole way, and surprised the medical officer in the process.

"Julie said our job was finished, so I want to see it. How long was I gone? They probably got her treatment near completion by now."

I spoke faster with every sentence. Defensively, Saav raised his hands.

"That's just that sweet, sweet medicine making you feel stronger than you are right now, so let's relax a little."

"I feel fine."

He called my bluff with a single look, and turned to the medical officer. When the officer noticed he was waiting for an intervention, he shrugged.

"He has healed well. If he wants leave, he may."

Saav sighed.

"Thanks, Officer...?"

"Olsa."

"Officer Olsa, thanks-"

"No, no. Just Olsa."

Saav looked at him weirdly, but nodded anyway. Turning back to me, he dropped his shoulders.

"Okay, but at least clean up first."

Moving to the end of my container, he reached down and brought up a large, dark cloth.

Tossing it to me, he headed for the door.

"I'll wait outside."

Olsa took a final glance at the monitors, tapped a button on my container, and followed behind Saav. Grasping the side of the container, I pulled myself up and slid over the edge. When my feet touched the floor, I almost collapsed, but another grasp of the container saved me. On a low table across the room was a set of clothes that looked exactly like what I was already wearing.

Once changed and mostly wiped clean, I stepped into the hall to find Saav leisurely posted against the wall. He greeted me with a nod, and gestured down the hall.

The academy was different from before. Fewer people were in the halls, and all passersby managed to be colder and more formal than before we left. They were nearly lifeless shells of people, somehow even more robotic.

When we got to the dark passages where Julie's treatment was being tested, I started to feel uncomfortable. Our footsteps echoed eerily, and it felt as though we were the only people left in the building. The entire time we walked, my eyes remained forward, avoiding a peek into the windows we passed. The image of the guy with the large blotches covering his body replayed in my mind, so I avoided witnessing anymore casualties.

I held my breath as we approached the lab. Saav opened the door, revealing a room that was just as quiet and dim as the hall outside of it. Salesti was hunched over a table, asleep, and he didn't move when we entered. But as Saav sat on the stool next to him, and I took the one on the other side of the table, he jolted upwards.

He looked spooked, but calmed when he saw who it was. When he spoke, his voice was groggy.

"I was just brainstorming something..."

I stared at the test tubes resting in a rack on the table.

"We're not here for anything specific. I just wanted to see the progress of Julie's treatment..."

"Well an officer took a trial and lived. He said he felt fine throughout the process and testing confirmed such so..."

He followed my eyes to the tubes.

"We just have to run a few more trials to make sure the results are guaranteed, and then we can move forward with curing the director."

"Can you show me?"

He nodded.

"Yes, of course."

He reached across the table and turned on the burner. The liquid warmed quickly. When things reached the level they were supposed to, he gestured for me to come around to the other side of the table.

After grabbing a magnifying glass and sliding it over, he signaled for me to take a look. With the magnifier focused and in place, the cells became clear as they calmly floated along. They still appeared to be oddly shaped, but their behavior was calm. They just slowly bulged into and out of different shapes.

"You're now looking at the damaged cells of the director."

He reached across the table and grabbed a tube with a clear liquid in it. Pouring it into the first one, he spoke lower than before.

"And these are the cells after the treatment is applied."

I held my breath, waiting for a drastic change, but it didn't happen. The cells stopped morphing, but that was it. They were still frozen into whatever shape they had already been in, and looked nothing like they were supposed to.

"Why aren't they going back to normal?"

"Well it's because this treatment doesn't reverse the director's illness, it simply stops it. That may not sound as exciting, but it buys us lots of time and keeps her from growing any worse."

I let out a sigh, and went back to the other side of the table.

"How long will it take to finish one that actually fixes her?"

It was obvious he didn't want to answer the question. For a moment, he didn't even respond and, when he finally did, he did so in a quiet tone.

"Well such a treatment could possibly be manufactured within a decade…Anything less would be a miracle."

I met his eyes across the table. For the first time, Saav spoke.

"So how long before this one is given to the director?"

"Assuming the rest of the trials go well, soon. Very soon."

I nodded my head, unsatisfied, but content. Looking back up at Salesti, I nodded once more.

"Okay."

Interlude V

From the Desk of Julie Winor

I sat in the banquet hall with Ruid, who was content with staring at me until I cracked and answered questions he hadn't asked. There were only the two of us, and the lack of distraction made it hard for me to ignore him. Beyond the towering glass that encased the room, a valley and forests abound across the land. It was calm, and quite a bit calmer than everything being experienced within the academy itself. Worse, everything in the building appeared calmer than what was being felt inside my own head.

I yearned to escape to the calm, simple world of outside. But, alas, an army of tables stood between me and the glass, while only one stood between me and Ruid. Finally, I gave in and looked him in the eye, which was all he wanted.

"I'm curious to know if you still believe this was a good idea."

"Don't be silly. He's my child."

I turned my gaze away as a pair of officers brought food over to us. The plates were steaming with a mountain of Rumin, and a cold glass of Okla was placed beside each. Desperate for an escape, I shoved a spoonful in my mouth and pretended to be more concerned with the food than I really was. But Ruid wasn't easily fooled. He knew me too well.

"Well I'm sure you know I understand that, Wuli. But that's not what decides whether or not something is a good idea. You should send him home. You've endangered him, and for what? A bit of contact? What if things don't go as you planned?"

He'd called me Wuli. It was a name I hadn't heard since just after my parents died, and it was one I'd forgotten since I became the Academy Director. Wuli had ceased to exist a long time ago. Wuli was someone who was vulnerable to the ills of the people around her. I was no longer Wuli.

I stuck another spoonful of Rumin into my mouth. When it was all gone, I blessed Ruid with another response.

"I have not endangered him by simply bringing him here. Allen is more than capable of adjustment, and I'm sure he will protect himself just fine. We've endured a few attacks and even won a battle, so I can assure you the academy itself will do just fine also."

The words had come out a little sharp, and Ruid grinned mockingly before taking his first spoon of Rumin. Within seconds, he swallowed it and reached for his cup of Okla. When the metal cup was placed back on the table, he resumed his prodding.

"So you consider escaping a win?"

"No, I consider a win a win. What are you really trying to

get out of me right now?”

He shrugged.

“So you’re saying you won’t send him back?”

“I’m saying I don’t need to.”

“And what about the bylaws you broke by bringing him? Will you rewrite those?”

I stared at him for a moment.

“Your extensive concern sounds more like Riv as each day passes. You’ve been somewhat of a stone for some time now, but you seem oddly obsessed with Allen. Why?”

His smile dropped.

“I am not a stone, and I am not “obsessed” with little Allen. I’ve merely calculated what should and shouldn’t have been. He was never meant to be here, and I’m sure you know that.”

“Oh, Anais. You’re a director in an academy that travels the galaxy and tries to play the invisible hand of fate to other societies. That is also something that was likely never meant to be, and if you’re logic is sound and fair, you’ll agree. If I must fix what I have done and where I stand, then you must do the same. So, if you always follow the guidance of nature and fate, step down from your position. Leave the academy and subject yourself to the cruelty of a more natural world."

He paused and stared at me. Rumin steamed from the spoon in his hand, and his eyes searched my face for any signs of my words being empty. But they were not, and I'd meant every one of them. When he saw how serious I was, he laughed.

"Wuli. The one who has turned the academy on its head on more than one occasion. It's the thing I love and hate about you. But, you're right. What should and shouldn't be is often a gray area and I will not attempt to dictate it to you."

He went back to eating his Rumin, but I'd lost my appetite. The room fell silent, and it was almost as if there were no longer a single person there. Not me, Ruid, or the officers standing guard at all of the doors.

After taking another sip of Okla, I voiced concerns of my own.

"What do you propose we do?"

He didn't even bother to look up.

"*My* opinion? You want *my* opinion?"

"Yes. The academy is facing a threat it has never seen before, and you are the combat director."

He placed his spoon down and rested his elbows on the table.

"Well, as much as Riv will hate me for this: I propose we do as you're already doing. Military vehicles are on the edge of completion and officers are training night and day. When you are preparing to face something you know nothing about, I don't think there's much else you *can* do."

"There's always more."

"And you're usually the one to reveal to the rest of us what that is."

For the briefest of moments, there sat Anais. The boy with the genuine eyes of admiration. He was like a ghost that would only appear for a second, before disappearing and leaving one to wonder whether he'd ever been there. But this time, it was different. He didn't disappear, and he revealed himself to me for as long as I'd hold the gaze. I found comfort in his presence, and in that moment, I knew Ruid would always be Anais. My old friend who was hardened, but the same nonetheless.

My gaze dropped to my plate, which was still piled with Rumin. With only another spoonful, Ruid was nearly finished. After scooping it into his mouth, he gulped the last of his Okla.

"Would you like to finish?"

When I shook my head, he backed out his chair and stood. He walked toward the large windows, and I quietly buzzed after him. A pair of officers cleared our table and, as we neared the glass, I suddenly felt smaller. Even within the academy, I'd been turned into someone that needed a chair to get to the other side of the room. I tried to push the realization from my mind, but the room loomed over me, and when we made it to the glass, it did the same.

Ruid stared out as the sun set over Avenur. There was a slight breeze in the distance, and the collective swaying of trees and fields of grass made everything look like a large ocean we could dive into if only we removed the window in front of us.

Ruid's reflection stared back at him, before both suddenly

turned to me.

"Do you remember the plans we used to make for all of this?"

He gestured toward the world outside, but I would've known what he was talking about even if he hadn't.

"Yes. We wanted homes over there, and training grounds over here..."

"Aircraft fields just behind there..."

When he looked down at me again, his grin was small, barely noticeable. But still, it was there.

"Ah, the dreams of children. I don't think this academy will ever grow into such a thing, but maybe it doesn't have to. What we have now is already well beyond what was intended anyway."

My eyebrows raised.

"I never let go of those dreams. I would still like to lead an academy where having a full society of our own is embraced, and children of Avenur aren't shunned for their existence."

"Becoming an actual society only brings on fear. If we were to do so, who's to say we wouldn't fall victim to the same things we aim to save others from? Even now, we're preparing for a war. In what book of the academy has it ever been stated that a war was fought against Avenur?"

I peered out at the peacefulness of everything lying around us. The academy was truly the only thing that didn't naturally fit with the land and air around it. But even then, that was another gray area. Without the academy and the generations of people who founded it, Avenur would be a desolate pool of fire like the other Andies. A place where nothing could exist.

I turned back to Ruid.

"I understand. I simply wish some things were different."

"I'm sure you'll make it so. You've done it before."

He walked off, but this time I didn't follow him. I stayed near the glass, where I was closer to the calm I yearned for. The setting sun cast an alluring glow over the world below it, and it shown brightest across the edge of the horizon. As I stared, it seemed to set more slowly, as if it were trying to give me another second of what I enjoyed so much. But the thought of such a thing was undeniably arrogant.

As large as the academy felt to those within it, we were only a spot on the planet, and a phantom in the galaxy. Placed in a valley and rudely built atop a forest, we attempted to make ourselves feel as though we were above the catastrophes we tried to keep others from. But in reality, we weren't immune. We were bigger than some things but, in the end, we were just as small and vulnerable to the things in the universe as anyone else.

twenty-two

I stood in the center of the training room, waiting for Julie. After giving me a few days to finish healing, that's where she'd asked me to meet her. No one else stood in the room. For a while, I thought no one would enter. But when the doors slid apart, she buzzed through them. She was accompanied by a tall and slender officer, whose black hair was tied up in a thick and complicatedly wrapped bun. The entire thing was weaved like a basket. When unraveled, it could probably pass her hips.

Julie smiled.

"I wasn't sure how energetic you'd be after spending so much time in the medical unit."

About five feet away, she stopped buzzing and pointed to the officer.

"This is my M.O., Ren Yeral. She'll be accompanying me seeing as I'm...in need of assistance."

A moment later, the walls dissipated, and we found ourselves in the middle of a small park. Two sidewalks crisscrossed each other, intersecting just below our feet. Trees were scarce, and there was a clear view of the streets bordering us on four sides. Weirdly, they were empty. There were no cars and no people. The park sat in a city center and, though buildings rose in every direction, everything was quiet. We were alone.

Julie sighed.

"Lovely."

At first, the area was foreign and unfamiliar. When it finally became something recognizable, I grew uncomfortable. I'd slept in this park before. But within so short a time of being away, I no longer fit within it. The trees, the streets, and the buildings were all insignificant, unimpressive, and far away. They felt like they belonged to a world I could never really return to.

Julie had buzzed down the sidewalk, so I hurried to catch up.

"I didn't know the training room could bring me back to places like this."

"It doesn't take you anywhere. It only allows you to experience a place an officer has already been."

She stopped near a park bench and gestured for me to take a seat. With her chair just on the other side of the bench's armrest, she looked around the park as if she'd never seen one. She was relaxed, and watching her brought a sense of calm to my own spirit. She looked at me briefly before turning away again.

"The simplicity of this world is so comforting. It almost makes me want to stay forever."

She turned.

"And that is why I brought you here. After enduring so much, I wanted to know if you wanted to return for good. We could even remove parts of your memory, freeing you of the burden of the academy's existence...Just like that, you could go back to being normal."

She paused and searched my eyes before quietly adding,

"I could make that happen for you..."

I looked away. Only a mere second passed as I mulled an answer, but when I looked back, Julie was nearly falling out of her chair in anticipation. Without saying a single word, she begged.

I took a deep breath and shook my head.

"There is nothing for me to go back to. I can't say I understand most things, but the academy has both pushed me away and pulled me closer. Even if you did something weird to my head, I'd probably always know it somehow."

"I know the feeling."

There was a short silence, but then she waved her hand.

"Stand up."

The world dissipated into darkness. It looked as though we were being sent into a void, but specs of light appeared, revealing the Grand Arena. Despite the crowd, it was silent. Above us was the blue band of the intel unit, with the violet band of combat just below. The only lights that were turned on were the ones tasked with lighting the stage.

The stage itself was empty. We'd arrived just moments before the directors would come out to fill it. Every mouth was sealed, and every expression stony. No one moved, and no one realized we were even standing there in front of them. They simply looked straight through us. It was as if we were ghosts, just like when Julie had shown me the small boy whose foot had been blown off.

In perfect unison, the crowd stood. A figure emerged onto the stage, heading for the podium. There were no other directors around. There was only her. She wore a combat suit, and her left arm was striped with a color for each of the academy's units. Her face carried an expression that bore a striking resemblance to that of Ruid. It was one that seemed to be perpetually angry or bothered. Nearly seven feet tall, her body was so thin, she would probably disappear in my peripheral. Her nose was close to non-existent, and her ears were two ridges that raised down the sides of her face. With limbs that were long and lanky, and hands that were large enough to palm my head, she was striking.

She reached the podium and paused. Authoritatively, her eyes seized the room. Her lips were tight, and her face hung low as if it carried the weight of all suffering. Unwavering, the crowd waited. When her eyes passed over us, I tensed up even though she couldn't see us. Even under the safety of a simulation, the intensity of her anger reached a level that somehow crossed dimensions.

She finally leaned toward the mic, looking as though she'd spit fire. There was a pause just after parting her lips and, when her voice finally came out, her words dragged. The sound of it was raspy, rough, and painful to hear.

"Heo. Sivv te."

Everyone immediately took a seat. Somehow, the movement was even more uniform than it was whenever Julie addressed the academy. As officers fell back toward their chairs, all necks remained stiff, and backs remained straight. No one glanced away from the stage, and knees only bent enough to allow sitting to actually happen.

My ears ached, and the room grew quieter. A pressure built inside of my head, and when it was finally released, the speech of the Director came out in words I could understand.

"I rise before you in a situation unfortunate…"

A woman appeared in the shadows of the stage's curtain. When she walked out into the light, I held my breath. It was Julie. A younger Julie that still carried the authority everyone had grown to know, even in her youth. As she walked, her eyes were straight, piercing into the back of the lady at the podium. But the Director didn't seem to notice.

"Our academy has felt a devastating shake. It was one that has affected us all. Going into effect immediately…I will be stepping down as the director of the Academy of Celestial Training. In my place will be-"

She turned to find Julie already standing there. It looked as though she hadn't expected it. The looks they exchanged were ones of hate. If it weren't for the crowd watching them, they'd have probably fought. But Julie's expression wasn't quite as angry as the Director's. It was only challenging. Not once did her eyes drop, and her fists slowly balled up as if she were in fact preparing to fight. But after a long, awkward moment, the Director turned back to everyone else.

"I will cede my post to Wuli Wino. She will be your decider. She will be your controller."

The crowd erupted into boos and shouts. Coming from the mouths of so many, it was a sound that snaked into my bones and grasped my skull. It was one of an absolute contempt, and part me felt as though it had been directed at me personally.

Older Julie's expression matched that of her younger self standing upon the stage. It was content and unbothered, and it hid everything that could possibly lie behind it. The eyes of younger Julie traced across the crowd, absorbing all that was being spat at her.

The director looked particularly happy with the response. For a second, a sly, small smile crossed her lips. She glanced at Julie, who once again gave her the death stare she'd gotten the first time. When she finally turned back to the crowd, her smile had fallen.

"It has been decreed. This decision is not to be undone."

Stepping away from the podium, she backed up and made room for Julie to join her. When Julie came and stood within inches of her, they eyed each other again. Silent to the ears of the crowd, the director's pursed lips repeated, '*It has been decreed.*'

They turned to face the room. All together, everyone rose again. The stripes on their arms changed, and Julie gained a stripe for each one the director lost. When the change was finished, Julie stood with a stripe for each of the academy's units, while the director stood with none.

When she stepped to the podium, outcries poured from the crowd, but they were much fewer than before.

"Please, be seated."

Reluctantly, everyone fell to their seats.

"My name is Wuli Wino, and I am your Director of Academy. Behind me is my predecessor, Sagenti Ilo...Though I wish there were kind words I could bestow upon her, there are none."

Again, the crowd erupted. Officers stood to their feet, and

some even stepped toward the stage. The noise was louder than it was before and, this time, younger Julie didn't react with a blank expression. This time, she looked confused and unnerved. As the ruckus grew and the noise became monstrous, her brows furrowed. When more officers maneuvered away from their seats, she grew angry.

"SIT!"

Everyone fell silent.

"…down."

She was still angry, but her voice had lowered. Her expression had also softened, but not by much. Officers began retreating to where they should have been, but some still silently refused. The few that took the longest looked around as if they were hoping more people would rebel with them.

"Ilo has tortured this academy and drained it of all it was destined to be. She's taught hate, impatience, and violence. She's stolen people we love, and tried to tell us they deserved it…And you believed it. You've believed that I am less than you are, because my birth broke from what was taught as acceptable.

You've even believed my parents deserved to die for it…"

The room became even tenser than before. I turned to Julie, but she didn't return the glance. She simply stared down at her younger self, fully entranced by what she was once again experiencing.

"…But that is not what I will teach. From this point forward, I am Wuli Wino, your Director of Academy. I am your teacher. I am your decider. I am your protector."

A random officer rose to his feet. He stood within the combat area of the arena, and there was a moment where Julie just stared at him. Her expression was one of gratefulness and, in the middle of their moment, two more people stood up. But as they did, the world around us dissipated yet again.

We'd been returned to the training room, but the tension remained. Next to me, Julie now sat with her hands in her lap and her eyes downcast.

"Moments like that are ones that constantly push me away while pulling me closer."

"Why were they so angry with you?"

"They thought my becoming director was the worst thing that could happen to the academy. I, an Avenur-born girl, was becoming Director of Academy. We're a place where having a child is seen as one of the worst crimes against our existence. It makes some feel as though we're becoming more like the people we try to protect, and being more like others equates to being just as weak as they are...how about I show you something else?"

We ended up taking a ride through the late afternoon. Most of it was spent with me staring down at the quiet, green land of Avenur. Ren Yeral sat in the front with a pilot I'd never met, while Julie and I sat near the back. Neither of us attempted to start a conversation, but there was a comfort in the silence. For there to have been so much that needed to be said, the comfort was oddly satisfying.

We were about to pass under something that was hovering in midair. It was a large silver orb with a few blinking lights around it, and the bottom of it was flat. Periodically, it would spray something into the air. I was the only one taken aback by it.

"What is that?"

Julie had been staring ahead, but she glanced over.

"It's an ATMOS guardian. We use it to maintain the environment on the planet. Without them, Avenur wouldn't harbor life."

Intrigued, I raised my eyebrows and nodded. Below us was a low mountain range that stretched for as far as I could see. It looked like a natural gate that separated a dense evergreen forest from a valley that produced nothing but grass. We were headed for the grassy side and, after we passed over them and flew about a mile in, Julie ordered our pilot to land.

Once on the ground, the aircraft's entrance was opened and the chilly air from outside blew in. The wind was so heavy, virtually every blade of grass was blown nearly flat. But there wasn't much else to see, so I just took a seat at the top of the ramp.

The air was refreshing. For a second, my thoughts and the world around me slowed. I closed my eyes and took a deep breath, and the effect was so strong I thought I'd fall asleep. Everything mattered less, and I found myself craving more of the fresh air.

"Careful, Al. Too much Zepyr air at once could put you to sleep."

I opened my eyes to the sight of Julie staring at me as she buzzed her chair over to where I sat. stopping just beside me, she peered at the valley as if it were the first time she was seeing it.

"This has always been my favorite place on Avenur. It's calming and makes me feel as though my worries are no more."

She stared with a faraway look in her eyes. Watching her made me crave for a peek into her thoughts, but I feared the things I'd find. She could be such a mysterious woman. The thought of knowing everything she knew actually made me uncomfortable. Even with the little I'd seen, there was too much.

I sighed.

"Are you afraid?"

"Of what?"

"Your illness."

She looked at me for a second without responding. It was a face I couldn't read, no matter how hard I tried. When she finally looked away, she gently shook her head.

"No. I think I've faced bigger problems. Why? Are you afraid?"

She dared me to answer with an affirmative. I considered telling her what she wanted to hear but, instead, I told the truth.

"I feel like I was only given a few minutes to experience a life with you, but soon the minutes will run out."

"You shouldn't worry so much. Enough Prasolin was obtained and the medical unit is working on something."

With an arresting gaze, she turned.

"I'm sure they're capable."

After a moment of listening to the wind, I understood why Zephyr was Julie's favorite spot. There was a weird sense of life in the empty, windy valley. It moaned and whistled, sounding as though it could tell an entire story if only I'd listen hard enough. It was calming and invisible, yet strong and graceful.

"I used to always try and picture what you would be like. But I never pictured this."

"Well, hopefully that's not too bad."

I shook my head, and things went quiet until I grew

curious again.

"What was it like?"

"What was what like?"

"Leaving the simplicity of home-or, my home, to come

back here. The day you had to leave us behind to come back to

this, and you stared at me, what were you thinking? I almost feel

as though I can hear you speaking to me sometime, from back

then, but it never makes any sense."

Julie's eyes dropped and her lips pursed.

"Well…"

Her voice cracked, so she stopped. For a moment, there

was nothing but the wind. Her eyes had watered a bit, and she

took a deep breath as a single tear fell and was blown into a wisp.

Finally, she turned again.

"I felt like I was leaving a part of myself. I wasn't excited to

go. The only thing it did was create an empty hole I can never fill."

The entire time she talked, she stared out into the field,

purposely avoiding the sight of me.

"But I didn't think it fair to separate you from your

destined normality because of my own decisions…bringing your father back with me would have been next to impossible anyhow. Most people, and things, on Avenur don't have families. Here, every person you pass is a remnant of a society or world that no longer exists, and it is that way by design."

She inhaled deeply.

"We don't take entire families. We're not a country. We're an organization of the broken, aimed at keeping others from breaking. That is who we are and, in my youth, I didn't have the power to change that. I barely have it now."

Turning, she reached out her hand, requesting mine. When I offered it, she gently pulled me closer and rested my hand against her face. In a way, it was as if she too were intrigued by my existence. I was as much of a dream for her as she was for me.

I closed my fingers, tightening my grip around her hand. Responding with a quick squeeze, she let me go and finally looked me in the eye. Though she remained silent, she smiled. It was a quiet, peaceful moment and, somehow, it answered every question I'd had.

When we returned to the academy, everything was quiet. The aircraft chamber echoed with every step I took. The buzzing of Julie's chair droned on as we moved, and could probably be heard from any of the platforms surrounding us.

As we waited for the elevator, she finally started talking again.

"Allen…there's someone I'd like you to meet. She's very-"

A lone patter of feet approached. They ran as if they were rushing to something important. The glass of the chamber gave a clear view of an officer coming around the curved hall, dressed in a dark gray combat suit. Just before he emerged around the curve, he slowed his pace. He was carrying something, but I couldn't tell what it was. Both Julie and Ren Yeral looked confused.

"Hey!"

Another officer came rushing after the first. She looked familiar, but I couldn't tell where I'd seen her. She had short, curly hair, and she broke into a sprint when the first officer ignored her. A closer look revealed the first officer to be my medical officer, Olsa. His expression was different from the first time we'd met. He was colder, emptier. Once there was no longer any glass separating us, he raised what he was carrying. Paired with the look on his face, his intentions were clear.

Julie nervously called out to the other officer still following him, reminding me of where I'd seen her.

"Talo..."

Olsa aimed. I thought he'd raised it at me, but he hadn't. Instead, he'd aimed past me. I moved when I realized his true target, but it was too late. The trigger was pulled, and the sound of a bullet echoed throughout the entire chamber.

twenty-three

He took another shot.

"MOVE!"

Julie cowered behind me and Ren Yeral. A couple of the ricocheting bullets were followed by the sound of Julie shrieking. Quickening footsteps echoed throughout the chamber just as the elevator's door opened. Julie was the first to be shoved in, with Ren Yeral doing her best to keep her covered. With my head down, I pulled my mask on and turned to Olsa.

Noticing I wasn't taking the elevator, Julie screamed.

"ALLEN!"

Her face was strewn with terror. Hand outstretched, she beckoned me to her, but I refused. Just before the doors shut, she yelled for me once more. But I'd decided already and, snatching my eyes away, I ran for Olsa.

Bullets thrashed my combat suit, but the barrage left no marks, and was cut off when Talo caught up to Olsa. In a flash, she grabbed him. Throwing him against the wall, she pummeled his face. There was a squabble for the weapon he carried, ending with it being knocked from his hands. As the gun slid in my direction, I hopped to avoid it.

Olsa dealt a few deafening blows of his own, and it was obvious Talo had felt them. Just as she was being flung to the ground, I ran up and tossed him aside. Stumbling a few feet, he dashed back into the fight. His swings were quick, and their power felt. Most were dodged, but a few landed across my face, stomach, and chest. He was skilled where I wasn't but, just as the hits began to take effect, Talo jumped in again.

The battle was intense. Two to one, Talo, Olsa, and I

threw blows one for one. Olsa easily held his own, but we fought with more ferocity. It was obvious Talo and I cared more. Sweat ran down my face, soaking the inside of my combat suit. The symptoms of exhaustion were shown, but oddly unfelt. Swing, swing, dip and dodge, swing. The fight took on a rhythm that became natural and wild. For a moment, we fought to music that wasn't there. It rumbled, cracked, thumped, and groaned.

There was an elbow to my chin and a punch to Talo's temple. We both rocked and stumbled for a second, which was all Olsa needed. Sprinting around the curve of the glass, he stopped at the nearest platform entrance. We caught up just as he was halfway down the platform and, again, battle ensued.

A string of blows brought us to the platform's edge. At one point, Talo fought while a fall to her death was only an exhale away. But she fought as if she hadn't even noticed.

Rushing feet spread throughout the chamber. Inside the curved hall, a swarm of officers appeared, and all ran to help. Within seconds, the hall was filled, and officers were coming onto the platforms. A few had weapons they used to shoot, while others ran for the aircrafts.

Only able to avoid the begging of death for so long, Talo slipped. Abandoning Olsa, I rushed to help. Olsa took this as an opportunity, and dashed for the end of the platform. There, an aircraft waited for him. Bullets decorated his path but, still he made it.

Officers rushed onto our platform. With extra hands, Talo was pulled up, while others shot at the aircraft. The offense had little to no effect. Underneath the spatter of bullets, the aircraft screamed to life.

Initially scraping the platform, it rose higher as it sped away. When it reached the end, it dipped over the edge, heading for the exit at the bottom of the chamber.

"NO!"

Talo's voice ripped from her throat. Charging, she broke through the small crowd of officers that stood nearby. I chased after her as she ran back into the hall and toward another platform. Other officers were already starting aircrafts throughout the chamber, and Talo and I caught the closest one just as it hovered from its platform. We leaped to catch the door before it shut us out, and rushed to empty seats.

Three other officers were already inside, but no one wasted time on greetings. We sped toward the end of the platform, and didn't slow as we poured over the edge. Other aircrafts did the same, but they did so at intervals that avoided a crash by a mere hair's width. Fortunately, the exit tunnel was large enough to accommodate the flow.

When we tore into the evening sky, Olsa was heading for the clouds. Shots rang out. With a single target, the bullets seemed to converge into a single weapon. Though academy aircrafts could take a beating, the assault was relentless. Battered, Olsa changed course, now aiming toward the ground.

Within moments, everyone caught up and, just behind Olsa, the other aircrafts formed a cloud that threatened to consume him. At the front of our own, an officer reached over and pressed a button on the dash.

"T23-194, this is your warning to land your aircraft. I repeat, this is your warning to land your aircraft...It will be your only one."

Nothing changed. The chase continued, and Olsa even sped up a little.

Our pilot sighed, annoyed.

"Guess we all needed the exercise."

Everyone spread out, widening the cloud that would wrap its hands around Olsa's T23. At the front, another switch was flipped. Electric currents pulsated and flashed near and around the aircraft, and the same was happening around most of the others. Soon, the currents converged. When it repeatedly reached for Olsa, his aircraft began to lose altitude. Seemingly, it was moments away from shutting down completely.

But in a show of determination, he banked. The movement was so quick, no one was prepared for it. A few aircrafts tried to move out of the way, but it only caused collisions. As crashes colored the sky, the skill of our pilot was the only thing keeping us in the air. Billows of smoke and flame formed an obstacle course that threatened a crash after every turn.

A few T23s fell from the sky, while everyone else spread as

far apart as possible. Olsa had sped ahead and was now heading for the clouds again. Angrier, everyone shot at once. This time, even the shooting managed to sound more coordinated, and it took on a beat that was felt as well as heard.

Olsa banked and curved, doing all he could to avoid sudden death. His skill was obvious, but everyone else cared more. They all began curving and banking in an attempt to cover every area he may try to escape through and, somehow, we ended up dead center of it all.

Aircrafts shot, banked, curved, sped, and screamed across the sky. Oddly, it was well coordinated. Like the walls of a moving maze that everyone had been forced to memorize, every movement became fluid and precise. But, being an officer of the academy, Olsa skillfully dodged every maneuver.

A voice crackled through our speaker. It was one that was tired, but also dripping with determination.

"Father Gol breeds no failure. He breeds no fear. You may chase. You may shoot. But you will never overcome us, for to kill us would be to kill yourselves."

The aircraft was tense. Everyone continued their swirling and diving maneuvers, until there came a tiny explosion across the belly of Olsa's aircraft. Abruptly, it was thrown backwards through the formation of T23s. It flipped violently and clipped a few other aircrafts as it fell. Narrowly, we avoided its path. With everyone in shock, one of the officers in our T23 grew hysterical.

"It's suicide!"

With a shake of her head, our pilot dismissed the outcry.

"No, it's not."

We rocked in another direction. Every move was precise, and just barely saved us from crashing into someone else. Free of the cloud of debris and other aircrafts, we chased after Olsa. One side of his T23 was covered in flame and, as it twirled, it created a ball that left a smoking trail behind it.

Below us was a field of rolling hills, bordered by a forest. We slowed as we got closer, but our fate was already sealed. Holding on tight, I prepared myself for the third rockiest landing of my life. Up ahead, Olsa crashed directly into the forest. He'd disappeared into the trees, and his location was only given away by smoke.

"Here we go…"

Our pilot turned us slightly to avoid a direct a hit, and succeeded. Relatively. With the aircraft skidding across the field, the landing wasn't much to wish for. We hadn't deployed any legs but, given our speed, they would've likely been torn off anyhow.

The T23 stopped sliding just before the edge of the forest. Talo was the first to unbuckle and dash toward the opening door. Everyone else had to rush to keep up. As she jumped to the ground and sprinted for the forest, she pulled on her mask.

The forest was denser than the one on Prasola. So much so, we hopped and jumped just as much as we ran. Everything went by in a blur, and no attention was paid to anything around us. All eyes stared in one direction, and we all ran for where the smoke was thickest.

If it weren't for my mask, I'd have been blind in the forest. But my path was clear and so was Talo. She was a spot that constantly zigged and zagged, moving so easily, it looked as though she had the whole forest memorized.

When we got to the area where Olsa had crashed, there was nothing but broken branches and fire. His aircraft was a mess of metal, and pieces of it littered the area. It had created a clearing in the forest, and we all slowed as we entered it. All except Talo. She ran to the aircraft itself and attempted to look inside. When I crossed over to her, she quickly backed away, frustrated.

Olsa wasn't there. She paused and looked around for a moment, before turning and continuing her manhunt. Not wanting to be left behind, I followed behind her. As we entered the forest, there were a few quick, successive beeps. After a moment of silence, an explosion rocked the forest. It had come from the crashed aircraft, and everyone still standing in the clearing had disappeared in it.

The force threw me and Talo to the ground. Rising, I froze at the sight of scattered body parts. Burned and tattered, they lay lifeless across the ground. A few officers had been traveling without their mask on, and evidence of it lay just beyond my feet. A couple of masked officers had only been thrown to the ground. They rolled over and coughed, but there was no time to stop and help them. Leaves crunched as Talo jumped to her feet and continued running. She hadn't wasted any time on checking on the other officers. After peeling my eyes away from the gruesome death, I chased after her.

She dashed through the trees even quicker than before. Slowing to a stop, I allowed myself a moment to breath. My mask was pulled off and dropped to the ground. The air was still filled with smoke, but it was thin enough to crouch low and breath fine. Talo's running echoed in the distance, but soon it faded to nothing. Exhausted, I was alone.

I panted, sweat dripping down my face. Even in the relative quiet of the forest, the world was chaotic. The sound of T23s still whirled overhead, searching for Olsa. Pulling to my feet, I started running again. No one else could be heard in the forest.

Eventually, I came to a creek. There was no telling whether Talo had crossed it, and there was no telling whether I or anyone else was even searching in the right area. Olsa had gotten away because he'd obviously prepared for all that had happened.

Stopping at the creek, I peered in both directions. There

was no trail of footsteps and no signs of movement. No splintered branches, no skids in the dirt, and no misplaced rocks. Everything was calm. As I began to leap over the creek, I stopped. There was a large, odd blotch in it. Noticing it was a reflection, I looked more closely. The blotch was watching me. Slowly, I looked to the trees above me. There, Olsa peered back before violently leaping from the branches.

I was forced into the creek headfirst. The flow of water along with the weight of a person was disorienting, and I flailed about as I tried to get up. The moment my head emerged above the water, I felt a breathtaking punch. It knocked me back to square one, and again I found myself fighting to get up.

After a slippery scuffle, I knocked Olsa down and rushed to dry land. The creek rose halfway up my shin, and I sloppily stomped around. Just as I reached the bank of the creek, an arm grabbed me and forcefully swung me around. The motion was followed with another punch to the face. Briefly, the world faded as I fell back onto the mud. With no time to think, I was met with a barrage of blows to the face. Each punch was executed mind-numbingly well.

Abruptly, Olsa was thrown off. There was a flash of water and mud, and it all covered a body that had jumped from the forest. Talo. She'd ditched the mask herself, and sweat dripped across her face. She was bruised, but she didn't show it. Blow after blow, she fought with a hate that could have made her a murderer.

The world spun, and my head throbbed. The only thing to be heard was splashing and the abusing of flesh. Talo wasn't letting up. A few times, Olsa gained the upper hand, but he never kept it. Even as the fight continued, he'd lost, and there was no arguing it.

Olsa lie on his back with his legs resting in the creek. He could've been dead, but he could've been alive. There was no telling. The only thing that was guaranteed was the way Talo wanted him. As he lay on his back in pain, Talo thrashed across the river, grabbed a large branch, and returned. Her face was twisted and dark. She stood over Olsa, breathing heavily. Bringing her hands as far back as she could, she swung the branch around and brought it down directly into his face.

I turned to the sky and dropped my head, sighing. If Olsa

wasn't dead before, he probably was at that point.

Interlude VI

From the Desk of Julie Winor

As my chair floated down the hall, I kept getting the urge to heave. Each time it happened, I'd come close to vomiting, but I'd stop myself. I begged myself to stay composed, but I failed to control it. I was nearing a breakdown that I constantly fought to keep at bay. But every time my mind wandered back to the image of the officer with his weapon raised to my face, another part of me broke down inside.

Never had I been attacked by an academy officer. The very idea of it was proof of the fact that I was losing. We'd been in a battle with an enemy I wasn't sure of, and not once had the academy been able to take a preemptive shot of its own. We just packed on more and more armor, hoping the next hit wouldn't hurt as hard as the ones before it. But each time, hope failed us.

I walked with five combat officers and Ren Yeral. They all walked with cold eyes that examined every inch of the hall, and even passing officers got the death stare. I didn't blame them. But for my own reasons, I chose to not look at the faces of passersby myself.

I heaved and felt a tear begin to rush down my face. I hadn't even realized my eyes had watered. I'd just been hiding behind my wall of officers while I did my best not to vomit. The wet of the tear only made me try harder. I knew I was beginning to crack at the edges. My storm was revealing itself. But, even knowing this, I attempted to hide it anyway.

There was a second where I successfully held it together

and thought I'd won. But I hadn't. My fingers buckled, and my chair stopped. Reluctantly, I let it all crash down. Nothing was held back. I wasn't sobbing or wailing, but I realized that within my second of composure, I hadn't been composed at all. Two more tears had silently fell down my face, and the wet path they'd left was still there. I could only imagine how I looked in that moment with my tears, my heaving, my wearied face, and my gray hairs. It felt as though everything I built was unraveling.

At first, none of the officers said anything. But then Ren Yeral kneeled beside me. When I caught a glimpse of her face, she looked confused. My eyes naturally darted to the ground, but I brought them back up. We just stared at each other. Seconds went by, and we just stared. The heaving stopped and there were no fresh tears. Just staring. After she'd found whatever she was looking for, she leaned over and grabbed both of my hands.

"Director, you have never failed us, and I'm sure we will triumph…But for us to do that, we're going to need you."

She looked around at the other officers that were surrounding us. Plenty had stopped and stood by purely out of concern. Surprisingly, none of the faces were ones of disappointment. They all looked concerned, genuinely so, but not disappointed.

Ren turned back to me.

"…this assignment's all yours, director."

She gave my hand a final squeeze before letting go. Within seconds, we were once again marching down the hall. Contrary to a few minutes earlier, I was rejuvenated. I didn't feel, "good," in any sense of the word, but I didn't feel as broken as I had before either.

A crowd of officers followed a few steps behind us. As I scanned the faces, I realized everyone we passed joined in. The sight reminded me of all the reasons I loved the things I did. Looking into the face of an officer, I nodded my head in acknowledgement. He proudly nodded back.

When we made it to the directorial meeting room, one of the officers grabbed the door and held it open for me. I nodded a thank you and went in, followed by a couple of the officers, including Ren. They all stopped and waited near the door.

Everyone else we'd come with simply stood guard on the other side.

Ruid stood up as if he were about to come over and inspect my wellbeing, but he stopped when the officers at the door lurched away from their post. The movements surprised everyone. For a moment, the room was tense. Slowly, Ruid eased back into his seat, and the officers went back to their positions.

He was clearly agitated.

"Officers prepared to drop a director? That's not who we are…"

I didn't respond to the comment, but one of the officers near the door did.

"I'm sorry, sir, but after today we're all a little tense. It's only a precaution…"

Ruid aggressively rubbed his hands together. I thought the situation would go from bad to worse, but it didn't. Instead, he exhaled deeply.

"I understand. But I can assure you none of the people at this table will ever hurt the director, so this is one area where I encourage you to fall back."

When I turned around to look at the officer, he was already staring in my direction. He wanted my permission. I gave him a slight nod, which he quickly passed on to Ruid.

"Yessir."

Everyone at the table stared at me and, for the briefest of moments, it was unsettling.

"Before we get started, I must say that I'd like for everyone to remind their units of our bylaws, decrees, and polices. Tension amongst and between our ranks will not be tolerated. I do not believe rogue officers will be the greatest of our threats, so allowing this to divide us will only tear the academy apart from the inside-out."

I paused to allow room for interjection, but no one spoke, so I continued.

"Director Numan, has your unit been able to obtain any information connecting this officer to those we encountered on Prasola?"

He shook his head disappointedly.

"His name is O-Olsa, but there is no information on his origin and his p-presence within the academy is only verifiable for the previous year. Beyond that, it appears he never existed."

I tilted my head in confusion and dropped my eyes, thinking. Someone had simply waltzed into the academy all on their own. It was laughable at best, but terrifying at worst. Given our strength, no one should have been able to come within a lightyear of our post, let alone within the building itself.

"What about our missing officers? Has connections been found between them and Olsa?"

Again, Numan shook his head.

"No ma'am. We've analyzed all of the d-data that was synced from that team's T23, but there's nothing that ties him to the situation."

He paused.

"…And I'm afraid it appears we will never have an explicit confirmation."

The revelation made everyone uncomfortable, so I tilted the conversation in another direction.

"Director Riv, what about my illness? Has your unit been able to uncover its origin?"

"No specifics have been uncovered. However, the virus does line up with the timeline presented by Director Numan. According to our studies, the illness first entered your body between ten and eleven cycles ago."

She looked just as disappointed as Numan had. The lead she provided wasn't as big as I'd have liked it to be, but paired with what Numan had also provided, it was a lot more than we had before.

"I can also tell you that after analyzing all methods of possible entry, it appears that you were poisoned through your drinking glass."

I looked down at the glass that sat on the table. Whenever Directors met, there were always glasses of Okla waiting for each of us. It was customary, and the glass had become such a typical part of my day. I never even questioned its preparation.

I pushed it a little farther away, purely out of comfort.

"Please continue your research. I trust that both you and

Director Numan will be able to provide us with more information in due time."

Both nodded in agreement, so I turned to Ruid.

"I'd like for your unit to ensure our new captive is watched and interrogated around the clock. The information he holds is our clearest path, so I need for you to assure me you'll be able to get us what we need."

He'd been zoned out while we spoke. When I looked over to him, he was tracing his finger around the rim of his drinking glass, but he stopped and looked up as I waited for a response. When he spoke, his voice came out lower and gravellier than I was used to.

"That is a promise I'd love to make, Director. But I can only make that promise if a couple of your…*officers,* don't kill him first. Given what's currently happening in combat's division three, I'd say we don't have much time."

He stared blankly, as if I myself were to explain his statement. The lack of words confused me, but it only took a moment to get the answers I wanted. I was looking at a person I'd known since I was a child. Though the expression of his care and affection rarely revealed itself in the same way, I always knew it was there. So, looking at his darkened face, I could see it. But I could also see something else.

For a moment, he had the glimmering eyes of the boy that would study me when we were children. Eyes that wanted to know everything I knew, and go everywhere I went. But they were also eyes that told me everything he knew, and every place he'd been.

No part of him wanted Olsa protected, and he chose to sit at the table while a few officers were doing the worst of the worst. His eyes told me that he didn't care, and it was likely he'd explicitly sanctioned whatever was currently happening.

Slowly, I maneuvered my chair backwards. Even as I watched him in horror, he didn't care. To him, nothing, not the missing officers nor my illness, was ever about the academy. It was about me. If he had our captive killed, it wouldn't be something done to protect the academy. It would be something done to protect, or avenge, me.

With anger and anxiety building, I left the directorial meeting room and rushed down the hall. The officers who had been waiting outside looked as though they were waiting for me to give them instructions or guidance. But, in that moment, I couldn't. I didn't have enough time to stop.

Once I was almost to the doors of Combat Division Three, I slowed to a crawl. I tried to listen for the sound of screaming or grunting, but the effort was fruitless given the thickness of the door. Part of me grew more anxious because I feared the quietness meant I'd arrived too late.

The doors slid apart. As soon as there was even a crack of space created, the noise it held broke free. There came the battering of flesh, and deep grunts that followed. Through it all was the huff of heavy breathing. Worst of all, there was the sound of more than one abuser.

The only officers in the division were Talo and Allen. Olsa sat against the wall in one of the cells. He produced little response to his abuse. In fact, he wasn't even bound by anything. Given the opportunity, he could stand and face both Talo and Allen. But I knew that wouldn't happen because neither of them would allow it to.

No one noticed me. It was as if they hadn't even heard the doors opening. Initially, I approached slowly, purely out of shock. But my mind reeled when Talo walked up to Olsa and stomped him in the chest. Such a stomp could have broken whatever was left of him. Given the minimal response from him, I was sure they already had.

My frustration rushed back.

"STOP!"

When they turned, their faces were wrought with surprise and a ting of guilt. There was even a bit of fear mixed in. Seeing them in such a way disappointed me. We weren't savages, and we didn't succumb to the tempting behavior that is brought on by war and hate. We were strategic, and we placed the future of the academy above our emotions.

But even then, I couldn't stretch my disappointment beyond a couple of seconds. We'd all neared a breaking point, but we dealt with it differently and needed to be reminded of what we stood for.

Going to Olsa, I glanced at Talo and Allen.

"Know when you've won the battle."

Neither of them responded. They just watched as I came within inches of the same person who'd tried to kill me not even an hour ago. I leaned forward and looked at him for a moment. I was afraid I wouldn't see any signs of life, but he was breathing. Even that looked painful for him though.

He slowly raised his head and looked me in the face. His hair was dirty and wet with sweat. Some of it stuck to his forehead, partially covering the scar that ripped through his eyebrow. He was battered and bruised, but the pain didn't seem to reach his eyes. They shone with an energy I wasn't expecting. They were fully awake and studied me just as hard as I studied them. But they were soulless.

Unexpectedly, he spoke.

"I haven't failed."

His voice was deep and rich, and his words echoed in my head a moment after he spoke. Part of me wanted to hear more, but part of me feared whatever he was likely to say next.

I backed away.

"Send him to the medical unit. Now."

As I floated toward the door, I looked over my shoulder to get another look at him. He was still staring, and I ended up looking him directly in the eye. He mouthed something as I left and, even without hearing them, the words rattled in my head. As I passed through the door and into the hall, they followed me. They attached themselves. Even when we were separated by distance, I continuously heard them.

"I haven't failed."

twenty-four

The mood in the arena was somber. Everyone sat with their backs straight and their faces forward. No eyes wandered, and no limbs twitched. The lights were dark, and the only thing lit was the stage. There were four empty chairs upon it, and everyone knew who would sit in each. As the directors finally began to cross, everyone stood.

Their faces were stone-cold. Even Julie's. They stood frozen in front of their seats. Everyone waited for Julie to approach the podium but, at first, she didn't. There was a moment where she stared at the empty spot as if she were apprehensive about it. Ren Yeral had accompanied her to the stage, but she'd stopped next to the unit directors. When Julie seemed stuck in place, she stepped forward to help. But then Julie surprised us all.

Taking a deep breath, she clutched both her armrests and stood. Her chair was left behind, and so was her apprehensiveness. The air in the room grew tense, and everyone feared she'd collapse. But she didn't. Ren Yeral remained in place, but her face was laser-focused on Julie. If anything went wrong, she probably would've teleported to her.

Julie paced herself to the podium. She walked with a slight limp, and every move looked like it required great skill. When she made it to the podium, she grasped both sides of it. Her eyes seemed to take in the details of every face that watched her. When she finally spoke, her voice came out low, but clear.

"Please, be seated."

The academy sat at once, and Julie waited for the commotion to die down. It was nearly instantaneous. With all eyes and ears on her, she continued.

"My name is Julie Winor and I am your Director of Academy. Seated behind me is Nuet Numan, your Director of Intelligence, Freda Riv, your Director of Medicine, and Anais Ruid, your Director of Combat..."

They all nodded solemnly as their names were called.

"Five hours ago, a battle ensued within our precious academy. We defended it well and our attacker has been sealed in captivity. However, a battle field is rarely left unscarred. In service to our academy, the lives of many officers were lost..."

Our emblem had been shown on the screen above the stage, but suddenly it changed. Photos of officers slid across it, and there were more than I'd expected.

"Their sacrifices will never be forgotten, and neither will the lives of our missing officers. As you all know, the annual Academy Banquet is scheduled to take place on the evening of tomorrow. It is a time we reflect on and honor our achievements and, as such, this year will also be dedicated to honoring the lives of those that have paid for the rest of us to live on."

Everyone hung onto her words as if they were the most important things to ever be said. Not a single person allowed their attention to wander to anything other than her, and the level of attention they gave was nearly zombie-like. It bordered on the edge of unnatural.

I watched as her mouth moved, but her words became silent to my ears. I just studied her, admiring the strength of her demeanor. When everyone stood to their feet, I blindly followed without knowing why. I just watched my mother, my once dead mother, as she commanded a room of thousands.

A group of officers lined up across the stage. Their faces were just as stony as those of the directors. They appeared in an endless stream, and all stood with perfect posture. There was nearly no space left on the stage and, with so many people, the directors were no longer visible. There was only Julie with an army of combat-ready officers behind her.

"I present to you the officers of Special Detail. Volunteering their service, they have agreed to serve as the extra eyes that will watch over our academy around the clock."

The room erupted in praise. It was the same cheers and claps that had awarded the Prasola mission, and the officers on the stage remained frozen as they humbly took it all in.

Julie turned to give praise herself, but her claps took on an odd beat. Within a span of seconds, she slowed with each one, until she was no longer clapping. The cheers of the crowd died down. When Julie turned back to us all, her eyes were wide with pain. One of her hands reached for the podium, while the other grasped her stomach. Her knees buckled, and she caught herself. But she only caught herself once.

I moved toward the stage just as she collapsed to the floor. The only thing that kept her from crashing into the ground were the hands of the Special Detail. The arena had fallen silent. The stage got further away with every step, and I nearly stopped when Julie's head lazily turned toward me. Her eyes were distant, yet somehow close. Her expression had become relaxed. She'd spoken without words, and they were all words I didn't want to hear. But no matter how hard I tried, I couldn't ignore them. In a moment of grief and sudden pain, her eyes had found my own and she, seemingly content, had begun to tell me goodbye.

***

I rhythmically beat my forehead against the glass that stood between me and the private room where Julie lay. A nurse was assisting her, blocking my view of her face. So, instead, I looked at her hands. Her fingers rested calmly at her side. Someone who was ignorant to the situation would've thought she was doing just fine. But she wasn't. In fact, her health had withered to the point where visitors weren't even allowed in her room, and medical personal sanitized themselves before passing through the doorway.

Standing a few feet away was Alora and Luna. They spoke quietly amongst themselves, but I could clearly hear everything they said.

"…maybe we should get him help? Just in case…"

Thump…thump…thump…

"No. He's going to be okay…"

Alora allowed her words to trail off for a few seconds before changing whatever she was about to say. When she spoke again, it was lower than before.

"Watching a loved one die never becomes easy, but it becomes bearable. You just have to make it so."

At the sound of the word 'die,' I stopped thumping my forehead against the glass. Instead, I just rested there. I didn't say anything, and I didn't walk away. I just rested there. I would've sat there for the rest of eternity, but the door to Julie's room opened.

Ren Yeral poked her head out.

"Director Winor wants me to sneak you in. But I beg that you stay next to the door to minimize any contaminations."

After I stealthily passed her and entered the room, she stepped out. She allowed us to be alone, but she didn't walk away from the door. A peek through the glass revealed she was still standing there, pretending to look over whatever was on her tablet.

The room was quiet. The only thing to be heard was the rhythmic beeping and humming of the medical machinery. There were multiple screens that hung on the wall around Julie's bed, and all displayed information I couldn't understand. As I studied them, a part of me regretted breaking the rules and possibly jeopardizing Julie's health even further. But another part couldn't help but appreciate the opportunity to even be in the same room as her again.

She didn't seem to be in any pain. The room was mostly dark, but a bit of light flooded in from the hallway and fell across her hair and face. Her short hair had thinned significantly, and her skin had dulled to a hue that was almost lifeless. It was strange. She'd been relatively fine just a few hours ago, but it was as if her aging sped faster and faster the closer it got to the finish line.

She hadn't moved yet, and it actually looked like she was sleeping. When I finally mumbled something, it felt as though I were saying it for myself just as much as I were saying it for her.

"Only the medical staff is supposed to come in here…"

"I know…But I'm still the leader of this academy…"

Her eyes dragged open. She took breathy pauses between each sentence and I juggled with the thought of telling her she didn't have to speak. Confined to her bed, she looked around the room as if it were the first time she'd seen it.

"This is far from what I ever pictured…"

There was another pause, and it actually looked as though she'd forgotten someone else was in the room. But then she spoke again.

"I'm sorry, Al. I really am…I never thought this is how it would happen…but I missed the mark this time and for that, I am sorry…"

Her eyes watered, and her hands trembled. She turned her head to the ceiling, and breathed deeply.

"You're not even the first person I've hurt. I hurt your father too…and not even he was the first…"

No words escaped me. I could only stare at her frail body, and when a lone tear finally fell, I had to fight from walking over to her. I was sure she was no longer strong enough to wipe it away herself.

She'd fallen silent but, after taking a deep breath, she continued.

"This illness has caused me to break so many promises. Most of them to myself…I was convinced I'd get you here one day and everything would be right but, *look at where we are...*I'm lying on a bed attached to a...machine that would forget to protect me if the power went out."

I did my best to not breathe too fast or make a move. I'd cry if I did. Someone was being snatched away from me for a second time, leaving me in a place I didn't fully understand. But it would be selfish to pretend as if I got the worst end of the stick. After all, Julie was lying in a bed struggling to breathe. I only had to watch.

When she closed her eyes and another tear fell, I backed up against the wall as if it would make her stop. The silence was suffocating. When she spoke again, she simply repeated her apologies.

"I'm *really* sorry Al, but...I don't think my body will hold on long enough for the treatment to be given to me..."

My breath left my body in a rush. I could no longer look at her, so I opted to look down at the floor instead. No words fell from my lips. When I looked back up, she had closed her eyes. There was a path down the side of her face that had been left by her tears, and again I juggled with the thought of walking over to wipe it. I knew there was to be no contact, but I had the unfortunate realization that it wouldn't matter anyway. I moved toward her, but then the door opened.

Standing in the doorway were a pair of eyes that lacked any sign of kindness. They spoke before the person's mouth did and, without saying anything, I was dragged from the room. As I backed out, Julie's eyes remained closed and she appeared peaceful.

Director Ruid waited for me in the hall. I expected an immediate scolding, but it didn't happen. Ren Yeral was no longer there, and Ruid only motioned for me to follow him. It was hard to pick up on how angry he was, primarily because he always appeared angry.

The walk was brief. Soon, came to a door that was labeled **DIRECTOR OF COMBAT**. He allowed me to step in first, before pointing to a chair in front of his desk.

"Take a seat."

His office fit his personality well. It was a plain white box that only held a large desk with a chair on both sides, and a lone metal pen. I assumed the pen never got used because there wasn't any paper in sight. As my eyes traced across the walls, I willed them to bear something interesting. But they didn't, and the cold emptiness of the room remained.

Ruid and I just looked at each other. Agitated, he scrunched up his brows, and sighed.

"Officer Winor, do you think you're the only person in this building that cares about the director?"

His face still wouldn't convey how angry he was.

"No sir."

"So, tell me, why would you make an unauthorized visit into her medical room, knowing it is currently open to medical personnel…only. Are you unaware of her condition?"

My downcast eyes served as an admission of guilt. He leaned back and rubbed his mouth as if he were trying to physically rub off his agitation. When he leaned back across the desk, his voice was low, almost sympathetic.

"I understand your desire to speak with the director. But right now, we must minimize vulnerabilities at all costs, which does include visitation."

He stared as if he were waiting for his words to sink in. Daring me to look up, the force of his glare nearly burned a hole in my forehead.

When he finally leaned away, he switched back to a voice that echoed with authority.

"No more visits. I'm also putting you on detail in Division Three tomorrow night. You'll be working instead of attending the banquet. Understood?"

There was a pause as I mulled over the thought of never seeing Julie up close again. When I looked up, our eyes met for a moment before I finally mustered a response.

"Yes sir."

twenty-five

The inner walls of combat division three were wrapped in a thick glass, sectioned off into white holding cells. The room was filled with the people the academy had arrested from various corners of the universe. They were intriguing to look at. Some looked like regular people, but others had a form all their own. With skin that was hairy or hairless, light or dark, hard or soft, they stood with a range of statures. They were big and tall, thin and short, and most combinations thereof.

But the longer I watched, the less interesting they became. The only one I found myself returning to repeatedly, was Olsa. He sat on the floor of his cell with his back to the wall. He was still bruised and stained with blood, but he'd been mostly cleaned up. The medical unit had even changed him into a fresh set of snow-white pants and a shirt. He almost looked like an asylum patient. For a while, we were locked in a staring contest. But then I grew bored of him.

The control center I sat at had multiple screens, a couple of which showed camera feeds from the banquet hall. The room was filled with tables donned with white cloths and extravagant floral pieces. Each piece contained flowers that were either blue, white, or violet, and officers were seated according to that. A matching light glowed from the center of each, making the intentions all the clearer.

Officers were dressed in an assortment of clothing. Using a variety of both color and style, they contrasted each other and showed just how different each of their cultures were. Some wore things that were thick and drab, while others opted for stuff that was thinner and more colorful. But no matter what was worn, they all still carried the intense aura of the academy.

A flip of a control switched one of the other monitors to a feed of Julie's dark medical room. She was calm, only seen in the light from her window. Shadows passed over her as people in the hall wandered about. A few of them passed slowly, even stopping. But, peacefully, Julie lay unaware of them.

Disturbing the silence, the division's door opened. Given the environment and what had happened, the noise was jarring. But it was only Alora. Like the officers in the banquet hall, she'd forgone her usual combat suit. Instead, she wore pieces of woven fabric. Like her body, the fabric was covered in lines and circles.

She stopped near the doorway, noting my surprise that she was even there.

"I thought it best if you weren't alone."

I nodded. She took it as her cue to join me, and was soon pulling out a chair at the control center. Her eyes stopped when they landed on the feed of Julie.

"So peaceful."

I remained quiet until a glance revealed her patiently waiting for a response.

"You don't have to stay here. I'll be fine."

"You will."

She stared blankly at Julie. Whatever was on her mind was just as well hidden as whatever was concealed behind the lines on her face. Giving up on reading her, I turned back to the monitors.

"Why do I even care? I'm a lot more familiar with her not being around anyway. Maybe this should feel normal."

"Some things go unbroken, even in absence."

It was hard to tell if she were talking to me or herself. After staring at Julie in wonder, she leaned back in her chair, finally bringing her attention back to the control center.

"A band of broken species, yet she's made so much of us. I've seen many deaths, but none this peaceful…she is leaving upon her own accord."

"Better would be her not leaving at all. What am I supposed to do here, Alora? I don't know this place like you do. I don't even know her like you do."

She shook her head.

"You know more than you realize. Even if you are not conscious of it, you have what you need."

She turned, lightening her tone.

"My induction preceded yours, which is why I trained with you your first day. Experiencing that with someone newer than me was just as much for my benefit as it was for yours. I'd never had a session where I was to be a leader, so working with you proved that I could be. I was ready. Soon, you will have such an experience yourself. It's inevitable. And when it is over, you'll realize that you've always had what was needed."

She paused.

"I too needed time to adjust. But I have, and that is what is important. Whether or not you yourself thrive or allow the director to leave is up to you."

In the banquet hall, Director Ruid rose from a table that was placed on a small stage at one end of the room. It had a golden tablecloth, and sat just in front of the window. On the other side of the glass behind it was a nighttime sky that nearly burst with stars and the wonders behind them.

Ruid headed for a mic that stood in front of the table. Once he made it, he waited a moment, allowing the room to fall silent. When he spoke, his voice carried his usual level of discontent. But somehow he managed to make it a level lighter than usual.

"Tonight, we honor the honorable and recognize all that your efforts have done for this academy. Your labor and dedication are things that many within the span of the universe will never know, yet despite this fact, I'm thrilled to say that I, your Director of Combat, have never witnessed any faltering of tenacity or bravery."

People stood and cheered. Surely, moments like these were the only ones that ever allowed the interruption of a director's words. When the cheers died down, and everyone was seated again, Ruid continued.

"As you all know, our most cherished Director Winor is not well enough to celebrate this evening but, even so, I ask that everyone in the room take a moment to formally recognize her presence and influence that has undeniably carried us."

Everyone, including the directors, rose and stood perfectly upright with their hands clasped behind their backs. It was exactly how we stood when we were chosen to take on a mission. After a moment of silence, Ruid thanked them and everyone reclaimed their seats. When the room was settled again, he continued.

"Now, I'd like for everyone to enjoy their night, and always remember: we will never fall, and we shall never perish."

The doors lining the perimeter of the room opened, and food was wheeled out by officers dressed in their combat suits. The seated officers clapped in appreciation.

On the other side of the control center, the monitor furthest away flashed with the word, 'acknowledge'. Just below it was a depiction of a planet. It was placed on a grid plane, and near the edge of the grid was a red dot.

"What does that mean?"

Alora's forehead scrunched.

"I've never seen this warning before…"

She hit a switch on the desk.

"Special Detail…I believe we have a problem."

After a moment had passed, someone responded.

"Already on it."

The warning message disappeared, so I turned back to the banquet. Everything continued just as joyous as it had been before. Officers just chatted and ate, blissfully unaware of the tension at the control center. After a few minutes passed, the radio attached to the main monitor crackled to life again.

"Security to Intel and Combat, craft's origins are unclear. Please assist."

Alora tapped a few options on the monitor, bringing up the camera feed being broadcasted by Special Detail. Everything was foggy and unclear, and the monitor repeatedly blinked. But once it became steady, my breath caught in my throat.

Taking up most of the frame was a ship bigger than any of the aircrafts I'd seen at the academy. It was large enough to carry the academy itself, and it was a mash of metal molded into shapes that could house anything from nuclear weapons to a small town. Lights blinked across it and it hung in the sky like a monster that would descend at any moment.

We peered at the screen, unsure of what to do. It flickered a few times, before the feed completely shut off. On the monitor that had shown the first warning message, there was now a green dot approaching the red one. Special Detail.

In the banquet hall, everyone was still unaware of what was taking place. Beyond the glass the directors sat in front of, the T23 that Special Detail had taken shown as a distant spark in the sky. Alone, it climbed into the sky towards whatever was approaching. Beyond it, a large mass could be seen, but it was faded and partially hidden behind the clouds. Its size made the T23 racing toward it look like a mouse attempting to face an elephant.

As my hands began to sweat, an explosion rocked the sky. The T23 was engulfed in flame, growing dimmer as it fell toward the ground. Briefly, the sky was colored in orange.

The banquet hall fell silent, and a few of the officers stood up. When the directors saw what was causing the disruption, they also rose from their seat. Ruid approached the window. Everyone watched as the ball of fire fell until it finally disappeared amongst the darkness of the trees.

In the distant sky, the faded view of the spaceship remained, and it loomed over in an eerie quietness. As everyone stood frozen, a few dots formed in the distance. As they got closer, it became clear that someone had opened fire on us.

Speeding across the sky were missiles, aimed directly for the academy. But, still, no one moved. Within moments, we were staring them in the face. One by one, they crashed across the glass of the banquet hall, causing fire and smoke to blanket everything outside of the academy.

Camera feeds around the building began losing power. Every monitor in front of Alora and I went blank, until everything left just turned off at once. No sounds were being made, and the building was cast into pitch darkness. After about five seconds of an enveloping nothingness, the lights and power returned.

When the banquet feed reappeared, people had started to move, but Ruid calmed the room with a single hand. Someone dressed in a combat suit with an Intel designation approached him from the side of the room. They whispered amongst themselves before Ruid shook his head and turned to face everyone. Anyone that was still seated quickly stood upon their feet, ready to take whatever orders he was about to give.

Donning his usual rugged expression of aggression, he was no longer in leisure mode. When he spoke, his voice bellowed across the room.

"SUIT UP!"

The room became alive with movement. Officers rushed in all directions. Garments were ripped off as people ran about, most of which was left across random tables. Everyone knew where to go and what to do.

The red dot on the 'acknowledge' monitor was no longer moving. Instead, it was stationary just outside the planet's atmosphere.

With a low voice, Alora called out to me.

"Al…"

Dragging my eyes away from the monitor, I looked up to see her standing and facing the rest of the division. Some of the cells were now empty. I rose from my seat and stepped forward once, afraid to move further. Willing reality to offer a single olive branch, I turned to Olsa's cell but, as expected, it was empty.

Leaving Alora, I rushed out of the division. Officers flowed in every direction. When I spotted Director Ruid, he was marching down the hall with Riv and Numan.

"DIRECTOR!"

As I fought my way through the other officers, the directors stopped. The hint of celebratory relaxation that had donned Ruid's face before was completely washed away. He now carried a look that almost made me want to turn around. As my words caught, Alora appeared and spoke up for me.

"Captives are missing…including Olsa."

Ruid gave us a quizzical look. As if he were measuring my competency, he took a moment to size me up. He turned away and, with his back to us, he raised his wrist to his mouth.

"Detail, this is your Director of Combat. There are captives unaccounted for. Change that."

The directors walked away, but then Ruid stopped again.

"I want both of you in the Grand Arena, ready to act."

After a nod, the directors disappeared. For a second, I didn't move, causing everyone to flow around me. They all wore emotionless expressions. Most showed no signs of fear or uneasiness. There were just faces determined to do as they were told. The firmness was both fascinating and frightening.

Just as before, gone were the emotions that made them feel like people. In their place, there was nothing left but a militarized sense of determination, and it was one that made them feel as far away as the ship looming over the academy.

twenty-six

The crowd in the arena gradually became silent. When the directors finally emerged, everyone stood to their feet. Only three of the four directorial seats were claimed.

A moment of sadness fell upon the room. It was usually the point where Julie would walk to the podium and began addressing the crowd. But the spot remained empty. Solemnly, Ruid took the podium. Looking out onto the sorrow of the crowd, he paused. When he spoke, his voice was heavy.

"Please be seated. My name is Anais Ruid and I am your Director of Combat. Seated behind me is Nuet Numan, your Director of Intelligence, and Freda Riv, your Director of Medicine."

Each somberly faced the crowd, choosing to forgo a wave as their names were called.

"It is my displeasure to present to you mission number 9-7-9. The assignment is located on K-138f...Our home. Officers, we are at war. Though we have our assumptions, details of our attacker are unknown, and we are unsure of their strengths and weaknesses."

He paused.

"However, this lack of information shall not serve as a hindrance. It is neither a barrier nor restraint on our capabilities, and we will *dine* on the miscalculations of their endeavor."

An energy in the room was silent, yet undeniably present. Every officer hung on the words of the director, ready to act as weapons as soon as the command was given. Next to me, Alora's eyes were focused and unwavering, and she sat perfectly still.

With a posture that was stiff, she fit right in with all the officers surrounding us.

"Due to the urgency of this mission, there will be no formal designation of captains. Officers are asked to proceed to the aircraft chamber, and the position of captain will be given to the first individuals to claim an aircraft. Remaining officers are then asked to sort themselves among teams accordingly, and wait for further instructions…"

Taking a moment to eye every inch of the crowd, Ruid raised his arms.

"I PRESENT TO YOU: TEAM MEMBERS NINE-SEVEN-NINE."

The room erupted into a roar that dwarfed the strength of any "cheering" I'd ever heard. It was animalistic, devouring every sense of humanity in the room. It rumbled into my chest and around my head. It was a sound that was initially petrifying but, within moments, you could easily find yourself joining in. I not only watched as the crowd of officers became one beastly entity, but I felt it.

Across the room, officers grabbed shoulders and threw arms in the air. I pictured Julie lying in her medical room, asleep. In the small, guarded square, she could probably hear all that was happening. With an arm thrown around my shoulder, and Julie in my thoughts, I added my voice to the throat of the academy.

The crowd continued even as Director Ruid leaned back into the mic.

"Assignment's all yours, officers."

Within seconds, everyone was in motion and heading down to the aircraft chamber. Officers poured down the hall and took whatever path to the chamber was available to them. Waiting on an elevator would've been a fruitless task, so most opted for the stairs instead. Depending on which division you'd been in, this could prove to be a common-sense choice, or a small journey.

Once Alora and I made it to the chamber, we had to travel to the lowest floor because the rest were full. When we burst into the curved hall, all the garage doors already had an officer standing next to it. It was obvious they'd be serving as captains. Some were even calling out to people passing by.

We rushed around looking for a captain with an opening. When we saw one, we ran over. He had red hair, and his eyes darted up and down the hall as if he were looking for someone. But they stopped when he noticed us coming over. Surprisingly, I found my voice before Alora did.

"Full?"

"Yeah, sorry. I'm just waiting for – her."

Another officer appeared, and they both jogged down to their platform's T23. Without a team to join, Alora and I stood in the hall with other team-less officers. Along the chamber's inner wall, platform doors slid shut as everyone filled each of the aircrafts. When they had all shut, Ruid's voice began filling up the halls.

"T23 officers on platform level one, you're cleared for exit. I repeat, you're cleared for exit."

A rumbling echoed from above us. A few moments after, a wave of T23s passed the level we were standing on. Counting the seconds, I estimated the time at which they'd be bursting into the night sky.

They'd burst from an exit tunnel into a world that was calm. But just beyond the realm of Avenur, our threat would hang. Given its size, it likely held smaller aircrafts that were prepared for battle. I could hear shots ringing out, and the swooping of academy aircrafts, but the tension of the moment blurred the line between reality and the feats of my imagination.

The academy would have the upper hand. We'd use the same formational tactics that had been used on Olsa. With so many opponents, the net would only be thrown larger. The other side wouldn't have the same level of team work. In fact, they'd scatter across the sky. But in a show of skill and coordination, our officers would bully them to the ground. We'd win.

Tearing the chamber from its heavy silence, Ruid's voice came over the intercom.

"ALL LEVELS ARE ORDERED TO EXIT THE CHAMBER. YOU ARE CLEARED FOR TAKE OFF."

Every aircraft revved to life, and the second level started its descent. One after another they dived for the exit tunnel.

Again, Ruid's voice crackled over the intercom.

"REMAINING OFFICERS ARE TO MAKE THEIR WAY TO THE WARSHIPS APRON, IMMEDIATELY."

Everyone moved at once. This time, Alora and I were able to get an elevator ride. The officers already in it gladly held the door, and then moved over to give us enough space to squeeze in. When the door shut and opened again, I was met with a place I'd only ever seen from the hallway.

It looked like a warehouse that spanned most of the building. Seven T46 aircrafts rested within it. Though they had appeared large the day Julie pointed them out, they were downright intimidating up close. While standing beside one, its control center was hidden from view, and the width of a lowered ramp was larger than the entirety of a T23.

Around them, officers dashed and scattered to complete preparations. A few were in the process of pumping shimmering shards of glass out of the floor. They glowed a mesmerizing red, and were immediately recognizable as the Prasola we'd nearly died for. Slowing my pace, I took a second to watch one of the officers attach a pumping handle. When he noticed, he gave me a questioning look.

Some officers carried tablets to explain information about the ships, while others simply used the scream and point method. As the new arrivals tried to get an idea of where to place themselves, various captains came over to point us in the right direction. One of them happened to be Saav, and he readily inducted us into his team.

He threw one arm around me and the other around Alora.

"How nice of you guys to come find me. We'll be using Aircraft Two."

He pointed and rushed off. Following his direction, we ran to the aircraft that was conspicuously labeled with the number two. Ruid stood outside of it, speaking with an officer. The guy had a tablet in his hand, which glowed with a blueprint of the T46. He was in the middle of giving a quick explanation of something, but the look on Ruid's face wasn't indicating an understanding.

Cutting into our path, Talo appeared. But without waiting to hear what she had to say, Ruid pointed in the opposite direction.

"Aircraft Four. I want you stationed with Director Riv."

"Which one are they carrying her in?"

"AIR. CRAFT. FO-"

"YOU KNOW WHAT I MEAN!"

Even with us only watching, the air became hard to breath. Every officer nearby stopped what they were doing. Angry, Ruid forced the tablet away from him. He approached Talo as if he were ready to toss her across the room, and there was a deafening silence between the two as they stood face to face. When he leaned close to her ear, towering over her, the tension was heightened when his voice came out both calm and threatening.

"Director Winor will be placed on Aircraft One if the need arises. Regardless, you will be placed on Aircraft Four. Now, leave."

He leaned away, looking her directly in the eye. When she didn't move, he added,

"If I were you, I'd move. Officer."

For a moment, her expression dropped and she looked hurt. But almost immediately, she switched back to anger. With an expression that was void of any sense of fear, she dragged her eyes away from Ruid and backed off. Everyone standing around slowly went back to what they were doing, but Alora and I were still frozen in place. When Ruid noticed us standing there, his expression alone was enough to defrost our limbs.

"And you?"

"We're uh, t-two."

He nodded. Going back to the explanation he was receiving, he freed us from his grip. Inside the aircraft, everything was just as sleek as the outside. Leading up to the central control area were multiple doors and small hallways veering off into other areas. Halfway to the front, a glass encasing was labeled, 'Emergency'.

In the control area, there were monitors and panels going around the perimeter. An island with a single seat filled much of the center area, and the central dashboard was located at the very front. It was complete with three seats for whomever got to DJ across its controls.

Luna stood over the shoulder of an officer at a monitor, and rushed over as we approached. Without wasting time on greetings, she pointed to each of us.

"Al, you are working left defense and Alora you are on right. I know it is all going to be new to you, but we are in an emergency and most of the work will be done up front."

She gave us no time to respond, and instead went toward a monitor. While she modified some controls, Ruid, Saav, and a few other officers flooded the control area. Also joining the team was Twoh, who sat perched across Saav's shoulders. I started to say something about it, but Ruid cut me off before any words could leave my mouth.

"Will these two be okay on defense?"

Luna grabbed my arm and guided me toward the station she'd just prepared.

"Yes sir. They'll do fine."

She handed me a headset and moved to another station. Ruid sat at the island, Saav and Luna were seated at the central controls, and Alora and I sat on opposite sides, ready to man the defense. I didn't recognize any of the other officers, but they all looked comfortable with whatever they'd been assigned.

Luna scanned the faces that had just arrived.

"Where's Ravi?"

Saav placed Twoh on the floor.

"He was reassigned and put on standby to pilot A1."

Standing, he addressed everyone else.

"Alright, the apron is clear and aircrafts 3, 4, and 5 are prepared to leave. We'll be leading the charge on this fine evening, so I'm going to need everyone's absolute best."

After receiving a few nods and a 'yes sir,' he took his seat. A few controls were flipped, followed by him grasping a lever that resembled the one in the T23. He pulled back on it, revving the innards of the aircraft. The noise caused Twoh to hide near his feet. Attempting to force himself even further beneath the dashboard, the creature nervously peeked out at everyone.

The sound of the aircraft roaring to life was accompanied by the identical sounds of the other T46s. As it rose, an alarm was sounded. It seemed as if it were ranging throughout the entirety of the building, and a computerized warning accompanied it.

"ATMOS: DEACTIVATED...ATMOS: DEACTIVATED...ATMOS: DEACTIVATED..."

A pinging sound rang at the front of the aircraft. Luna responded by reaching over and tapping on one of the monitors. Suddenly, a portion of the windshield donned the face of an officer who looked to be sitting in the combat unit. Breathing heavily, he jumped straight to the point of his call.

"Director, there are currently no captives found anywhere in the academy. Including the ones that were initially accounted for. Captive A147 was seen entering Director Winor's office, but was gone when officers searched the room."

Ruid aggressively rubbed his chin. Leaning back and then quickly sitting up again, he sighed.

"Send a detail to search the underground facilities. It is possible that they're hiding out in there."

When the call ended, Luna turned.

"Who's A147?"

"Olsa. Maybe the Winor kids should have killed him when they had the chance."

As I turned to ask Saav what he meant, Ruid cut in with instructions.

"All flight captains are ordered to initiate their climate shields. Officer Talmani, security will find A147 and the other captives, I just need you to fly this ship."

"Yes sir."

Saav flipped a control on the dashboard, and a thin blue film appeared across the exterior of the aircraft. He then surveyed a monitor in front of him before leaning back and grasping the steering handles. Luna flipped another switch on the control board and a portion of the academy's wall was pulled inward a few yards, before sliding away to allow the T46s an exit of the building.

The only sign that there'd been any discord in the harmony of the planet was the war that was taking place in its airspace. Aircrafts chased and shot at each other, and periodically one would fall from the sky. In the background of the chaos and death was a distinct orange horizon. It seemed to be growing and fast approaching. At the sight of it, I grew uneasy.

"What's with the horizon?"

"Well, like a regular horizon, that's heat. But unlike a regular horizon, it's heat from this planet. ATMOS is down so our temperature is rising as Andies One returns to its natural state."

Saav turned.

"Fun, right?"

He answered his own question with a snort, and accelerated the aircraft. Faster than I could blink, we were out of the academy. We were the first team outside, followed by everyone else. It felt as though we went from 0 to 300 in four seconds, and I found myself grasping for something to hold onto.

Once we were high enough, the "horizon" became clearer as it expanded and slithered its way over the planet. The orange glow violently ripped its way through the trees, and everything it touched was consumed by it. Oddly enough, columns of fire were sparse. But, even then, evidence of the heat's presence was terrifyingly clear.

Interlude VII

From the Desk of Julie Winor

I lay in my medical room in a world that was hazy and nearly silent. Every word uttered in my presence had begun to sound like mere whispers that were said in a dream that was created in the mind of someone else. Nurses rushed in and out to check on me. They wouldn't say much while they were in the room, but I could tell that it was out of necessity and not out of negligence. Everyone already knew I was well within the grasp of death, but it was as if they were also under the impression that I'd already left. Each nurse that entered came in and spoke softly, as if my ears and mind were full of an innocence that needed to be protected. As if I'd become the most delicate thing they'd ever encountered.

Even as the ATMOS alarm sounded, they all pretended the noise wasn't there. I'd have loved to tell them that I was still the leader of the academy, and was aware of what was happening, but my mouth and the muscles in my face no longer belonged to me. I was neither able to speak nor move. I could only watch and listen, and my lack of abilities made me feel as if every ounce of my identity was being ripped away. Left behind was the carcass of a leader that now felt the waves of a debilitating guilt.

Someone had gripped their hands around the throat of the academy, and I'd failed to protect the people I had a duty to. It was a thought that manifested itself into a physical pain, and there was nothing I could do to curb it. The feeling of helplessness was something I banished from my life a long time ago, and I rejected its very existence and refused to fall victim to it. Yet, my last act would be entirely spent in it. Helplessness.

Snatching me from my thoughts was the sound of someone entering my room. When the door opened, four medical officers came in. One of them happened to be Ren. There was a sense of urgency in their arrival, which was unsurprising, but there was also a sense of excitement. Everyone quieted themselves as they entered, quietly shutting the door behind them. They stood over me with two on each side, trying to contain a happiness that I found strange.

Ren leaned over as a tear began to fall.

"Director, the medical unit has done it. We will be able to reverse the effects of your illness, but we must start treatment immediately."

I wanted to grasp her hand, but I couldn't force the muscles to move. After a second of my failure to react, I realized I didn't have to. The officers understood just fine, and Ren moved out of the way to allow another to get closer.

This one carried two syringes. Reaching over to my

infusion pump, she attached the first one.

"We're going to give you the first treatment, and then we must move you into Aircraft One due to an emergency. Every treatment following this will be issued every twelve hours, and this will go on for a span of eight precycles."

She looked down to see if I'd taken it all in, before shaking her head.

"Okay, Director."

She pressed a button on the infusion pump, and everyone remained silent as the first syringe was emptied. When the device beeped, signaling a completion, she attached the second one and the process was repeated. The attachments in my arm were then removed, and my bed was wheeled out of the room.

As we ventured down the hall, officers ran back and forth past us. Respectfully, all acknowledged me even if I hadn't the energy to nod back at them.

I found myself staring up at the hall lights, which reminded me of the last time I'd paid attention to such a thing. It was the day I birthed my first child. Even with the happiness, the sadness, the pain, and the pleasure, it was exhausting. But I wouldn't undo it, given the chance. While the small child fidgeted in my arms, I beamed at him.

"Allen? Allen? Are you afraid, little Al?"

Below the surface, I'd felt a wave of despair. I knew he was something that didn't really belong to me. He belonged to a world I was only given the privilege of visiting. He was a product of the things that surrounded me, and so he was something that I'd also have to leave behind.

Returning to the present, I looked around as the nurses and I neared our destination. The T46 warehouse was mostly empty. Four of the seven ships had already left, and two were in no state worthy of leaving the ground.

Aircraft One was in the center of the room, ringed by several T23s that would serve as escorts. As we approached, the captain of the ship, Officer Talmani, rushed over to us. Adhering to expectations, he nodded to me before addressing anyone else.

"Hello, Director. We're going to switch you to another bed so we can strap you down inside the aircraft."

He paused as if I'd object, before nodding once more. He then signaled for some of his team members to come and get me. I was moved and strapped into another bed, and it was quickly wheeled into the aircraft. Fortunately, I was locked in place in the control center, rather than pushed into a closet off to the side.

When everyone was situated, Officer Talmani started the aircraft, and we began to rise. The escorts that surrounded A1 also prepared to leave, and Talmani spoke as he switched on the climate shields.

"I must warn you all, our home may not be so pretty at the moment."

He opened the large exits in front of us, and a devouring heat entered the room and bled across its interior. The aircrafts were safe due to the shell of the climate shields, but I feared the building itself was now a loss. Putting forth my best effort, I took a deep breath and lay quietly.

twenty-seven

I ripped my eyes from the destruction and brought my attention back inside the aircraft. The island in front of Ruid now had a hologram of the terrain below us, and it changed as we flew. The sky had darkened due to the sheer amount of smoke, and seeing further than an arm's throw became a task on its own. Most of the air was filled with patches of white and black, but it all had an orange inner glow.

Thunder rang out, but there was no rain in sight. There

was only smoke, fire, and lightening, which flashed closer and closer. At one point, we entered airspace that was clear. The smoke around the area enclosed it like walls of marble, and it periodically flashed with the blue of lightening. The thunder rumbled louder as we climbed toward the upper wall of it, until finally it beat so loud I felt the strength of it quake within the hollows of my ribcage. It was one of the most surreal things I'd ever encountered.

For a second after, the rumble stopped. I dragged my soul back into the confines of my body, but I was only allotted a single moment before the light and noise returned. This time, it rang louder and closer than any of the previous instances. As if it had served as an introduction, a few of our attackers emerged from the smoke. Their aircrafts were near replicas of our T23, just as they had been on Prasola.

"Alora and Allen, pick a weapon, mindful of the target potential, choose an unchosen target, and click launch."

I looked down at my monitors to see what Saav was talking about. The top monitor displayed the view that was seen from the front of the aircraft, and the bottom monitor displayed a simple menu with the option to choose a missile type. With the pressure building, my mind raced to make a decision before we were blown out of the sky. Choosing a random option, I clicked three of the opponent aircrafts and clicked launch.

The missile shot from the bottom of the T46, and split into three pieces that took out the aircrafts I'd chosen. Each target was consumed in smoke, but more burst from the seams of the clouds. They approached like a swarm of bees. This time, Saav didn't ask for my and Alora's help. He just reached across the dashboard and started flipping a few switches himself. The four missiles that were dispatched were bigger than what I'd used. Each flew into a different part of the swarm, and exploded into a ball of fire that hungrily ate at every aircraft within its reach.

We dived toward the ground, just missing the destruction. Within seconds, the war below us was revealed. All around, there was nothing but fire, smoke, and a sky that echoed with the sounds of bullets and explosions. It took the world I previously stared at in awe, and turned it into something that was blackened and burning to the point of being unrecognizable.

The aircraft's radio crackled to life.

"Directors and Officers of Avenur, Aircraft One has officially left the ground. I repeat, A1 has officially left the ground."

Saav turned to Director Ruid, who only gave him a nod. Cutting through the destruction, we were curved back in the opposite direction. Soon, we were coming up behind the mountain where the academy stood.

The site of it left a sense of sadness. It had fallen victim to the war that lay around it, and was now nothing more than a shell of what it used to be. The glass of the banquet hall had shattered into the building, and wisps of fire escaped through any opening available. With the limited number of aircrafts, I was sure there hadn't been enough space for everyone. The thought ate away at my mind, and I had a split second of wonder over what would happen to everyone that hadn't been devoured by the attack.

Ahead of us was another T46 surrounded by a team of T23s. It was approached by seemingly every academy aircraft still in action, and soon there was a cloud of T23s and T46s surrounding it. Coming up fast were opponent aircrafts, but some of our own sped off to stop them from getting closer. Easily, they shot them from the sky. As we all climbed higher toward the large ship resting just outside our atmosphere, I held my breath.

The sound of thunder shook the world, and soon we were once again within the grasps of the clouds. Lightening flashed and the rumbling continuously grew until, suddenly, it fell silent. The clouds were dark and dense, hiding all that was within them. When another sound finally came again, it sounded as if all the air was suddenly being sucked away. It grew until there was a horrific flash of lightening that lit up the entire sky. The aircraft was rocked, and for a second I thought it might crumble into a thousand pieces. Though it only lasted a second, the force of the lightening swung around a second and third time.

Briefly, the aircraft was suspended in place. But then we fell. Every second felt like the drop of a rollercoaster, and it seemed to last for hours. As the seconds crept by, our fall sped up and the force of the drop became noticeable on the aircraft itself.

Everything shook violently. Wishing for an escape, I closed my eyes and gripped my armrests.

The chaos of the fall receded, and everything slowed down. The aircraft had restarted. Even though we were no longer falling, no one spoke. Across the control center, a few monitors came back on, and reports were read.

The only lights that were on were the emergency lights. Other than that, most things were dead. Except the climate shield. Fortunately, it appeared to be working. No one was injured, but everyone was shaken, and no one knew what to say. We all just looked around and accepted the fact we hadn't become a pile of wreckage.

Ruid took a long, deep breath.

"Officer Ulmanh, please, give me a status report."

Luna finished pulling herself together, before turning back to the dashboard. For a moment, she tapped a few controls and skimmed over whatever appeared on her monitor.

"…The current was too much for the aircraft, so it is making a safety landing. There is no way to override it."

Ruid sighed.

"Talmani, safety report."

Saav hit a switch on the dash.

"Aircrafts One, Three, Four and Five, sound off."

There was a long pause, and for a second I thought no one would respond. But then voices came in one by one.

"Aircraft Three, safe and accounted for…Aircraft Four, safe and accounted for…Aircraft Five, safe and accounted for."

The absence of a response from Aircraft One nearly stopped my heart.

"What about Aircraft One? Why didn't they respond?"

Saav saw the urgency on my face, and requested another response.

"Aircraft One, this is Officer Saav Talmani, please sound off."

There was a short silence before a response was finally given.

"This is Officer Ravin Talmani, our ship didn't fare well under the shock and nurses are scrambling to assist the director…she's not breathing."

I snatched my headset off and stood to my feet, looking around for a sign of what to do. Cautiously, Luna stood up.

"…Allen…"

I rushed to a monitor showing feeds around the aircraft, and tapped around until the world beneath us was shown. The other T46s were already landing, and ours was quickly closing in on the ground. Accepting the first thing that came to mind, I shook my head and ran to the emergency exit I'd passed when I first entered the ship. Luna called out my name in protest, but I tried to ignore her. When the calls didn't stop, I grew angry.

"I'M GOING TO GET HER!"

Everyone in the ship stared in shock as I walked away from the control area, rushing to the emergency exit I'd passed earlier. But I chose to give them none of my attention.

Making it to the exit, I searched the thick glass for a button to open it, and began beating on it when I didn't see one. When the glass finally slid away, Luna appeared down the hall. But just when she started to speak, Ruid emerged and interrupted her.

"Al…"

"Let him do it."

I stopped. It was shocking to hear him showing any level of confidence in me. Every interaction I'd had with him consisted of him looking at me as I were beneath him and everyone else. But when he saw me stop, he only nodded his head, encouraging me to go on.

I pulled on my mask and entered the exit. The encasing was large enough for five people to stand in, and I searched the area for something that would give me a way outside. The glass wall slid shut again, and a red light on the opposite wall turned on, accompanied by the whining of an alarm. A corner of the floor jerked away, revealing a clear path to outside. The climate shield stretched across the hole, but light wisps of smoke and flashes of fire still rose from it.

I stepped forward and looked down. There was a ladder that would take me to the very bottom of the aircraft, but it was a dead drop after that. Analyzing how far of a drop it would be, I paused. It didn't seem that far away, and I could hear the legs of the aircraft deploying as we neared the dirt.

I glanced over my shoulder once more. From the other side of the glass, Luna silently watched. As she stepped closer, as if she were contemplating pulling me out, I turned away and started climbing down the ladder. I waited at the bottom and, just after the aircraft touched the ground, I took a deep breath and dropped outside.

The ground was dry and solid, and a bit of dust kicked up and blew away. For as far as I could see, there was nothing but rock and dirt. There were no signs of trees, grass, or water. Everything appeared barren, and lacked any signs that anything worth seeing could have ever been there.

The sky was dark and orange, filled with nothing but smoke and ash. The sheer amount of it blocked off the view of anything further than where clouds would be, and the barrier left an odd feeling in my stomach. Some of the smoky air even reached the ground, limiting visibility before everything just vanished behind a haze.

The air flowed toward a large wall that was far off. After a moment of looking at it, I realized it was a mountain range. The range looked vaguely familiar and it didn't take long to realize I was standing in what used to be Zephyr Fields. Julie's favorite place.

A few T46s rested in the distance, so I began running toward the one that was closest. The run was wobbly at first, but I quickly gained my footing. I breathed heavily. I was afraid of what I'd see, but I slowed my pace as I saw a large '04' written near the windshield of the aircraft. There was another T46 further away. I hoped to see '01' written somewhere on it, and my heart leapt when I did.

As I ran, the faint sounds of aircrafts screamed out behind me. Nervously, I slowed. At first, the only thing in view was the mountain range and the heavy air blowing up the side of it. A dark cloud of dust was forming above it, and I became convinced that I was only hearing things. But then three dark aircrafts burst from the cloud.

I stopped. All were heading in my direction. I wanted to run, but there was no place to hide. As their bays dropped, and their weapons deployed, I stood frozen, waiting to be gunned down. But they passed over me. My arms were thrown in front of my face, but no bullets came. Slowly, I lowered them. Wondering why I'd been spared, I looked around in confusion.

Still off in the distance, Aircraft One lay still. Dirt and dust blew around it, obscuring it. But its presence was obvious, and the aircrafts that passed over were aware of it. Disturbing the calm, the attackers shot. Their bullets created a line leading up to Aircraft One, and it became more pronounced as more attackers got closer.

My mind raced, and my feet failed to keep up with it. The aircrafts traveled much faster than I, and I watched in horror as they took turns rhythmically pattering A1. More approached from behind. When a squadron of six came to assist the first three, I pushed myself harder.

They began circling back around. Every shot taken was successful, and the front of A1 fell toward the dirt as its leg buckled from the assault. When it crashed to the ground, I got a better look at everyone inside. Most of the officers were surrounding Julie, and they were attempting to hold up her frail body as they tried to help her. The few officers that weren't helping were frantically pressing controls on the dashboard.

The only thing that was still working was the climate shield, but it was beginning to wither from the damage. As it did, the faces of Ravi and the other officers twisted in fear. When it finally flickered away, there was a large crack that tore across the glass of the windshield and, fearing the situation had grown beyond my control, I slowed to a stop.

Everyone in Aircraft One must have heard the crack, because their heads turned to face it at once. The only pair of eyes that ignored it was Julie's. She stared past it and directly at me. I began breathing even faster as I stared into her unmoving face and, for the first time since I'd arrived at the academy, I saw fear.

Like a cruel joke of fate, the glass of the windshield abruptly burst away. Everything slowed. No one in the aircraft was completely covered in a combat suit, and I watched as the heat of the planet licked its way into the aircraft and consumed everything within it. Julie's weathered face lay unchanged as it darkened to gray and black, and her lips, wrinkles, and the tips of her ears were red-hot as the heat spread across her body and devoured all that she was.

The muscles of my face trembled and twitched. Within seconds, A1 became indiscernible within a ball of fire. It was chaotic and heart stopping, yet it all happened in a silence that managed to be barbarically melodic. I fought to keep myself together, but the pressure became too much to withstand. Something disconnected, and I stopped breathing. My face stopped twitching, and my breath became nonexistent. Suddenly, nothing mattered again.

twenty-eight

I fell to my knees. As I sank lower, I willfully allowed the world to exist as it was. There was a sense of comfort in giving up on the fight for control, and I basked in it.

Aircrafts roared behind me. Dust and smoke was blown around but, still, I wasn't brought back to the reality I'd somehow escaped. In my head, there was nothing worth giving my attention to. There were no aircrafts, no dust, no fire, and no war. There was only Julie.

My thoughts took me back to the day I'd arrived at the academy. Julie had looked at me as if I were the greatest wonder of the world. Her words had caught in her throat, and she'd been overcome with something at the mere mentioning of my name. She'd stammered as if I were something of a legend that had suddenly been proven to be real. But now she was no longer with me. Her life had been snatched away when she was at her weakest, and I'd watched it all happen.

"Your director…"

Someone yelled, speaking as if their words were swords. My mind was slow to process it. Part of me thought the words were nothing more than a figment of my thoughts. But, when my head lazily turned, there was a single person waiting for me to respond.

Olsa.

He was dressed in the gray combat suit he'd worn when he first attacked Julie. Ready for battle, he stood with his hands out. As I rose to my feet, his posture stiffened. He took a step forward and, when he spoke, his voice rang with a controlled anger.

"...headed a place that was nothing more than a stone in the flow of the universe. You, and everyone else, owe us your appreciation. In the name of my father, I have succeeded for all that breath."

I started toward him. My intentions had to have been clear, but he went unfazed. In fact, as he continued talking, he came toward me too.

"I've removed the stone from the river and, now, all is as it should-"

I swung for his face, jamming his words between the creases of my fist. The swing carried a strength I'd never experienced, and it left part of his mask barely intact. Any stronger and the glass shielding his face would have burst away and the heat of the world would have consumed him, just as it had done to Julie.

He'd fallen backward, and was fumbling to regain his footing. Rushing, I dropped my weight on him, and attempted to do away with his mask. I wanted the glass to burst away, and to watch as his face blacken to something that, within moments, would blow away in the wind. I wanted to see his eyes as they watched in fear. But, no matter how hard I tried, his mask wouldn't reveal the things I wanted to see.

Punch after punch, it held on. I willed my arms to deliver a blow much like the first, but none did. Every one of them seemed to get closer and closer to the flesh of his face, but none got close enough. Once he regained himself, I was quickly thrown to the side.

He stumbled a little before rushing toward me. I rolled out of the way just as he lunged, and sloppily gained my own footing. As I breathed hard, he pointed an agitated finger.

"DO NOT DEFEND WHAT YOU DO NOT UNDERSTAND!"

We both ran for each other. This time, blows were dealt one for one. Across the face, in the stomach, past the temples and into the side, fists landed wherever they could. All around us, dust blew past. The sky was still an unclear sheet of orange, and there wasn't much to be seen in the distance.

As Olsa and I continued to fight and wrestle for our lives,

Saav's voice entered my mask.

"No worries, Al. We're almost there."

Olsa held off my swings with those of his own. But, just as I began to get the upper-hand, bullets poured from the sky. Separating us, they all fell around Olsa. Above us, Academy T23s shot passed as they were chased by opponent aircrafts. The sound of bullets surrounded us in every direction, and a few crashes and explosions could be heard near the mountains. The dust and smoke grew thicker and, with every crash, the light of the explosions grew dimmer.

Olsa frantically looked around, before turning to me. Giving me one last point of the finger, he dashed away. I tried to follow behind him, but lost my sense of direction and, seconds later, an aircraft in the distance rose into the sky.

A T46 began landing beside me, and I hurriedly rushed to it. Determined not lose Olsa, I kept my eyes on his aircraft as I boarded my own. A climate shield stretched across the entrance, and I rushed through it before the T46 even touched the ground.

When I made it to the control area, all eyes were on me.

But as I snatched my mask off and took my seat, everyone quickly turned back to their stations. Luna took the longest to pull her eyes away.

When we rose from the ground and broke through a sheet of orange fog, I got a clear view of a fight that had reignited in the sky. There was no coordination and no formations. For as far as the eye could see, aircrafts just dipped and dived, shooting at targets that weren't perfectly clear.

My eyes darted around the mayhem, determined to find a single aircraft. When I spotted the one I believed to be Olsa, I pointed.

"THERE!"

Saav followed the instructions without question. Soon, we were dipping and dodging past bullets and aircrafts alike. Causing us to bank even harder were columns of orange dust and fire that twisted up from the ground. The world was tearing itself apart, but I failed to register most of it. I only thought about Julie and how bad I wanted to catch Olsa.

He'd dipped around a column and then dipped around

another one. As we followed, a gust of dust and dirt blew over us, and the air became too thick to see through. For a few moments, we flew with no idea of what we were headed for.

At the front of the aircraft, Saav clicked across the controls before turning to Ruid.

"Sir, they're retreating."

"CATCH THEM, DAMMIT!"

With Ruid's words mirroring my thoughts, Saav tipped the T46 upward. We sped toward whatever lie above us, unsure of how close we were to crashing into something. The smoke and dust had become so thick, we were flying blind.

A few T23s followed behind us, and their presence was only made known by the familiarity of their lights. As we continued to climb, no one spoke. The only sound to be heard was the quiet rattling of things inside the aircraft, paired with the patter of debris hitting against the windshield.

Twoh still sat near Saav's feet, and he began to whine, but no one paid him any attention. Everyone just kept their eyes focused on the windshield, prepared to jump into action at the first sight of an aircraft. Sweat poured down my forehead, and my breath became slower as we neared what should've been the outer limits of the planet's atmosphere.

The smoke lightened up. Ahead, the light of the moon and stars broke through. The noise of debris grew louder until, suddenly, it stopped. We were no longer trapped between the hands of smoke and dust, and everything beyond Avenur had once again become clear. But there were no opponent aircrafts. As we continued to speed away from the planet, everything around us was nothing more than a lonely, dark, space.

The only thing I could do was stare blankly at the spot where I'd anticipated Olsa to be. Everyone else frantically hit buttons to figure out a course of action, but I did nothing. Once again, I just found myself in a state of shock that stopped me from moving.

"Officer Talmani, we need answers. Now."

Ruid's voice was a mix of tiredness, disappointment, and his usual agitation. It was almost as though it were mirroring everything I felt going on in my head. He'd slumped down a little in his seat, and he stared at his hand as he rhythmically beat against the table. He wasn't hitting it that hard but, still, the veins in his arms protruded in a way that almost looked painful.

"Officer Ulmanh, please, get me a status report."

After taking a moment to study what was on her screen, Luna read what she saw.

"We are currently operating at 40% efficiency. Our level of fuel will be able to carry us for 4 years, but the last two would be spent operating purely off reserves. 80% of our weapons have been deployed, and our climate shield is only hours from requiring a recharge."

Ruid sighed. Leaning across his island, he flipped a switch of his own.

"Directors, what do you all suppose we do?"

There was a pause before any of them responded. When someone finally did, it was the voice of someone I'd never heard speak. In fact, other than Julie and Ruid, the other Directors had both been silent mysteries to me.

"Seeing as there is no returning to Avenur as of now, I

propose we retreat to the Orweiian outpost."

There was a pause as Ruid thought over the suggestion. Another voice came through before he could respond.

"I s-second the suggestion, Director."

Rubbing his chin as if he could rub off his despair, Ruid sighed again.

"Then it has been decided. We will retreat to the Orweiian outpost."

He then looked over to Saav.

"Officer Talmani, get me a safety report."

Saav reached across the dashboard.

"Aircrafts Three, Four, and Five, sound off."

As they all accounted for their officers, the mood of our control area dropped even further. Everyone knew there would be no report from Aircraft One, ever. It was a thought that physically weighed me down, causing me to slump in my seat.

Once they were finished, Saav moved on to everyone else.

"T23-112 through T23-546, sound off."

"A112, safe and accounted for."

"A113, safe and accounted for."

"A178, safe and accounted for."

"A226, safe and accounted for…"

Their voices rang one after the other, and soon it became too much for me to bear. I stood to my feet and rushed into the hall that led away from the control area. I wasn't sure where any of the doors led, but it didn't matter. The only thing I wanted to do was get away from the voices that would never say the one thing I wanted them to.

The hall was dark, and smaller halls led away from it. Turning down one of them, the door closest to me slid open as I approached. Behind it was nothing but a small room with a bed and sink. Contrary to the hall, the room was bright. Everything from the walls to the thin sheet on the bed was white, and my dark, dirty combat suit was a stark contrast to everything I stood around.

I dropped backwards onto the bed, and stared up at the ceiling. The light stretching across it was nearly blinding but, truthfully, I wasn't really looking at it anyway. My mind was elsewhere. Even though I lay in a quiet room, away from everyone else, my thoughts felt as though they were moving a thousand miles per hour. Soon, it began to feel as though I were growing too big for the room I sat in.

I shut my eyes as tight as I could. In that moment, if I squeezed hard enough, maybe everything around me would fade away and disappear. Maybe I'd find myself within the walls of the training room, and Julie would buzz over and explain everything that had happened. But, maybe, I'd open them and find myself in the same position I'd been in before I closed them.

My breathing quickened, and I could feel my insides starting to erupt. I breathed harder to suppress everything within and, soon, I did. I breathed more slowly and, reluctantly, I opened my eyes. With disappointment, I found myself still laying on the bed within a room that felt as though it were moments away from collapsing in on me.

There was a knock at the door and a second later, it slid open. Saav stood in the doorway, and his face was plain, nearly emotionless. For a moment, we both just stared at each other. But then I turned back to the blinding light above me. Allowing the door to slide shut, Saav stepped into the room and fell against the wall. Sliding down until he came to rest on the floor, he sighed and looked at nothing in particular.

But then he looked at me. There was nothing I could say in that moment but, luckily, there wasn't anything I really had to say. Instead, Saav spoke. When he did, his voice came out both low and husky.

"We're going to find them, Al."

I only stared in response, and Saav took this as a sign that I didn't believe him. Resting his head against the wall, his eyes watered as they darted up to the ceiling. When he brought them back down to meet mine again, he repeated himself.

"I promise. We're going to find them."

I turned back to the ceiling and sighed. Just as before, the light above me blocked out everything that was nearby. My eyes grew glassy, but a tear never fell. In that moment, there were no emotions that could be described. There was only a closed-in room with a light that beckoned me to a place that was calm, safe, and simple.

From that point forward, we sat in silence. Together, we just absorbed as much of the quiet as we could. But sitting around and doing nothing couldn't last forever. So when Saav stood up and left the room, I did the same.

The control area had become just as quiet as the room we left. Everyone still sat at their stations, but no one's movements were frantic. No one even seemed particularly concerned with what they were doing. Luna sat where Saav had been sitting, and she gave up the seat as he approached. With a nod, he thanked her and regained his piloting duties.

Everything outside the aircraft was mostly dark and desolate. But the stars that were there were stretched for as far as I could see. We were traveling through the trans-universal highway, though I hadn't felt the effects of moving so fast. It could have been due to the technology in such a new craft, but it could have also been because my mind had been moving a lot faster anyway.

As I stared at all the nothingness outside the ship, Saav

cleared his throat.

"Approaching the Orweiian outpost in 3...2..."

Everything slowed down. All the stars that were stretched contracted. A large sphere came into view, and it was the size of a small planet. But most of it looked hollow. There was a clear, netted, shell that formed the outside of it, and the inside of it was split into two halves that contrasted each other.

It was hard to see in a single look, because it would constantly flash in and out of view. At one moment, everything would be perfectly in place, but in the next it would all become a distorted mess. Whenever it did this, everything I'd previously seen would look as though it had melted and been pushed to the outer edges of the sphere. It would become almost completely clear, revealing nothing but the dark nothingness behind it. But then, it would all return.

The top half was made up of land that was brightly lit, and it looked as though it was a section of Earth that had been cut out and placed inside. There were hills of green that gave way to forests that went on farther than my eyes could reach, bordered by the clear shell of the sphere. Instead of coming to an abrupt stop, a bit of the land rose up the side of it.

Near the center of it all was civilization, but we were too far away to make out the details. It was as if it were nothing more than a toy that sat on a sidewalk, and I was looking at it from fifteen floors up. There were tiny buildings, and some of them rose up as if they'd grown from the land itself, but the space wasn't crowded.

The bottom half of the sphere was the exact opposite of the top. There was no land, and it wasn't nearly as bright. It was mostly parts that were strewn together and seemed to be holding up the life on the other side. There were a few large arms that reached from it and connected to openings on the shell of the sphere, and these were what we headed for.

Once we were close enough, the nature of the outpost revealed itself. There was a climate shield stretching across the openings, so large that all T46 aircrafts were able to pass through at once. T23s followed like worker ants, and soon we were passing through a tunnel much like the exit tunnel that had been at the academy. Only, this one was much more massive.

There were lights that ran the length of it, but it was still dark. In fact, the light of the aircrafts shone just as bright, if not more. It began to curve, and up ahead it broke into four separate paths. We led the charge, so everyone readily took the one that Saav chose.

A few moments after, light flooded the tunnel. Up ahead, an entrance appeared as a dot in the distance. When we finally poured out of the tunnel, it was angled in a way that felt as though we'd just come up the ramp of an aircraft.

We found ourselves in a place that looked like a larger version of the warships apron that had held the T46s. But there were only T23s parked across it, and some of them looked a bit old. The ones that weren't were slightly modified in a range of ways, and a few of them were even painted in a variety of colors.

Fortunately, there was enough space to park the T46s in the center of it all. Around them, the T23s simply took whatever space was left over. As everything powered down, no one spoke. With the monitors shutting off, and much of the control room falling to darkness, we all just stood and sauntered into the hall that would lead us out of the aircraft.

When we neared the exit ramp, a person came into view. The color of her skin was like that of a peach, and her nose was nonexistent. She didn't have any hair, and her ears smoothly rose and fell from the side of her face. She was dressed in a combat suit, but it was different to that of everyone that had just arrived. There was no reptilian pattern, and it had a utility belt around both her waist and a thigh.

But the most striking thing about her was one of her arms. Everything below the elbow had been replaced with a prosthetic, but the outside of it was clear. Within it was a blue energy that glowed and flowed like liquid, and it all disappeared behind the covering of a glove.

She stood with her hands clasped in front of her. At first, she was silent. But as we all exited the ramp, a small smile came to her lips. She looked at no one other than Director Ruid, as if he were the only one there. When she spoke, her voice was smooth.

With eyes that said too much while also saying too little,

she greeted Ruid.

"Nice to see you, Director. We've all been waiting."

End of A1

Next in series: Prince of Prasola

Visit avenurian.com!

Here you will be able to:

Access supporting texts

Be put into an academy unit

Access data on previous missions

View, add, or edit wiki entries

View announcements

View future early release information

Participate in forums

Letter to readers:

To those that trusted me enough to embark on the journey told in this book, I thank you endlessly. Even to those that briefly read the back cover or simply glanced over the front, I thank you. This work is by far my longest-running project to date, and the book you hold is the culmination of more than 4 years of work. I am proud of it, and I am grateful to anyone who grants it even the smallest sliver of attention.

To anyone that crosses this page, I'd like to say something that may be a cliche, yet is all too real: Follow your heart and feed your dreams. I cannot say that I was always 100% sure that I would get this far with this book and this series, but I continued even when the dream felt too far away. I encourage others to do the same, because I believe we owe it to ourselves to fully seek our desires for the future. With every action you take, know that you always have the power to make the negative voices in your head dine on their miscalculations. No matter how hard the mission may be, or how many initial battles you lose, the assignment is always yours, and it always will be.

With much love, I will see you all in the next one.

-Kei Khani

Have you reviewed this story? Got a theory you want to share?

Good or bad, long or short, I'd love to read it! If you have posted

something about this book that you want me to read, send a link to

reviews@keikhani.com. Please only include a non-shortened link

to your post, and a short message. For safety reasons, I will be

unable to open any attachments, so please do not include those.

For more information on the series, visit:

avenurian.com

keikhani.com

jkhannans.com

'avenurian' on social media sites